THE
BLUE
WASHING
BAG

W0008361

MARY CLANCY

POOLBEG

Published 2020
by Poolbeg Press Ltd.
123 Grange Hill, Baldoyle,
Dublin 13, Ireland
Email: poolbeg@poolbeg.com

A catalogue record for this book is available from the British Library.

ISBN 978178199-731-4

www.poolbeg.com

About the Author

Mary Clancy was born and raised in Tipperary town. Later moving to Cahir, she spent many happy years rearing two of her four children, Denise and Adrian, before settling in Kildare where she now resides with her husband Michael and her sons Michael and Fionn. She spends much of her time in beautiful Donegal.

Mary is an Honours graduate in Social Studies (BSS) from Trinity College, Dublin. She holds an MA in social work from TCD and the National Qualification in Social Work (NQSW). She holds a post-grad in Mediation and Conflict Resolution.

Mary began writing poetry as a young teenager but, finding her poems rather dismal, she set them aside. Moving away from her social work career a few years ago allowed her the opportunity to wind down, finding the perfect distraction: writing.

She is inspired by stories from the past – stories about women in Ireland finding their way in a patriarchal society.

The Blue Washing Bag is her debut novel.

Acknowledgements

To each of my dear friends who have supported me over the years – friends in Tipperary town, Cahir and Clonmel.

To my special friend, who read the first manuscript, urging me to go ahead with such gusto. You know who you are, Missus.

To the lasting friendships that I have made, since moving to County Kildare many moons ago. I thank you for the pleasure of having each of you in my life.

Thank you, Besties, for the laughs and good times shared.

To my Donegal friend, Rosemary, who has listened to her fair share and much more.

To my darling husband, Michael, for his continued support.

To Adrian, Michael Jnr and Fionn, my three fine sons, thank you.

To my sister Anne and brothers, Adrian and Gerard, from whom I learned much about the nuances of life. Thank you.

To the dog in my life. Yes. Coco. My most adoring fan.

To Paula Campbell, Poolbeg, who put such a smile on my face when I read those words "I would like to offer you a three-book deal …" From the beginning I wanted no more than to hear those words from Poolbeg.

To my editor Gaye Shortland for the way in which she has embraced my story, offering suggestions without changing my voice. Her attention to detail is wonderful, having the perfect blend of professionalism and a great personality. Thank you, Gaye.

Last but not least to Conor from whom I learned the craft of writing while attending one of his courses at the Irish Writers Centre, Dublin, where I met my wonderful supportive writers' group.

Go raibh maith agaibh go léir!

Dedication

I dedicate this book to the brightest stars in the sky
– who are never more than a thought away.
Mary Teresa, my mother.
And my daughter most precious, Denise.

Chapter 1

The Blue Bag

Sunday April 4th, 1965

A blue canvas bag was left down gently outside No 1, Church Street, Ballygore, on a mild Sunday morning in April 1965. The road was quiet. Mass was still going on. The baby inside was asleep, all dressed in blue, swaddled in a blanket of the same colour. A bright mulicoloured scarf had been used to secure the top of the bag, looped through the eyelets around the rim and tied tightly in a bow, letting in enough air while holding the baby securely inside.

The woman who had left the bag there had done so very quickly, quietly, pausing just for a second before passing between two parked cars and crossing back over the road running past the church. The line of empty parked cars had provided a screen as she put the bag down. There had been no prying eyes.

Following his instructions, she turned her head away as she passed the corner shop on her left, past the glass-panelled door. Faded plastic crates lay upside-down on the ground outside, newspapers on top. She set off along

Church Avenue which led off Church Street, keeping her scarved head down, aware of the houses on the far side of the road. He had warned her to keep her wits about her. But there was no one else to be seen on the street, except for the woman herself, Molly Payton. Nervous, yet slow and measured as he insisted.

Having walked for a minute along Church Avenue, Molly looked back over her right shoulder. Before quickly turning on her heel. Back towards the bag. Heart pounding. Unable to walk away. She could not leave her baby there alone. Not until she was fully satisfied that it had been safely found.

She heard his words in her head: *"Don't dare turn around to look back. Or stop for anything. If you do, I'm gone and you're on your own. And you can tell them whatever you like but you won't be believed – and I will find you! Is that clear?"*

His threat had left Molly in no doubt as to what he would do to her if she opened her mouth. She wouldn't. But she couldn't leave, not just yet. She walked steadily back towards her baby, one last time, just to be sure. Even though he had warned her not to.

"Remember, do exactly what I said," he'd fumed as he left. *"Keep your bloody head down or turn it away if you come across anyone at all. Get back over to the car as soon as you leave the bag down. No stops. Jesus Christ … I can't believe I'm agreeing to this … in broad bloody daylight! I should have got rid of it myself before daylight as I'd planned. The timing was perfect. Now look where we are. Jesus. I must be as cracked as yourself."*

Yes, she had stood up to him in the end. For the sake of her baby. And she would stand up to him now, though she was tired, so tired. Weary. The way he had roared at her. He just wanted her gone. And immediately. She kept

2

her head down as she passed by the houses once again, mindless of the danger she was placing him in by returning to the bag. To her baby.

The original plan had been to leave the bag, just before daylight, at Father Mac's gate on Church Street – a long street running from the top of the hill, down past the school, the priest's house and the church, then past a row of gated houses before meeting the main street at the bottom. He would drop her off and then turn up Church Avenue, the only road off Church Street, straight across from the church. He would wait for her there at the gate of a small scrap-metal yard which was screened from the street by a low wall and some thick shrubbery. He'd said it was foolproof. Even she could surely manage it. They'd get away with it. Unseen. He told her the bag would be found very soon, probably within minutes, when Pat Waters came to get the keys to open the church well before first Mass. But it had to be timed to a T. Precisely. And quietly. Not a sound on the street. Curtains closed. The place in darkness.

She remembered him mentioning Grace, his wife. Saying that he'd even managed to get rid of her and the children for a couple of days, so that he could slip in and out of the house in the early hours without suspicion. All the hurtful words he'd thrown at her. *Crazy. Mad. Lunatic.* But Molly was used to hearing those words and much more and not only from him.

But she had panicked at the last minute and couldn't go through with the plan.

There had been no sleep for her the night before. Up all night pacing the floor, waiting to hear his key turning in the lock well before dawn. Feeding the baby.

When he'd pulled up outside the flat, her red suitcase ready in the hallway, ready to be put in the car, her heart almost stopped. She stood stock still, staring at her door until it opened. Then she panicked. Begging him. Insisting that she was too scared of the dark herself, let alone leaving her baby out there, even if it was only for a few minutes. Telling him that a fox could get it, or a cat could sense the warmth in the bag, sit on it and smother it. All too much. He tried to calm her, saying that he would drive back to check it was OK after he'd dropped her to the flat. She hadn't believed him. She knew he wouldn't do that.

She had changed her mind. And his foolproof plan had fallen apart.

When she'd refused to leave, he'd tried to grab the bag from her. Roughly. He said he would take the bloody bag to the priest's house himself. That they had to get it done in the dark. *Now.* Before daylight came. The streetlights around the area were bad enough, he said. Creating shadows. They wouldn't be seen. But she wouldn't let go of the bag, finding a strength that she knew he didn't believe was in her. But it was. Like a vice grip, he said. No, she was not letting go. The baby was crying. She was crying. He told her to shut up and shut the baby up – he couldn't think straight. She tried to run out the door with the bag, not knowing where she was going, out to face the darkness that she was so scared of. But he'd stood with his back to the door, shoving her and the baby back. Wiping the sweat off his face with his sleeve. He had tried to keep her quiet, losing patience with her. He said the neighbours might hear the commotion through the walls though he'd told her before that they were deaf and the walls very thick.

Eventually he sat behind the net curtains, at the window

in the front room, in the dark, knowing daylight was near, his hands holding his head. He heaved heavy breaths.

Then a glimmer of daybreak. Panic.

"We're fucked," he said, his teeth clenched together. Talking through them. Grinding. *"Now what? You fucking madwoman! I'm ruined. Ruined."*

She thought he looked like a wild animal.

He seemed to calm down when she promised to leave on the train as planned, without her baby. She would follow his next plan. Whatever it was.

"No fucking good," he'd said, wiping his hair back off his forehead. "We'll be copped. Too many eyes and ears out there in daylight."

Molly got down on her two knees, him standing in front of her, her swearing on her child's life that she would get on the train, leaving her baby behind her. But not until later. Not until the baby was found and safe. Failing that, she had bravely told him, she didn't care what happened to her. Or him.

It was his turn to pace the flat.

Molly regained some sense of control. She would leave, she repeated, once she was sure that the baby was found. Safe.

Picking up the baby to feed, she sat in the shabby armchair and opened her blouse. The baby instinctively searched for and found the nipple. Her milk had come in. She told him that she'd put what she could into a bottle in the bag. For the journey, she said.

"Enough," he said. *"Let me think."*

Pulling a pencil and a few sheets of paper from a drawer in the old sideboard, he sat at the table and began to write, ignoring her.

As the baby fed, she sat there awkwardly holding a darning needle between her fingers, licking the black wool thread, trying to put a shape on it to thread it through the needle.

After some time he threw down the pencil, pulled an upright chair over beside her armchair and showed her the paper. He'd drawn a map for her with numbered notes down the side.

"So here's the plan. I hope you're bloody satisfied?"

"I don't want –"

"*Just shut up and listen.* I will put the child in the bag in a while, cover it and put it into the car. The old couple next door will probably sleep late as it's Sunday but in any case they're used to seeing me in and out of here. The old one on the other side is as blind as a bat and deaf with it – and the shop below here is shut on a Sunday. You stay put. At five to eight sharp leave the flat and start walking – as if you're going to early Mass. Meet me at the school above the church, at quarter past eight *sharp*. There should be no one at the school at that time on a Sunday and the high wall of the park runs along across the road – so I can pull in beside the wall. If there is anyone around I'll have to drive on and come back. So *wait*. And don't panic. Got all that?"

"So I'll leave here at five to eight? What if the baby wants a feed?"

"Jesus, woman, it won't be that long!" He glared at her. "So when I see you coming I'll put the bag on the road between me and the wall, where you'll walk by and pick it up. If the coast is clear. *Only if the coast is clear, mind.* And I will drive off if you make a scene. Got it?"

She nodded.

"Right. Walk down the hill quickly. Leave the bag in front of the first house past the church. Cross the road and walk past the corner shop and up Church Avenue. Do *not* look back. I'll be waiting in the car – in the spot in my original plan – in behind the shrubs where O'Brien keeps the scrap metal. If there is anyone around, *don't come near the car* – sit on the low wall there and *wait* until the coast is clear. The last thing I need is some nosey one telling Grace that her car was parked in where it shouldn't be. *Do you hear me?* It's bad enough that I have to hide like a bloody rat, without you messing things up again." He stopped and stared at her. "Jesus! This is all pure fucking madness. I can't believe I let you talk me into it. Crazy. I should have just put it on the bloody train with you! That would have been less risky than this!"

He was fuming and she was afraid that he'd attack her. His well-thought-out plan had been ruined. By her. She couldn't take in half of what he was saying … just enough to know that there was no way out.

Molly had done as he had told her to do. Followed his directions, walked to the school where she'd picked up the baby. She knew she had to hurry before the baby got hungry again. So she did. Feeling every bit of his anger. But at least she hadn't left her baby out in the cold dark night. Alone and unprotected.

Now she straightened herself up as she continued on her way back towards the church. Feeling dizzy, she stopped and stood still at the corner shop. Feeling that she had messed up, but in her own way defiant.

The parked cars were blocking her view but if she stretched her head slightly to the right she could see part of the blue bag. It was of some comfort to her. She waited. She remained where she was for now. She didn't know what else to do. At least it had given her a few minutes more, where she could keep her eye on the bag. On her baby.

Any fear that she might have felt was not obvious to her now. Even though she had not followed his orders by going straight back to the car.

Aware of the sound of her heartbeat, pounding in her chest, she ignored it. Dismissing the aching cry in her heart. Molly Payton was doing what she had always done. Feeling the shock and letting it go, to a place deep within, from where there was no escape.

Without drawing attention to herself, she remained standing where she was, waiting for the church doors to open. She might have just been waiting for someone to come out from Mass.

The large doors opened. The crowd at the back of the church were on their way out. Rushing out and down the wide steps, heading for the gates. The others would follow.

Molly stood, erect and steady, looking straight ahead.

She had always felt uneasy at the thought of being in the middle of a crowd, any crowd. On this occasion her uneasiness didn't register with her as much as it had at other times.

"Morning."

"Grand morning."

"Morning," they said, as they walked past her.

She didn't respond. She didn't look directly at them.

It was just the norm, people greeting each other after Mass.

She wrapped her loose-fitting brown coat around her, the same coat that had hidden her pregnancy so well.

With her beige headscarf tied under her chin, she was little different to any of the other women of her age in the town. Molly Payton didn't draw attention to herself. She had of late worn a little red lipstick. On this occasion she hadn't bothered. She'd only worn it because he'd said he liked it. Her pale face was drawn, her grey eyes small and deeply set.

The Sunday papers lay on their plastic crates behind her at the shop door, as more and more people gathered at the corner.

"Morning."

"Grand sermon."

"Morning."

Different voices, different tones, all saying the same things.

Molly was by now amongst the crowd. Noise. People everywhere, passing each other, rushing to pick up their papers. Standing outside to chat. Chain-smoking cigarettes, as if they might never have another. Burnt matches being cast aside on the footpath. Men coughing, laughing at the same time. Women whispering, passing on what gossip they had.

Blind to the tragedy in their midst.

She was feeling vulnerable and childlike away from him. Waiting for someone else to take control. To take over. Hoping. Her face didn't display how she was feeling.

Some of the people were heading down Church Street, others had turned for home in the other direction up the hill, more walked past her over along Church Avenue.

She crossed the road and joined the people heading towards the bag. She would try to act as surprised as the others.

Surprise was not an easy response for Molly Payton.

Two men walked straight past the bag without paying any heed.

The women walking directly behind them stopped in their tracks. The bright-blue bag had caught their attention.

Within seconds a small crowd had gathered. The women tut-tutted, wondering what was in it. It looked out of place. Each having their say.

One supposed it was a bag of kittens. A bag of pups. No, it wouldn't have been left there – too near to the church. Much too fancy to be a bag of rubbish. A hoax to draw attention? Fool's Day had passed just days before. Others advised caution – it could be something dangerous. But no one dared to take it on themselves to get close enough to take a look inside. Women looking behind them, waiting for someone brave enough to do it.

By now people had no choice but to spill off the footpath, out onto the road. A few of the drivers who had cars parked outside the gates had been smart enough to move off quickly. The rest had to wait for the crowd to disperse.

Car horns tooted impatiently. *Move*.

People were moving around about in all directions. Coming in and out of the paper shop, wondering what the commotion across the road was about.

"What's going on over there?" they asked.

Some people walked on ahead, not wanting to be seen to be nosey. Others were too big in themselves to be concerned. Or, to be seen standing alongside people that they wouldn't consider to be their equals.

Molly stood amongst them, people shoving up against her. Relieved that there wasn't a sound coming from the bag. She would have to walk away soon. She would keep her side of the bargain. The baby was safe.

He had done well to convince her that she had no choice other than to leave her baby behind her in Ballygore, where 'twould go to a good home. With two parents. She knew that if she took it away with her, it would be taken from her and end up in a crowded children's home. And she wasn't having that. The thought of putting her baby into one of those places horrified her. A home that could never be a home.

She knew all about those.

Staying in the town with the baby was never an option. She couldn't look after it. Even if she could, she didn't have the money. She couldn't work in Ballygore and mind the child. And it would ruin not only himself, but his family also. "Big people," he'd said. He would hold her fully responsible. She was beyond thinking about the consequences in that regard.

She had no options.

Following orders, doing as she was told, she had seen it through to the end.

Time to turn and walk away.

Being well used to feeling low, this was different. The secret hiding place behind her heart didn't seem to be as secure as it had been in the past. It was letting her down. She felt a deep overwhelming heaviness. She wanted it to stop. She was unsure if she was even breathing or not. The feeling would not leave her. But it was too late for all that now.

Refusing to allow another thought into her head, she eventually succeeded in encapsulating her pain.

It's all for the best, it's all for the best. She repeated his words in her head. Believing them. She took a few seconds to force a long deep breath out of her mouth.

Molly had psychologically handed her baby over to the crowd. In the midst of the group standing around the blue bag, she felt a sense of protection from them. The sensation was a familiar one, one that she had easy access to. As the trials of her past echoed through her, she regained what strength she could muster, allowing whoever was around her to take control. Feeling and acting much like a spectator herself, she had succeeded in detaching herself from the situation.

She was once again on her own. Handing everything over. Releasing. Letting go. No longer feeling any sense of responsibility. And no more orders to follow.

Breathing out easily, she slipped gently away from the scene, across to the road where she knew he'd be waiting. She walked on this time, without looking back.

Putting her hand into the pocket of her loose brown coat, she felt for the crumpled bunch of tissues which held the brown plastic bottle of pills. Expertly flipping open the white lid, she took out a couple of the small green-and-grey capsules, aware that she had already taken more than her dose. It didn't matter. She needed something strong to distance herself from him. Her mouth was bone dry, but she managed. She was well used to it.

Moving in a slow, rhythmic fashion, oblivious to what was going on around her, locked into her own world, she walked along Church Avenue.

She got as far as the low wall, the shrubs thick behind it. He'd be waiting for her behind the shrubs, car well-hidden near the gate leading to a place used for storing scrap metal.

The flowers on the shrubs were beginning to sprout, putting their energy into displaying their blooms for the takers. She'd always found it difficult to tell one from the other. She didn't need to, she just breathed in the scent.

She sat on the low wall, forcing herself in between the spiny stems that pushed back against her. She closed her eyes for a moment. It was reminiscent of a time long ago. The moment passed.

She was just doing as she had been told. She waited.

Two women were coming towards her. Too early for next Mass. Strolling along as if they hadn't a care in the world.

Pretending not to notice them, she turned her head towards the shrubs but from the corner of her eye she saw them squint as they looked ahead.

"What's going on around the church?" one said.

They paid no heed to the vacant-looking woman, sitting uncomfortably in amongst the shrubs on the half-wall. Quickening their steps, they hurried past her, on towards the church.

Checking again to make sure the coast was clear, Molly stood and walked in around the shrubbery, towards the green Volkswagen.

The driver was behind the newspaper, his face well hidden.

Opening the passenger door, she sat in. She could smell him. The strong scent of aftershave.

She said nothing.

His face said it all. "*What kept you for Christ's sake? I was just about to leave.*"

Childlike now, hoping for some words of praise, she lowered her head as he started the engine.

Emerging onto the road, the car turned left, heading towards the railway station.

The medication had begun to take effect. She had been

successful in removing herself from the reality of her surroundings. Everything had slowed down for her. From the outside, her movements had slowed to a point where she appeared lifeless. Small eyes stared ahead, into nothingness.

She looked down at her hands. Detached. Sitting there on her lap, small pointed ringless fingers, unresponsive. Feeling no connection, she couldn't move, just stare.

For Molly Payton there was no fear now. No discomfort. No feeling.

She did well to rely on her pills once again, now that she was no longer pregnant. Knowing that as long as she kept taking the medication, it would take care of her. No human being had ever given her the space, or the peace, that the pills had given her.

She could hear his voice in the distance. Warbling. She offered no response. No effort. No need.

He spoke in short bursts. "We'd better hurry up or we'll miss the damn train – there's only the one on a Sunday – I hope to God no one copped you."

No response.

He rattled on. "'Tis all the one anyway – 'twould be your word against mine."

No response.

"Forget it now – the infant will be well looked after. How would you have looked after it? You can barely look after yourself. 'Tis all for the best."

He kept talking. She ignored him, hearing words that were of no interest to her now.

Suddenly, he leaned over towards her, as if to catch her hand. He didn't.

Tossing a thin roll of banknotes, tied with a dirty

yellow elastic band, into her lap, he said, "Take that. It'll do you until you get sorted up there. Say nothing."

Her hand clasped the notes, more out of obedience than understanding. She wasn't of the mind to figure it out.

In the past few weeks towards the end of her pregnancy, when she had been more coherent, she had been shown her sad reality. This man, who had made her smile, feel wanted, hadn't a kind word to say to her now. Loving him, relying on him, believing in a future with him. It had all meant nothing to him. Nothing.

She was afraid of him, terrified in case she might upset him. Hours ago, he had shown his true colours – wanting to leave her baby alone on a dark street. He wasn't the same man that she had met when he had rented the flat to her.

Now, sitting in the car with him on the way to the railway station, awareness of her situation was dimming. She was without regret. Without blame. Removed. Despondent.

A blurry picture in her head. A warm baby, a daisy and a tune.

She began humming to herself, gently rocking to and fro in the seat. Without letting go of the money, she placed her clasped hand over the motif of the daisy, which she had stitched to the sleeve of her cardigan, in the early-morning light, before leaving the flat.

She sensed that he was staring at her. Looking at her as if she was a stranger to him.

Unable to focus, she let it go.

Her humming continued. Hauntingly. In tune. Silently singing the words in her head as she hummed. Over and over again.

"Daisy, Daisy, give me your answer do
I'm half crazy all for the love of you.

15

It won't be a stylish marriage,
I can't afford a carriage.
But you'll look sweet upon the seat
Of a bicycle made for two!"

It was her one comfort and would remain so. Closing her eyes, the impact of a trauma hidden deep inside her. She was aware of where she was headed. It was a fact that didn't concern her. Having had her chance at independent living, it was not for her.

Molly Payton had turned thirty on the day she left her baby at the railings of the house next door to the church gates in Ballygore.

Chapter 2

The Widow Nail

Mrs. Rose O'Neill straightened the jacket of her black crepe suit as she walked out of Mass and down the church steps. She did the same thing every Sunday morning as she left Mass – checked and straightened her clothes, brushing away some imaginary dust with her hand. She carried out this little ritual on purpose, in order to avoid making small talk with the locals.

Rose was basically a shy woman, who covered her social awkwardness very well by exhibiting an air of aloofness, a calm confidence. She liked to keep herself to herself, impeccable in her formal dress, grey-streaked hair held neatly in a bun at the nape of her neck.

Neatly folding her black mantilla, she placed it carefully in the zip pocket of her slim black-leather handbag.

Then she noticed that there was a crowd gathering around the railings of the house next door to the church. Rose O'Neill would have usually walked away from such a spectacle but, for some reason, she felt the urge to see what was holding up the crowd.

Walking towards them, she saw they were standing around what looked like a bright-blue canvas bag, which was sitting firmly on the footpath,

The locals knew her well to see. Behind her back, they referred to her as "The Widow Nail".

It suited her, they thought. Ever since her husband died, the woman had never been right. "Tough as nails," they said.

Rose had lost her husband John P twenty years before, just five years after they were married. She had come back from the shop one morning to find him, as she thought, asleep in his armchair. Failing to wake him, it soon became apparent to her that the only man she had ever loved was dead. A massive heart attack, they had told her. He had been the same age as herself, thirty-six years old.

It had taken her years to get over the shock. When the day came that she did accept that he was gone, it changed little for her. Rose would mourn her kind, gentle husband for the rest of her life. There would never be another fit to take his place.

The insurance had paid out well – he had thought of everything, leaving her comfortable. She didn't need to go out to work.

In the early years after he died, she had kept herself as busy as she could – going to Mass every morning, returning home to clean and polish the house until it shone.

Late afternoon, she could be seen heading back down Church Street towards the graveyard behind the church, to tend to the grave of her beloved. The locals would comment that "even a leaf hadn't a chance of hanging around that grave for longer than it took the Widow Nail to come back to get rid of it".

After tea, she'd light the fire, listen to the news on the radio and read her book while settling down for the night.

In later years, as she became known for her clean living, she had been approached by the District Nurse to take in small children who needed a home. Rose would look after the smaller babies, until a longer-term home could be found for them. She didn't ask questions, taking her role very seriously, never opening her mouth about any baby in her care.

This tall straight woman gave the babies the very best of herself, the part which had scarcely been seen since the day John P had passed – the part which was rarely on show outside of her own front door. Outside, Rose continued to portray an air of stern respectability, being quite successful in keeping her distance from people.

And today was no exception.

As the crowd saw the Widow Nail coming towards them, they stood back a little, none of them knowing this woman well enough not to show her some level of respect.

It was known in the town that she had no children of her own, but she had been seen at times pushing a big navy pram around. Strange sight for the locals, who imagined Rose to be lacking in any sort of warmth, especially in caring for a baby. People knew that the babies weren't hers, but no one dared to ask who owned them. All they knew was that she was pushing the same pram for years and the babies didn't seem to be getting any bigger. They sometimes joked that the widow's pram contained no more than a doll.

Rose now gestured with her hands for those closest to the bag to part, which they did.

She said nothing. As she bent down to take a closer look, the crowd went silent. Tugging gently at one end of the scarf tying the bag, she opened the bow. Then she used the backs of her hands to push the sides of the bag out fully.

Those closest to the bag gasped in surprise, their eyes and mouths wide open.

Inside was a tiny baby, lying there, all wrapped in blue.

Rose took a deep breath, before turning to face the women whose eyes remained fixed on the baby.

Without hesitating, once again she took over.

"Will one of you run to the sacristy straight away for Father Mac? He'll know what to do. There's a phone there – he can call the nurse. Quickly, run!"

She had scarcely finished her sentence before three of the women took off to call the priest.

Lifting up the small bundle out of the bag, she could smell the baby powder. She could see the baby was breathing and appeared to be sleeping soundly, unaffected by the hustle and bustle surrounding the blue bag.

When she noticed the huge nappy-pin that had been pinned to the baby's cardigan, she couldn't help but smile. It secured a soother, as well as a small clear plastic envelope containing a holy picture of the Virgin Mary.

The baby was the most beautiful sight that she had ever seen.

Some of the people around her found their voices.

"*Aah*, it's a little boy, all dressed in blue!"

"A little boy!"

"Poor little thing!"

It didn't take Rose's experienced eye long to notice that this baby had been kitted out carefully, by someone who had cared enough to do so. And he had been left in a spot where he would, without doubt, be found within minutes.

As she cradled the infant in her arms, waiting for word from Father Mac, she noticed a small motif of a daisy on the right-hand sleeve of his cardigan. It had been roughly sewn on, with coarse black wool thread which was completely out of place on the otherwise perfectly groomed baby.

Nobody else seemed to take any notice of these details. Even if they did, they kept them to themselves.

Rose's mind was now working on overdrive. It was the weekend. The local nurse would be called out and the infant checked. All going well, Rose would offer to take the baby home, until the mother could be found, or until the court determined the baby's future. It could be for hours, days, or weeks – but it didn't matter. She felt in her gut that this baby would come home with her, knowing well that she was a first choice for the district nurse. And the social workers. Hadn't they told her often enough? And most of the time she believed they meant what they said.

She prayed silently that this would be the case on this occasion. *John P, please let me be the one to look after this little one!* Now it was out of her hands and in the hands of the Lord and those of her husband. Whatever about the Lord, Rose felt sure that John P would not let her down.

Even though she had cared lovingly for every baby that she had looked after, she had never allowed herself to become too attached, as then giving them back would be too difficult for her. But this little one had already such a great effect on this tall stoic woman that she feared losing all control of her emotions. She felt she had no choice in the matter – she was already drawn to this baby. Waiting for the priest to arrive, she couldn't control the way she was feeling. Smiling down at the infant, she was aware that those around might have noticed that she was showing her soft side. She needn't have worried – the powerful wave of emotion that she was feeling was not visible to the crowd. Even so, it distracted this normally self-controlled woman and she quickly tried to regain her composure.

Holding the infant securely in her arms, she heard Father Mac's deep voice in the background.

As the elderly priest was being ushered through the now dispersing crowd, a car pulled up. Nurse O'Dwyer had arrived.

Within minutes Rose, Father Mac and the nurse set off in the black Cortina with the baby, on their way to Rose's house. As Rose would be taking care of the baby for the moment, it had been decided that it would make sense to take the baby there. The nurse would check that all was well.

As the car pulled out, those left behind talked noisily between themselves, some of the women attempting to identify other women in the town who may have been pregnant outside of marriage. Most of the men had walked on. It wasn't of interest to them. The ones left behind held on to their own theories.

Shortly after, in Rose's warm kitchen, the baby was put into her arms by the nurse who had found a bottle of milk wrapped in a thick white towel at the bottom of the blue bag. The milk smelt fine, the baby was fed. The women had decided that it was only right to use the milk, which was most likely the mother's own.

Later, as the baby was checked and then changed by the two women, Father Mac turned his back to them and looked out the window, admiring Rose's back garden as a comfortable distraction.

And then ... it became apparent to the women that the infant was not a boy but a baby girl, who had been dressed head to toe in boy's clothes. In blue.

"Well, I never!" said the nurse as she gently cleaned the baby's bottom. "Look at you, a little miss, and you all dressed up in blue!" The infant's deep-blue eyes flicked back and forth, responding to the light. "Whatever the reason you're dressed up like a little boy, I can't imagine, but you are just so cute in blue!"

"Father!" Rose called. "It's a girl!"

The priest came forward. "Really? How unusual!"

"Let's get you dressed, little one," Rose said to the baby and set about putting on a clean nappy.

"Just thinking here on my feet," said the nurse, "it may well have its advantages for this little mite, when word gets around that it was a boy in the bag."

"How do you mean?" Father Mac asked.

"I mean that this little girl need not to marked for life as 'the baby in the bag'."

"Ah, I see what you mean," said Rose.

"Indeed," said the priest. "In fact, if journalists got hold of the story – which no doubt they will – and could identify the child, it could be most unpleasant."

"So you, little miss, might just be better off if nobody knows it was you," said the nurse.

Rose nodded her head in agreement. "I wonder was that why she was dressed in blue? To stop the tongues wagging?"

"People are good at that," said the nurse. "And why would we be complicating matters for this little one, no more than a few days old? Why would we be shouting from the rooftops that she is, in fact, a girl? The poor mother knows all right what she gave birth to."

"Indeed," said the priest. "Poor woman."

Rose shook her head. "Are we all agreed then – to keep the fact it was a girl secret?"

All three nodded in unison, as if they had been cast under a spell.

"But, of course, this also means we must not broadcast the fact that the baby has stayed with Rose," said the nurse.

"Agreed," said Father Mac.

The white-haired priest leant across Rose to speak directly to the infant, his voice lowered to a whisper, a far cry from the deep formal tone that he used on the pulpit.

"Now listen here, God's little child. Whether you're a boy or girl, it seems to me that you're not exactly an official member of the fold as yet. So, according to the rules of the Church, I shouldn't really be blessing you until after your baptism. But you look like a child of God to me, so here is the Sign of the Cross and we'll do it back to front. And we won't let on to the bishop."

The women smiled at the ageing priest as he dipped his thumb into the holy oil in a small brass box and made the Sign of the Cross on the baby's forehead with his thumb.

"And, just in case that you think it went unnoticed by me that whoever left you outside the church wanted you raised as a Catholic – it didn't." He pointed to the little holy picture.

He then fell silent, musing on the fact the baby was to remain with Rose, at least for now, or until her mother was found, which all three knew was highly unlikely. It was all too rare for a mother to come forward, once she had made the heart-wrenching decision to abandon her baby.

"On second thoughts," he said, "would it not be better to baptise her here and now, rather than Rose having to come publicly to the church with her at a later point?"

The women agreed.

"And a name?" he asked.

"Daisy," said Rose, pointing to the daisy motif on the little cardigan. "Her name is Daisy."

"Oh, I'm afraid it has to be a saint's name," he said apologetically. "But Daisy could be her middle name."

"Then I'd like to call her … Jean … feminine of John," said Rose. "What do ye think?"

"Perfect," said Father Mac with a smile.

Rose left the room and brought back a white crochet blanket as a christening robe.

"This will do for now, young Daisy. No point in making a bigger fuss than you can handle."

And so the baby was quickly baptised, quietly, in the warm kitchen by Father Mac, with Rose and Nurse O'Dwyer as witnesses. Rose's good cream jug was used to pour the holy water over the baby's head.

The strong smell of pipe tobacco was as evident as ever from Father Mac as he put on his coat to leave. The baby's secret would be safe in the hands of these people, he thought. Safe, at least, until any other information came to light which would merit the facts being made public.

He told the women that his next speech from the pulpit that morning would refer to the infant found near the church. He would say that the baby's mother, if she was found or changed her mind, should come to him as her first port of call and her identity would not be made public.

Meanwhile Nurse O'Dwyer would report the finding of Daisy at the Garda Station and document it herself at the clinic the following morning.

The priest and the nurse left the house. They were both of the mind that Daisy was in the best place she could be for now.

Chapter 3

The Boy on the Wall

The boy with the red curly hair, in the tweed short pants, crept along the high wall. It was Sunday and the boy had no notion of going to Mass. He couldn't go now anyway. After missing Mass again last Sunday, it was too late. The harm had been done. Had he missed just the one Sunday, he might have got away with it – confessed in Father Mac's confession box. But he hadn't and the Devil was after him now.

Each Sunday for four weeks, George Doyle had mitched from Mass. He had left the house at the usual time, in plenty time for the first Mass. The eight o'clock. Why his mother insisted on him going to the eight o'clock, he had no idea. It was just a habit, and eight o'clock Mass on a Sunday it was for him. Walking in through the front door of the church, making sure that he was well seen, keeping to the left, he would sit at the end of a pew close to the side door, squeezing in if necessary. Then, when everyone suddenly rose to their feet as the priest came out on the altar, he would slip out the side door. It was foolproof.

People didn't take a bit of notice of him – they were all too busy struggling to their feet and staring at the altar to notice him. As long as he was seen going in the front door of the church, he was there.

Every Sunday, when George arrived home after Mass, the quizzing would start. He was well able for it.

"Well, Georgie. Who said Mass? Was it Father Mac or the new man?"

"The new man."

"What was the sermon about?"

"Ah, Mam, shur what would a twelve-year-old lad like me know about sermons?"

"And who'd you meet?"

He had no trouble answering this one. He always took note of who was there before he slipped away.

"Well, Mam, Mrs. Waters was there with her son. And I saw the Connors woman and Johnny Welsh. Terrible strong smell of pis – I mean *wee*, I said wee – off old Johnny. I nearly puked, Mam."

"Ah, Georgie, shur that poor fella has a bladder complaint for years. He has no one to look after him, only himself."

His mam had insisted on calling him Georgie – she said that it sounded more like a child's name. He knew that his mother hadn't been too pleased when she had found out after his baptism that George was more of an English name. She'd been led to believe that it was the name of a Roman martyr who gave his life for his religion, but afterwards Father Mac had explained that the fellah's proper name was 'Georgios'. George was really glad she hadn't called him that. She blamed his granny for persuading her to use the name in the first place.

He knew now that his twelve-year-old soul was damned, no matter what his name was. And his mother rarely took a break from telling him all about the damned.

She wasn't half as bad as his granny though. When she came to visit, she didn't hesitate to share all her woes and fears of hell with her grandchildren.

"Oh, the Devil is all around you, Georgie. Sometimes you'll think it's God asking you to do something, when it'll really be the Devil trying to cod you."

"But, Granny, what's the point in ever listening to God so, when it might just be the Devil? Why would you bother?"

His protestations fell on deaf ears. She wasn't interested.

"Georgie, he could even fool you into thinking it's God calling you, by using the Lord's own voice. Imagine! Because he knows well that no one would listen to him otherwise. And he can appear just like God, you know."

Having no other choice, he had to pretend to listen. All this God business had him confused.

"God is the only one to fear in this life. Be afraid of no one, Georgie, apart from the Almighty."

And God (or the Devil) was all around him, and there was no getting away from it.

A large framed picture of Our Lord, with a bleeding heart, hung on the wall, halfway up the stairs. He hadn't noticed it so much when he was younger but all of a sudden it stood out. His granny told him it was the guilt, when he'd asked how come the picture stood out from the wall all of a sudden. Looking at the bleeding heart, guilt seemed about right, he thought. So they were all doomed. But his mother said it was just because his granny had painted the frame in gold. Anyway, the look on the face of Our Lord was enough to scare the daylights out of him. There was no avoiding it – no matter what angle he looked at it from, it stared right back at him. He had looked at it from above, from below, and sideways in order to avoid the gaze. Nowhere was safe. Even when he was climbing the stairs with his back to it, he could still feel the brown eyes, boring straight through the back of his head.

His granny would look straight up at it, making the Sign of the Cross as she went by. And she prayed up at the red Sacred Heart lamp over the mantelpiece, even though the small picture of the Sacred Heart there had long since disappeared.

He couldn't escape from it. The whole lot gave George the creeps.

Most nights his mam insisted on tucking him into bed. She'd say, "Georgie, cross your arms over your chest before you sleep so if the Lord should, God forbid, take you during the night, you'll be ready for Heaven. Oh Jesus, God forbid! Your granny always told us that as children. Doesn't bear thinking about. Jesus! But there you go, love!"

He was never sure if his mam's use of the Lord's name was praying or cursing.

George blamed his granny for doing to his mother what she was now doing to him. Lying awake at night, these little chats scared the life out of him but he was by now so scared of God that he wouldn't dare mention it to his mother, or he'd never hear the end of it.

George Doyle lived with his mother and younger sister Susan in a cottage, just a half mile from the town, out towards the Hill Road.

He hated living outside of town as they had to walk

everywhere. His mother didn't have a car, and even if she did she couldn't drive it anyway. And money was always tight. It wasn't that it was so far to walk. It was just a nuisance, especially in the rain.

His mother had a habit of scolding him, every time he waved a car on. "Always remember, pride suffers pain, Georgie."

Not entirely sure what she meant, he took it whatever way it sounded to him on the day.

At least the school and the church were at their side of town, which his mother supposed was a stroke of good fortune.

There was a battered old bike in the shed that had belonged to some old granduncle. Definitely, the kind of bike that only an old man would be seen up on. The battered seat was cracked right down the middle. His granny said to put an old cap on it for comfort. To avoid piles. No way would he do that. Bad enough to be marching around in hand-me-down clothes, besides cycling around on a bike fit for nothing only the junk yard. No. Georgie wouldn't be caught dead up on it. It was definitely for emergencies only.

All the same, the family were seldom stuck for a lift when they needed one. Most of the neighbours around them, in the bigger houses, had cars. They were well used to setting out towards town, knowing that most of the passing cars would offer them a lift.

Sometimes it depended on George's mood. He could take a notion and wave a car on when they slowed down to pick him up. It depended largely on whose car it was. He liked to think that he had a choice when it came to accepting a lift. It gave him a certain advantage over them. Finding out that his mother had to walk into town after being ignored by a particular driver, George would wave that car on, without acknowledging the occupants – confident that he recognised the cars as they came behind him, by the sound of the engines.

George hated the fact that his mother cleaned houses. He hated it more that she washed and ironed clothes for people. And knowing that she was called 'The Washerwoman' didn't help matters.

He would hear her swearing to Jesus as she sorted through the clothes. She insisted that she was praying, but she used the Lord's name quite a bit, he thought.

The smell off the clothes would be enough to set her off at times. *"Jesus, Mary and Joseph!"* Sometimes she retched as she scrubbed the clothes against the ribbed-glass washing board. Her hands would be as red as the carbolic soap she used.

George would feel embarrassed when one of the lads in his school would call to the door to collect the washing. Or deliver it. Most of the callers were all right, but it didn't stop him from feeling uncomfortable as he took in the bags at the front door. One funny look was all it took for him to be vexed.

George knew what he wanted to be when he grew up. He wanted above all else to be a journalist, or a detective, and in that order. He was just about all right at school and hadn't a notion on how he was going to become either. But he knew he would. He dreamt about being successful – when his mother wouldn't have to be dependent on people's dirty washing to get by. They wouldn't be dependent either on others for a lift into town. George would have his own car. A big car. A white Ford. Or a black Rover.

His granny said that he had notions well above his station. Well, his granny didn't know everything.

Each Sunday his mother walked him to the front door, dressed in his Sunday best. Castoffs. Always castoffs. His favourite thing was the mustard-coloured sleeveless jumper his gran had knit for him some years before. At least it fitted him now. He loved to wear it. No one else could claim it had belonged to them at one time or another. Unless of course the wool had come from someone else's knitting bag, which in this case it probably had.

The cuffs of his white shirt would be rolled up to deny the length of them. His wool pants, shortened, held up with braces. George cared about how he looked.

His mam had the habit of wetting down his hair with holy water, taken from the font on the wall by the front door. *Yeuk!* He didn't like it. It wasn't always holy. He had seen her filling the font with tap water, especially when his granny was calling. The base of the font looked as if frogs had laid their spawn in it. All green and slimy. But it was better than her spitting on her hand to flatten his hair down, like she was also likely to do. He hated that more. Then he would be handed a clump of toilet paper to blow his nose before being ushered out the door.

His mother always went to a later Mass on Sundays because she'd spend the morning cooking the Sunday dinner and then let his sister keep an eye while she was gone. Well, she said she went to Mass anyway. After seeing her blessing herself with the tap water from the holy water font when his granny was around, he wasn't too sure. For all he knew she could have been mitching from Mass herself. And she could be affected by the Devil, as well.

Lately, he was more certain than ever that the Devil was after him. Out of the blue, all these weird thoughts had begun to appear in his head. He couldn't shift them though they couldn't be normal. His face reddened at the thought of it.

Georgie crept along the wall, to get to his usual spot, where he had full view of the corner shop across the road. As well as any activity around the gates. He could see more than enough. And he had a great view along Church Avenue, which ran away opposite the church gates. His view to the left down Church Street was blocked by the church and the trees prevented him from seeing much up the road towards the school but, all the same, it was a perfect hiding spot. Easy to get to, easy to leave, out of sight. There was nothing to be seen behind him in the graveyard, as the trees were full and heavy behind him. So he didn't have to feel on edge as he sat there. But the best part of the whole lot was that nobody could see him.

Creeping along, parting the foliage of the soft bushy trees, he thought he heard something. He stopped to take a look.

Johnny Welsh was having a leak up against the wall below. Once he saw who it was, he crawled on. He was safe. Who'd be bothered listening to Johnny Welsh? They wouldn't stand beside him for long enough to hear what he was saying, with the smell off him.

George was at his happiest hiding away, watching the goings-on around him, taking notes in his small pocket notebook. Much of it mightn't be that significant, but it didn't matter – he just loved being there on his own, taking it all in.

When he was younger he had tried to get some of the lads to play detective with him. It hadn't worked out. They preferred kicking a ball. And George preferred sitting up on walls, out of sight, watching people.

He settled himself down on the moss-covered stone. At least it was dry, he thought. The Sunday before, he had gone home with a wet patch on the seat of his pants. He'd said nothing about it. If his mother had spotted it she'd have grilled him about where and when he'd been sitting on wet ground and would have suspected he hadn't gone to Mass. Plus, she'd be giving him that horrible thick red medicine, to ward off a cold.

Georgie was now well hidden by the heavy foliage of the trees. Ready to spy on whatever he could. All quiet now, with the church doors shut and Johnny Welsh gone back in through the side door.

Then he peeped out between the leaves, thinking he recognised the sound of an engine. He had. The green Volkswagen came into view and he watched as it came down the hill and stopped to let a woman out, then drove on past the railings down Church Street towards Main Street. It was his neighbour all right. The next person to pass the railings of the church was the woman, carrying the same kind of familiar blue bag that the Keoghs would bring to his mother with the washing in it. It struck George that Davie Keogh had taken his business elsewhere. The sneak. He didn't give it a second thought.

The woman by now was out of sight as she walked down past the gates.

After five minutes or so, he heard the loud distinctive sound of the same engine as it appeared, coming towards him, over along Church Avenue.

Mr. Keogh must have driven down Church Street, along the Main Street, and up Paul Street before turning right again onto Church Avenue. He had gone around in a circle. What was he doing now, driving in behind the half-wall with the tall bushes? There was nothing in there – only the gates to O'Brien's scrap-metal yard. The low wall had been built and covered in big shrubs to hide the state of the yard behind it. His mother said it was to keep Church Avenue looking respectable. But his granny told him it was built to hide the yard behind, to stop people from robbing the place.

Whatever it was, the car had gone in and didn't come out again. But maybe Keogh was mitching Mass himself, he thought. And now the same washerwoman who had passed earlier was in view again. She looked odd. Walking up and down as if she didn't know where she was going. And no washing bag.

George noted the facts in his notebook: the woman, the driver, the date, the Mass time. Most of what he could see got a mention in his notebook. The colour of the woman's coat and a mention of the blue washing bag that she was carrying. He'd figure it all out later.

He wondered if he had been seen. Was that why the car was circling around? He thought maybe not. Georgie figured he wasn't that important.

He guessed that the new washerwoman was just waiting for someone to come out from Mass, maybe to give her a lift home. That must be it. He was more interested in watching where the car was going anyway, than watching that woman with the blue washing bag.

He decided to stay put for now. There wouldn't be much else happening till the crowd started to leave the church.

Some mornings from his hideout he had a right laugh, as he watched the so-called respectable men and women of the town surreptitiously slipping a newspaper or two under their coats from the wooden crates, outside the wall of the shop across the road. Then walking off without paying. Maybe the Devil was in them too.

All was recorded in the notebook. Later, he would do as he always did before the light was turned off in his bedroom that night – write a proper record of what he had witnessed, using the notes he had taken as a reminder of the events of the day.

Nothing much escaped George Doyle – outside of the church, that is.

Hearing the doors open, he watched the usual back-of-the-church crowd begin to spill out through the gates. The usual lot swarmed over to the shop. He kept a keen eye out but didn't spot any newspaper-thieves. Still, it was fun watching their carry-on as they milled about, smoking and eating ice creams and gossiping about each other behind their hands. He wished he could hear what the gossips were saying. Some of the lads from school were there too and he got a special thrill from spying on them when they hadn't a clue. Aha! There was Jimmy Curtain robbing a paper.

And then he heard raised voices. He looked and saw people at the front gates of the church pointing down the road as they got into their cars. He couldn't tell what was going on as the church building was blocking his view. Then the crowd across the road began to look over at something and point too.

He was annoyed that he was missing out on something, but he couldn't move and risk being seen. Anyway, he had to stay put and wait for the green Volkswagen to drive out from where it was parked.

But still it didn't appear. He waited. And then he saw the washing woman walking up Church Avenue. And she stopped and sat on the low wall in front of the place where the VW was parked.

This was all very strange. Where was she off to?

Quick as a flash, he slipped down off the wall and moved fast out through the gates. Then, having a clear view of Church Avenue straight ahead, he saw the washing woman take off again, in behind the bushes where the green Volkswagen had gone.

He stood stock still, fascinated, and then watched the two heads taking off in the green Volkswagen, heading in the other direction.

The thought struck him again that Davie Keogh had been hiding, not bothering with Mass.

Adults are just too weird, thought Georgie, shaking his head from side to side.

Ignoring the crowd gathered at the far side, he turned right and ran away home up Church Street. His stomach was grumbling. He wondered what his mother had cooked for dinner. Roast chicken with stuffing and gravy, he hoped.

"Well, Georgie, how was the sermon this morning? Who did you see?"

He answered as always.

No need to mention to her that he had seen Davie Keogh with a new washing woman.

Chapter 4

The Womaniser

Davie Keogh put his boot down hard on the accelerator as he left the railway station. Having dropped Molly Payton off to meet the Dublin train, he couldn't get back on the road quickly enough. He couldn't believe that it was over. After the ordeal she'd put him through that morning, he'd never felt such relief. Now all he had to do was recover. No point in raking over what he could do nothing about. Too late.

She had certainly exhausted his patience. The whole business was risky enough without the woman backing down at the last minute. He'd taken plenty of risks in his life but this could go down in the books as the most memorable. And the most dangerous if he were found out to be linked to such a scandal.

At the station, he'd been afraid that she might balk again and he mightn't be able to get her out of the car. Darting his hand across her to release the door handle, he had got out and swung her red suitcase from the back seat.

"Hurry up!" he said abruptly as she slowly climbed out. "Get the ticket there at the glass hatch on the left. Use the money I gave you. Your brother will be at the other end. Off you go. Now."

No response.

She had followed his directions, walking on towards the platform, head down, bright red suitcase in hand.

He waited, needing to see her actually get on the train.

"Oh Christ!" he exhaled deeply as the train finally left.

Davie wasn't a man to let a woman get the better of him in any sense, but on this occasion it had been more than trying. At least it had all gone according to plan in the end. Or so he hoped. No point in thinking otherwise, he decided.

"Oh, a close one all right. What was I at, having anything to do with that one?" he said aloud.

Finding out she was pregnant, looking as if butter wouldn't melt in her mouth! He hadn't seen it coming when she'd tried to pin it on him. But as Grace would say, "There's no smoke without fire." Anyway, he had dealt with it now. He knew plenty poor fools that had been caught out and destroyed for life. But not David Keogh.

He sighed with relief as he drove up the long treelined drive towards his home. He remained in the car long enough to put order on his thoughts. Never again would he be landed in such a mess, after the fright he had got with that crazy woman. He could have lost it all. No – he *would* have lost it all.

He looked around him, admiring the elegance of his surroundings, watching the rays of the sun as they peeped through the trees wherever they could. It never failed to amaze him that the house was in fact in the town, but once inside the gate it would be easy to believe that you were deep in the countryside. A line of maple trees at both sides, sheltered, ready to blossom, fully awakened from the cold of winter. The white house standing tall and mighty in front of him. *Maple House.* A two-storey white Georgian house, eight windows to the front, including the large stained-glass half-moon over the door. He never tired of admiring it. Or talking about it. Definitely one of the grandest houses for miles around. He was one lucky man and he knew it. Taking a pine air-freshener from its packet, he hung it off the rear-view mirror. Job done. Grace had a nose like a sniffer dog, but he knew from experience how to throw his wife off the scent – literally. "David, did I notice a scent in the car, like a cheap cologne?" Always having something to complain about. "David, those cheap air-freshener things from the garage are just so overpowering." She would get rid of the cardboard pine air-freshener anyway, the minute she sat into the car.

His wife was never one to directly accuse – just a subtle hint to take note. He couldn't figure out if she was second-guessing him or not. Grace was no pushover and that was for sure.

"Thank you, God!" he prayed aloud, shutting the door of the Volkswagen before heading in the front door. At least he had the sense not to use his own car this morning. That would have really stood out. He had sold a number of Volkswagens in the garage. A common enough car. Grace had taken the bigger car, of course, on her trip with the children out of town to visit her sister.

Whistling no particular tune, he threw the keys on the marble-top table.

41

A hot bath and a whiskey were called for before Grace got back later.

David had first had contact from Molly Payton when she had written to him enquiring about the ad in the For Let section of the local paper. He had met her in the hotel a week later. He hadn't asked her many questions. She seemed decent enough. She said she would be looking for a job locally in a shop. He told her to search the local paper and the shop windows. A plain timid woman, from what he could make out.

He had sensed that there might be something odd about her when he saw her but, after making small talk with her for a few minutes, she seemed all right. She wanted the flat for at least three months and she wanted to rent it on the day.

When he told her that the flat needed a few bits and pieces, she appeared anxious. She began to fidget with the handle of the red suitcase that sat beside her on the floor. He quickly added that the flat itself was in good shape. He told her that work needed to be done, mainly on the stairs and the downstairs hallway – a few panels and a bit of floor covering. Nothing much. And just a few odd jobs to be done inside the flat.

He told her that she could move in straight away, as long as she didn't mind the intrusion of him being in and out to sort out the place. It would be mainly in the evenings, he told her. Letting go of the suitcase, she seemed to relax.

"OK, so."

Her reactions were measured, but he had her attention.

"Look, if 'twas anyone else, I'd be charging them

twenty pound a week. For you, miss ... fifteen a week and that's the very best I can do. I'll be losing money but what about it?"

She nodded.

It was obvious that the woman was desperate. She hadn't even asked to see the place.

"It's just between us, mind. Shake on it and we'll seal the deal. I'm a gentleman, so there'll be no spitting on the hand."

Failing to respond to his attempt at humour, she accepted his handshake.

"Fine, Mr. Keogh."

Watching her face relax, he could see that she was pleased. She said that it was always nerve-racking negotiating a deal for a new flat. Wondering how many flats she had moved in or out of, he decided that it was none of his business – but he would be keeping a good eye on her.

"If it's all the same to you, Mr. Keogh, I'll pay you for ten weeks in advance. I have the money with me. It's in my case."

She would move in the same day. He asked her about the rest of her belongings. She said that they would be sent on. He asked no more. The arrangement suited them both. Davie had the measure of her. He didn't need to know the details. Unusual to say the least.

Opening the suitcase, she removed a paper bag.

Where was she going with an old brown paper bag, full to the brim with small banknotes? None of his business, he decided. He asked her to put it back in the suitcase, telling her that she could hand it over at the flat. Safer. He couldn't help thinking that the red suitcase looked too new and too shiny for this woman.

She'd been right about one thing – decent flats were getting hard to find. He would have the place well sorted in the ten weeks and he'd have the place upstairs more or less ready also. If she hadn't paid up again by then, the flat would be let out to the highest bidder. Davie Keogh didn't do emotions.

He walked with her to the flat. The weather was warm and balmy. It was a short walk. He didn't ask how she had come to town. He didn't want to know.

There was a small hardware shop on the ground floor. He explained that the flats had their own front door. Opening the door, he led her in. A familiar pine air-freshener from the garage hung from the cable above the naked light bulb.

"Lovely smell," she commented.

The dirty cement floor on the hallway didn't seem to have any impact on her. Stepping over the pile of neatly stacked skirting boards, she offered no comment.

They mounted the narrow stairway to the first floor and he led her into the flat.

The small kitchen at the back had been painted yellow. She said she liked yellow. Small window. He'd get her a curtain. A gas cooker sat neatly behind the door. A small fridge. No room for seating. She said that it was everything she needed. The sitting/dining room was to the front. She could look out on the street. She said she liked to do that. A shabby armchair. The sofa was burgundy velvet, a few bald areas visible from under the arm-covers. She seemed to take no notice. A small table at the window. Two painted wooden chairs. A wireless in the corner. A small gas heater in front of the open fireplace. He showed her how to use it. The gas cylinder was nearly empty – he would bring her a new one. It was August – no need for it yet – the weather was warm.

In the small bedroom she asked if the wallpaper was new – he didn't answer. It was white with small yellow flowers, overlapping at the skirting-board – he would trim it for her. The single bed was soft and springy, a pink candlewick bedspread folded neatly on top. The nightstand held a small lamp on the shelf below – if she needed it.

There was no wardrobe – there was no need, she told him. Her clothes would fit nicely in the chest of drawers.

She said that she was pleased with her new home, assuring him that it was more than all right for her – adding that the short-term let was fine as it was getting harder to find a place and she was more than relieved to have secured this one.

From that first day, she made no demands of him. It was the perfect let.

Molly continued to tell him that the flat was grand. She praised him for the work that he was doing, as if it were a favour just for her. She expressed her gratitude at every opportunity.

There were no complaints about noise from her, or the upheaval of him arriving in whenever it suited him to do this job and that. After the first week she invited him to have a cup of tea with her. He did. They sat at the table behind the front window, one facing the other. It became the norm.

It hadn't been long before she'd got a job in a small sweet shop on a side street. She told him she had worked in different places over the years. She said she'd moved around quite a bit. He wondered but didn't ask.

The job hadn't lasted long. Walking in one Saturday to find her sitting alone in the dark room with the curtains pulled, Davie nearly jumped out of his skin. There hadn't been a sound as he let himself in. She was rocking to and fro on the armchair. She said her job was gone, that Mrs. Deasy was closing the shop as business was down to near nothing.

After that, she hardly left the flat.

He didn't care as long as she kept paying her rent. And she did. Where the money was coming from he couldn't imagine, unless the red suitcase was chock-full of it.

Gradually, the boundary between them had softened.

It hadn't entered his mind that he might end up in bed with her. She wasn't his type. He liked women who were bold. He liked face paint, red lips, low tops, a good bit of flesh. Excluding his wife Grace who was in a completely different category. Well got and inclined toward snobbery, with the appearance to go with it.

Grace would see no reason to consider Molly as someone who might catch her husband's eye. His wife knew what he liked – hadn't he hinted at it often enough? Talking to the wall – it made no difference. Grace was Grace.

When he began to leave his new tenant little gifts, she responded as if he had handed over the flat to her. Innocent at first – a small home-made apple tart, made by Grace for the garage, or a packet of biscuits. An old lace curtain, for the bottom half of the kitchen window.

Once he had the sense that she was easy with him, he left her more personal gifts. Gifts he had bought for Grace which were tucked away at home. Expensive gifts. He hadn't forgotten the look on his wife's face when he'd presented her with his attempts to jazz her up a bit. She never wore red lipstick or lacy underwear. A plain black slip would be the most she would wear in that line. She'd made him feel like a right fool. She could hardly contain her laughter when he'd handed her the sexy lingerie. Looked at him as if he were mad in the head. Handing him back the fancy boxes, suggesting he return them. Well, he hadn't returned them.

Taking the fancy underwear out of the box at the back of the high shelf, on his side of the wardrobe, was without guilt for him. Layered in the soft red paper they had been bought in, he removed two of the items. There would be no questions asked – the subject matter would be much too delicate for Grace. If she were to go poking around she would assume that he had sent them back or got rid of them. He'd be ready with an answer.

Molly Payton received her gifts with great appreciation. His wife had never shown him such gratitude.

Davie began to feel more like the man of the house in the flat in Spring Street than he had ever felt at home in Maple House. He felt respected.

And he never copped that she was expecting until a couple of months before she had it. He couldn't believe it when she mentioned the baby, circling her belly with her hand – the way he'd seen Grace do it. She looked just the same. Plump enough around the middle. He couldn't believe that he hadn't noticed. But that was the end of the tea. And the gifts. And all that went with it.

His first instinct was to keep well away from her after that but, after a few days, he realised that would be the wrong move. She was like a bomb waiting to go off and he had to keep an eye on her. Defuse the situation. And deal with getting rid of the threat.

Davie would tell Grace that she was born with notions. Delusions of grandeur. It hadn't helped matters that he'd moved into the family home that she'd grown up in. Her parents had moved to a bungalow. Downsized. He couldn't believe his luck at the time. They'd married quietly to avoid the scandal. Grace had been pregnant.

He was well aware that Grace's family looked down their noses at him. Some days he thought that Grace did too. To think that he'd always been in awe of them in their grand house, driving around the town in their fancy cars. And the ordinary Joe Soaps nearly drooling, gaping at them with their mouths open. And her crowd with their heads up in the air. The old one with her fancy scarf tied along her jawline – the same way that Grace wore hers. Not in under the chin like a normal woman would wear it. Toffs, the lot of them.

But Davie had a plan: he'd make enough money to make them all eat their words. Slowly. Even Grace. Being constantly reminded of her parents' pedigree hadn't helped. Purebreds on both sides, she'd tell him. Crème de la crème. Never feeling good enough around them, working every hour that God sent, to prove to them that he wasn't just one of the common Keoghs, from Martha's Park. Yes, he knew well what they thought of him.

He was looking forward to the day when he would tell them all where to shove it. And he would. The day when he wouldn't be seen dead driving around in a small car – or indeed the garage cars. He would own his very own Jag. And he would make sure that his wife had the best car that money could buy.

With the upkeep of the flats and houses in town, as well as buying and selling used cars in the garage, things were looking good. Upping his game by getting involved with Thornton, the local solicitor, had been a real stroke of fortune. Thornton steered clients in his direction or advised him of a property that might be on the cards for renting or buying. If a client had no links left with the town, apart from a vacant property, better still – such property could often be acquired below market value. A quick sale. Between the two of them there was good money to be made. And they were making it.

Davie knew that they were never going to be bosom buddies – Thornton always seemed to have one up on him. Finishing his sentences for him. Or cutting him off mid-sentence, not bothering to let him finish whatever he was telling him. At times treating him more like an employee than a business partner, making him feel inferior. That said, Thornton had the knack – he was a shrewd operator – advising certain clients of a local firm that he knew of. Mentioning squatter's rights, explaining the consequences as he went, the difficulties involved with vacant properties, owners that were sued for unsafe buildings.

Yes. Davie was sure that his future was looking bright. He kept his eyes and ears on the street. People moved away. People died. As soon as he heard through the grapevine of a house or flat about to be vacated, he was in like a shot. Buying up whatever he could, doing them up. More money to be made. Thornton held the deeds for the properties in his office.

Davie didn't bother Grace with the details of his business dealings, particularly about the flats. There was no need. Hadn't she reminded him often enough that it wasn't a woman's affair to be getting caught up in that sort of stuff? She had enough to be doing looking after Maple House.

And there was certainly nothing much to be had in

looking back to where he'd come from. A council house with six of them in it. He had walked away from all that and he'd show them, too, what he was made of. One fine day.

In town, though, he felt like one of the men that mattered. Amongst his own kind of people. Head held high. No feelings that he was out of his depth. He belonged. Five foot nine, a snappy dresser, black hair oiled at the sides, sideburns shaped to the last, far from overweight and at thirty-four with his finger in a lot of pies.

Davie had always liked female company and that certainly hadn't changed. As long as Grace had free access to a healthy bank account, and no scandal at her door, he figured that she would leave well enough alone.

The hotel bar in town was a man's bar anyway. Basic enough. Grace or her kind wouldn't be seen dead inside the door – this he knew to be a blessing in disguise. The local women who frequented it remained in the snug, ordering their drink through the hatch. And Davie enjoyed a prime view.

The married ones were usually a safer bet – just out for a bit of fun like himself. He would flash the cash, offering to buy a drink here and there. At closing time, he might offer a lift home.

Sometimes, if he was in the mood, he'd trail behind them, slowly, offering a lift along the way. If they were drunk enough, it was easy. If they were smart enough, they walked on. Davie Keogh loved the chase and the one-night stands didn't complicate his life. Nothing wrong with having a little fun on the side. And plenty of pine air-fresheners in the glove compartment.

Chapter 5

The Children's Home

Life had never been easy for Molly Payton and her twin James. Their mother had died in the workhouse hospital, leaving her illegitimate twins with no one to care for them. Living proof of their dead mother's grave sin, they had been brought to the children's home in Dunrick by the parish priest in the summer of 1940. They had been five years old.

James being the stronger of the two in every sense, she depended on him. Remembering little of her life before the home, her memories faded altogether in time. James had always made sure that everything was bearable for her ... until the day he had disappeared without warning from her life. The world as she had known it had collapsed. He had vanished into thin air. The shock to her eight-year-old system would be irreparable.

The black car had disappeared down the driveway without drama, the boy crying quietly in the back seat.

The head nun had called Molly into the office.

"Molly Payton, I have something to talk to you about. And you may not like it. James has been boarded out today, to a grand home. We thought it best to avoid a scene – so off he went. They wanted a boy, who would grow up on the farm, not being blessed with a son of their own. He'll get a good start and isn't that what we all want for him?"

There was no response from the child in front of her.

"He's not going to be far away. The Bates are fine people. I'm sure they'll sort out a visit for ye, when the time is right."

Molly just stared at her. She had no voice. No words. Having heard enough to realise that James was gone, she couldn't follow what the nun was saying to her. When she heard the dull moaning sound, she was unaware it was coming from herself. She lost all awareness. Her childhood as she knew it had just been snatched from her.

Standing up and pointing towards the door, the nun said that Molly should count her blessings. She was lucky to have a roof over her head. Shoes on her feet.

Her moaning turned without warning into a piercing scream.

She stood in front of the nun, unable to move, continuing to scream.

Feeling uncomfortable with the reaction from the child, the nun put a determined arm around Molly, not to comfort her but to usher her out of the room.

Molly struggled, escaping her hold and darting out the door. She ran through the building and locked herself into one of the toilet cubicles.

Refusing to come out, she was left there.

"Have a good think now, child, about how you're

upsetting the entire building. When you're ready to be reasonable we will deal with you."

The outside door to the cubicles shut with a loud bang.

She was left there until the following morning, when the caretaker was told to get the door open and remove her.

What they found in the dark-green toilet cubicle, after taking Molly out, was not to be spoken about. For the first time in years, the toilets were off bounds for two days. The strong smell of disinfectant permeated the building. Afterwards, the lower sections of the cold damp walls were brighter in patches than anyone ever remembered them to be.

Under orders from the Reverend Mother, the caretaker had gently wrapped the naked child, who was bleeding and covered in her own excrement, in a coarse grey blanket that had been removed from her bed.

"Take her to the Sisters' scullery, Denis, and leave her there on the floor. Whatever you do, don't forget to open the back door – we don't need the foul odour going through to the Sisters' kitchen. Stay with her until Sister Angela comes to clean her up."

The Reverend Mother stared at the child in exasperation as she issued her orders.

"Is this the thanks we get, for giving up our lives for the protection and welfare of you children? Ungrateful child!" She turned to the caretaker. "Denis, not one word is to be uttered about this. *Do* you understand me?"

"Aye, Mother, I saw nothing … as usual."

"There's no need for the 'as usual'! You have a job you wish to keep – or don't you? Well, do you?"

He wished that she would stop talking. Her voice unnerved him at the best of times. The very look of her unsettled him. Her long narrow face, her thin lips. A cold, spiteful being, covered from head to toe in religious garments. A wolf in sheep's clothing.

"I can imagine the face of your wife, if you were let go because you couldn't keep your mouth shut. Wouldn't that be a real shame?"

"Yes, Reverend Mother." There was little or nothing reverend about her.

"Enough then, keep your lips sealed. Go and do the job you are paid to do. Off you go."

Once again, Denis carried out his work as ordered. At least this time the child would recover, or so he hoped. One thing was for sure, this poor child was going nowhere, even if he left her outside the front gate. Her vacant eyes looked straight into his own.

"Now, now, child, you'll be fine. They're sending Sister Angela down to take care of you. She's a softie, talks to no one but herself most of the time. She might be away with the fairies, but she's one of the good ones here."

Denis wasn't too bright a man, but he knew well enough that whatever was going on for this child was more than the usual stuff.

Obeying the orders that he had been given, he placed the child gently down on the black stone floor. Making sure that the grey blanket covered her completely, he opened the back door to let some fresh air in. He left by the same door, finding himself unable to carry out the rest of the order. He'd had enough of the Sisters for one day.

Let them come and sort it out now, he thought

Molly was unaware of time passing. She lay without moving on the cold stone floor. There was no sign that she recognised Sister Angela, when the low-sized chubby nun arrived to tend to her.

Sister Angela was known to have her own troubles. She talked to herself incessantly, her arms swinging by her sides as she walked, as if she was on army parade.

On this occasion, the nun was silent as she took the child gently in her arms, holding her close to her. It didn't matter that there was no response – there was none needed.

Molly began to shiver, even though she was as yet wrapped in the blanket. Not bothered about protecting her own clothes, the nun wrapped the wide sleeves of her habit around her, to comfort her.

Then she rose and closed the back door. Lifting the child in her arms, she carried her into the Sisters' kitchen and placed her down gently on the rug in front of the stove.

Once she saw that the child had warmed up, she filled the basin in the sink with warm water. Reaching above her, she felt around for the bar of lavender oil soap and the wash cloth, belonging to the Reverend Mother.

Moving the child gently over towards the sink, standing her on the blanket, she tenderly washed Molly's thin body from head to toe. Placing the child's hands on the edge of the sink to steady her – watching as the congealed blood turned into watery red liquid. Emptying the basin, she watched the now reddish brown water drain away. The child had managed to harm herself while locked into the cubicle. The weapon, which must have fallen from Molly's hand into the stone sink, a rusty nail. The nun picked it up, said nothing and put it straight into her pocket.

Never being able to stand up for herself, or for the children, Angela felt a sense of moral decency as she looked after her charge. Reverend Mother didn't need to know she'd be washing her hands before meals in a washcloth contaminated with blood and excrement.

"Good enough for her, the witch!" Angela said aloud as she placed the washcloth and soap back where she had found them. Blessing herself in mock repentance, she repeated the exercise three times … just to be sure she was covered.

The nun wrapped the child in a warm clean towel, before putting the stained blanket in the bin outside. Knowing where to find the softer blankets hidden at the back of the hot-water tank, she took one out.

Angela was usually left to her own devices, particularly when there was a task to be carried out which would be considered on the delicate side. Many of the other nuns turned their noses up at tasks that she had no problem in doing.

Having dressed her charge in the best of the clean underwear and nightwear, from the clothes bin in the laundry room, she took her by the hand, up the back stairs, to the two-bed sick dorm.

The weight of the soft blanket had warmed the child's body by the time the nun left.

Molly didn't know how long it was before the door opened again and Sister Angela was once again by her side.

"Here, child, sit up, drink this – 'tis just a little tea I made up for you," she whispered, her mouth close to Molly's ear, while helping her to sit up.

A tin eggcup, small enough to keep in the pocket of her habit, big enough to hold her brew.

"Come on, sit up now. Swallow it all down in one go. It's bitter, mind. But it'll make you feel miles better. It will soon put a stop to all that old worry, and fretting."

Molly opened her mouth slightly, allowing the nun to place the small tin cup to her lips. She tasted the bitterness as she drank the tea. It smelt bad but she didn't mind. It wasn't difficult for her to place her trust in this odd but kindly nun.

The little nun with the warm amber eyes leant closer to Molly's face. "Oh, they all think I'm batty and, do you know, some days I'm sure that I am. But I'm not so batty that I don't see what's going on here around me. I do things my way, and they're half afraid to confront me."

Sister Angela rambled on, putting the small empty cup back in the slit pocket of her habit, the child barely understanding what her elder was saying to her.

"And I will let you in on another little secret. Do you see that drop of tea I gave you, dear? Well, I take a cup every day of my life, two some days. I make it myself from the plants. But you must keep it to yourself – we don't want to be giving them too much information."

She had chosen the ingredients carefully.

"You'll feel sleepy in a minute or two, so try to forget about your twin, dear. Within a few days you will settle. "They don't want the girls, only the boys, you see. They're better workers on the farms. Get on with it all, as best you can, and I will keep my good eye on you, I promise."

Off she took again, arms swinging by her sides in marching sequence.

From then on, most days, Molly was given a cup of special tea, the ingredients carefully selected – determined by her mood.

If the nun was not available, there was always a cup waiting for her on the following morning. The pain of losing her brother could finally be held at a safe distance.

The nun had been interested in the healing properties of medicinal plants ever since she could remember.

Believing herself to be a healer, in her time she had tried and tested as much as anyone had ever done. Good and bad. Reading everything that she could get her hands on. Through trial and error, she had learned how to use the correct doses to respond to the challenges of her own condition.

Knowing the properties of every growing plant around her, she was a natural. When it became clearer to her that things were not always quite as she had understood them to be, she didn't have to look far in the wooded area around the convent to get her hands on what she knew would help her.

Under the guise of foraging for wild herbs and edible mushrooms for the convent kitchen, she knew exactly what to look for. And where to go to find them. Nobody questioned her, half afraid that they'd be poisoned by her. Sister Angela left the toxic ones alone, safe in the knowledge that she knew where to find them, confident in her capabilities to use them if the time arose. If she had to, she would.

In her time she had tested the less toxic plants on particular sisters. Plants with sedative properties. Tested. Plants to liven up dormant energy. Tested. On cruel sisters who had lost any sense of decency, cold women, spiteful women who had got on the wrong side of her – nothing too toxic – just a rumbling reminder here and there. Gastric reminders, the messages she sent having the desired effect.

Sister Angela could be found at sunrise on the coldest of mornings, carrying her wicker basket, her pocket-knife sharpened to slice through the toughest of stems. Foraging for leaves, roots, seeds, bark and stems, identifying them all, sticky-backs clinging to her skirts, rummaging through briars and bracken – just doing what came naturally to her.

The voices had kept her company for as long as she could remember. She liked some of them – they were good company and made her laugh as she went about her business. She enjoyed the laughter, having learned over the years to tone it down when she needed to. There wasn't too much laughter around the other sisters and that was for sure.

Her tinctures toned down some of the louder ones. Others just refused to leave – returning at the most inappropriate of times. When she forgot to take her brew, all hell could break lose. The voices would babble on, giving her orders, telling her things. She could tolerate most of them by ignoring them – but not others which at times were overbearing. Shouting at her, making her say things out loud, getting her into trouble. Planting thoughts in her head that she couldn't cope with. Seeing pictures. But she knew how to shut them all up when she needed to rest.

She dried wild mushrooms in the winter – they were easy to locate, with their bright red heads and white spots. Others were brown and so small the caps looked like tiny pixie hats. She knew exactly what to take to make her feel as detached, or alert, as she wanted to be, living most of her life amongst the sisters, without being overly concerned with many of the events going on around her. Using her talent against the thought of parents, who had forced her into a life of confinement, to avoid the shame of having a daughter who was at best ... different. Now she would help young Molly find her own peace.

Whether the child needed a vapour or a tea, the nun would make sure she had it.

* * *

The child became less alert than she had ever been, less interested, her movements slow and drawn out. Her eyes the eyes of someone who had known no life, seen too much, or seen nothing at all. Molly didn't question anything. She took whatever potion that she was handed. It became a ritual.

The other children in the home, who had known her since she was a small child, accepted her as they found her. They got used to the new more sedate Molly – no longer playing games with them when outside, once a day, she paced up and down, staying close to the wall. She would pace all day, if she were allowed, while the other children ran around, delighted to be out and about, enjoying the freedom with each other.

Some of them would call her when the bell rang at the end of their playtime.

"Molly, come on, it's time to go back in!"

The child would never refuse to do as she was asked. Keeping her head down she would follow the others back inside. Sitting at the same place each day, she ate her meals quietly, finishing every morsel, never commenting on whether she liked the food or not. She ate it regardless.

It was well accepted by nuns and children alike that Molly Payton was as she was. She was doing fine, as long as she didn't cause trouble.

* * *

At thirteen she was referred to the psychiatrist. Having changed from the small meek child, who always did as she was bid, to a child who had lost what sense of social skills she'd ever had. Listless.

Sister Angela had kept her promise – she had taken care of Molly as best she could.

But it had become more trying for Angela as the child was getting older. Molly was no longer a small biddable child – she was growing, getting stronger, becoming obstinate at times. Refusing her tea or throwing it back at the nun. Angela knew that the time was coming when Molly should see the doctor.

She was a herbalist after all, not a medical doctor. On a clear day she began to fear that she might be doing the child more harm than good. She believed in the power of the earth to cure all ills but she wouldn't be around forever to look out for Molly. When her own time was up, where would that leave the child?

She needed to put a strategy in place to be sure.

The nun made it her business to plague her superior, suggesting that a visit from the doctor might be advisable, in order to keep the girl on the straight and narrow.

"Sister, will you please stop your constant waffling about the Payton girl? She's done perfectly well these last years, without any doctor. For the Lord's sake, another three years to get her to sixteen and we can send her on to the laundry. Enough of it now. Maybe it's yourself, Sister, who needs to see Doctor Wilton?"

Sister Angela was not giving up, deciding to up her game. She had a persistent streak when it came to her getting her point across.

"Mother, the Payton girl is upsetting the younger children – she's telling them to take off their clothes at mealtimes. And have you not noticed the smell in the hallway? There's been a few 'accidents'."

The nun knew that finding the child locked in the toilets, naked and smeared in faeces and blood, some years before had been too much for the Reverend Mother. Her background in the leafy suburbs of Dublin didn't lend itself to the harsher facts of life. A gentle reminder would do her no harm at all.

"Mother, I don't wish to bother you again, but it appears that the Payton child is causing a bit of a stir at night. She's removing her clothes in front of the other children."

The appointment was made within the week.

No need to mention the healing plants, especially not to the doctor.

Assessing Molly, the consultant made his diagnosis. He was in no doubt that Molly Payton had a mental disorder. His report stated:

Molly Payton has presented as being removed from all reality, living in a world of illusion and imagination. She presents as dazed, taking no interest in her evaluation, indicating a gap in her contact with ordinary life.

With a history of irrational behaviours, this child has been diagnosed with psychosis. Iced baths can be used to calm her when necessary. Lobotomisation may be a suitable treatment in the future. I am of the opinion that this girl does not have the ability to live independently without the support of the Sisters.

To be followed up every six months or by appointment, referred by the Reverend Mother based on her own observations or those of the Sisters.

Signed
Mr. Oliver Wilton
Consultant Psychiatrist

Sister Angela wasn't told that Molly was to be seen by the doctor. She had strengthened the dosage of the sedative plant, just in case.

It had been her plan to wean Molly off the brew – once she knew that the girl had some chance of making it without her. It didn't happen. She was never sure enough or confident enough to take the chance. Doubling the dose was the best she could come up with – if the child was spitting some of it out, or refusing to finish it, a stronger dose made sense. It seemed to work in calming her down.

The kind-hearted nun didn't look for help when she first felt the tightness in her chest. It had been enough to stop her in her tracks. Taking it as the sign that it was, she carried on.

Knowing instinctively that her system was weakening, she accepted her fate. Nature had always been her close confidante – she trusted that her time on earth was coming to its natural end.

As Sister Angela became frail and less active, Molly would wander around looking for her, expecting her dose of tea. It was not unusual for her to find the nun sitting on the damp earth, easy in the company of her beloved wilderness.

The good-natured nun had one more job to do before she went. Taking the child with her whenever she could, she pointed out the plants and herbs to her, showing her the ones to avoid at all costs. Explaining the properties of the bark, the roots, the leaves, the seeds. How to make a vapour. Exasperated. Telling her the best places to find them and when to go looking. Trying to explain what to take depending on how she felt her mood was. Pointless. Of no use. Molly seemed more bewildered than aware.

Angela saw that the girl didn't have what it took to

distinguish one plant from another, not to mind recognise her own moods. She wasn't taking it in. Any of it.

Growing more feeble and less inclined towards foraging in the wood, she saw no choice but to teach Molly how to make the tea using what dried plants she had. When she was able she would collect and prepare as much as she could for the girl. Molly was fifteen when she handed her the bag of crushed dried plants. A small wooden scoop was inside. She gave her a simple instruction: one scoop – no more.

Sister Angela passed away without warning. They found her outside lying in the beloved earth which had been her soulmate. A smile on her face. They buried her in the nuns' cemetery at the back of the home, in the same earth that had yielded its bounty to her.

There had been no mention of her death to the children until after the burial, when her name was mentioned in the refectory prayer. Molly Payton was almost sixteen years old.

Chapter 6

Signing Her In

The day James Payton had been moved without warning from the children's home in Dunrick had been the last day of him being close to anyone, until he'd met Peggy Dundon. By then the memory of his time in the home was no longer strong enough, or sharp enough, to recall with any feeling.

Once he had settled at Bates farm, he had been called to do jobs at six each morning. Cold mornings. All seasons. Straight out to the well for water for the house, back out later to feed the animals and wash down the yard before school.

Evenings were no better. After school he had his work to do on the farm. If the work wasn't done, there would be twice as much waiting for him on the following day, hail, rain or shine. Once the basics were catered for, there wasn't much else to be had. Bates was a hard taskmaster. His wife Nuala wasn't much better. A cold woman. He had worked as hard as any farm labourer for people who had promised to take good care of him. But they had used him instead as a work horse.

He left school after primary school. There was no discussion. Bates had told him he was as thick as two planks.

His childhood had lacked warmth and all that went with it. Turning seventeen had opened his eyes for him when he'd met Peggy at a dance, getting his first sense of family life. The warmth around Peggy's kitchen table had been a real eye-opener. The family chatting, raising their voices to be heard above each other, the girls laughing so much they'd nearly choke at times. Mouths wide open. Passing the food around. Going for seconds, just because they wanted them. Real atmosphere.

Married at nineteen, James Payton belonged to a family at last. He was working hard, taking extra work on neighbouring farms, finally being paid for his labour. Being appreciated for the hard worker that he was. Gradually distancing himself from the Bates altogether. Leaving them behind. They'd taken enough from him. He owed them nothing.

The hackney driver drove the car slowly in through the gateway and up along the gravelled driveway of Ultan's. Cautious, he took a long pull from his cigarette before throwing the butt out and quickly rolling up the window.

James Payton had noticed the look on the driver's face. He thought that he saw him grinning to himself. It didn't faze him though. He was well used to people being uncomfortable around Molly. And that included his wife Peggy.

Looking around him, he knew what Peggy would say if she ever saw this place.

Saint Ultan's psychiatric hospital was as bleak and miserable from the outside as it was on the inside. The window bars were barely visible through the heavy growth of ivy, which had long since taken hold of the building. Barbed wire sat coiled along the high wall and broken glass had been set, spiked into the concrete to inflict injury on anyone brave enough to attempt escape. There wouldn't be too many scaling the wall from the outside, James thought.

He knew what was facing them once inside. He had been here for each admission with Molly ever since he had found her at the laundry. Visiting her during her stays, being there to collect her when he got the calls. She had no one else.

But he hated the place.

Doors kept shut. Locking out the world. Bare walls. No flowers. No shelves to put them on. High ceilings. People walking as close to the wall as they could. Staff that could at times be mistaken for patients. Wayward staff taking medication themselves to ease the burden of the maddening cries. Overburdened staff, some long since devoid of compassion. Wards without visitors. Bathrooms that held on to pungent smells. Cracked, bubbled paint where dampness had set in. Many shades of muted green, none of which were linked to any sort of joy. People wearing ill-fitting clothes. Clothes that were delivered twice a year with no other function than to cover.

Patients given the amount of medication to bring them down to a state where they would conform. Or up to a state where they could function. Those whose gait left them undistinguishable from catatonic patients – except that they moved.

Monotone calls of distress. Wailing. Patients passing each other all day every day – without recognition of the other. Hurrying, rushing along but going nowhere.

James got out, opening the back door for his sister, taking the red suitcase from the boot. It was all too familiar. Damp silence.

"I shouldn't be too long," James said to the driver.

"All right, take your time. I'm not in any hurry."

Not expecting that he would be waiting for any great length of time, the driver stared after the couple that he had just brought in from the station. Strange pair. Not one word had passed between them on the way – no noise at all, aside from the faint noise of the woman's constant rocking. The psychiatrist would have his work cut out for him, trying to figure out which one of these two to admit. That was for sure. Sniggering, he watched the odd pair walk arm and arm up the stone steps. One just as bad as the other. The boys would get a right laugh out of this when he told them.

Leading his twin sister towards the crackled green door, James took his cap off and pressed the brass doorbell.

"Hello, Matron. You're expecting us?"

He ignored the heavy odour that hung in the air – overpowering disinfectant, mingling with less favourable smells.

Molly said nothing. Submissive. Walking forward, following her brother.

The matron led the twins through the hall, locking the office door once inside.

"We'll get on with it so," she said as she lifted a faded pink paper file from the drawer to the side of her desk. "Bring me up to date. Tell me how Molly has been doing since her last admission?"

James was taken aback. He hadn't expected this. The matron's tone was less than welcoming. Usually, when he brought Molly back, she'd be taken straight to the ward. He hadn't figured on being questioned in the matron's office.

He had less information about Molly than he knew he should have. Molly wasn't normal and that was that. He was here with the belief that they would sign her in for good this time.

Nervous, in case the matron would take it out on him, his voice quivered. He was uncomfortable around women with high-pitched voices. A legacy from his time with Nuala Bates. Screaming at him. Frightening the life out of him.

"The first I heard from Molly was three days ago, asking me to meet her from the train station. I called yourself first – then I went to Doctor O'Sullivan on Friday for the letter. And here we are."

The matron took her eyes up from the file, looking over the rim of her glasses at him.

"We didn't know what to do. She was rambling on the phone, saying she was coming back here, she couldn't manage. I thought I heard someone coughing in the background. The wife maintained that she was probably handed the phone and told to ring me. We hadn't heard a word from her since she'd left our place. She'd stay with us when it suited her over the years – then off she'd take again."

Looking over at his sister, he saw she seemed oblivious to the conversation.

"'Twould be fine for a few days, Matron. She seemed to be doing well and we were pleased when she told us that she was moving down to Ballygore. She was doing great, weren't you, Molly? And now this … barely a word. All I'm getting is the stare. We thought, with all that shock treatment, it would have bumped her out of it. We –"

"Right," said the matron, flicking through the file in front of her.

He could tell that she was growing impatient with him.

She said that she was in no doubt that the registrar upstairs would sign Molly in as a permanent patient.

Molly's brother looked at her with eyes that he knew showed his shame and helplessness.

He kept talking, trying to avoid questions that he didn't have the answers to.

"She stayed with us this time and never spoke a word, humming the same old song all the time, rocking backwards and forwards. Even the hackney driver outside was giving us queer looks. And Peggy the wife said she didn't get a wink of sleep last night, knowing that Molly was moving around next door."

Molly began to hum the tune that had settled in her head. In her heart. Oblivious to her surroundings, unable to register the conversation, she began to rock forward and backwards, forward and backwards.

Feeling braver now as the matron hadn't gone too hard on him, James continued: "Matron, she's better off here in Ultan's. We won't be worrying that she'll turn up at the door. And she hasn't much of a clue whose company she's keeping. And she always seems to have a ton of money on her, wherever she is getting it."

He looked directly at his sister, barely remembering the time years ago when he would have protected her at any cost, finding it difficult now to feel any real attachment towards his twin, who seemed to have completely lost her mind. He could take no more.

"Well, we never knew what to do. She'd be back on top of us before we knew it. Then gone again. We had no clue how to manage her. But she seemed to be much better when she took off this last time. We got up one day and she was gone. Her post-office savings book empty, left on the table. Peggy's new suitcase. Gone." James scratched the side of his head.

Molly had stopped rocking. She stared ahead, behind them, towards the wall.

"How was she doing with her medication?" asked the matron.

"Molly was not going to trust me, let alone my asking her about her tablets. We left it up to herself to go to the doctor and the chemist. She's no fool, you know, when it suits her. We couldn't be keeping tabs on her."

"Mother of God! But the reason you thought Molly was cured was that she was probably taking her medication correctly. Which meant that she was functioning well. It happens. They think they're fine and then stop taking it altogether. Because they have no one looking out for them." Matron sat up straight. "There's no point in saying much more."

"I know Molly was always different. When we were young, I don't remember taking much notice. Like I told you, we were separated when we were eight and the Bates took me in and kept me as long as I worked my backside off. There was no warmth there. I have plenty of warmth, Matron, with Peggy. All I have ever known is loss – and Molly too. But I can't lose Peggy. And I'm afraid that I will, if Molly stays in the picture." Ashamed, his head hung low.

"Very well. There is a bed ready for her at the top of

the house. I agree that we have no other choice. Molly is not able to live on her own. I will note on the file that neither yourself nor your wife are equipped to look after her. It is unlikely that there will ever be a time when the registrar will see fit to declare otherwise. Although with all the changes that are going on with this review and that review, only time will tell. Sign here and here, and the doctor upstairs will do the rest."

Taking the pen from her hand, he signed the form.

Molly didn't move. She remained in the same position. There was nothing to suggest that the conversation between the matron and her twin had registered with her.

The matron picked up the phone to make a call.

The knock came to the door within minutes and a nurse and orderly entered.

"Molly, you remember Nurse Cahill? She will take you up now and settle you in."

"OK, Molly," said the nurse, staring at the seat of the chair as Molly rose.

Molly took the arm offered to her while the male orderly picked up her suitcase.

Molly Payton walked out the door, leaving a fresh bloodstain behind her on the seat of the wooden chair.

James opened his mouth as if to speak.

The matron spoke first, having already noticed the two dried milkstains on the front of Molly's thin white blouse, noticed that her breasts had appeared engorged, swollen and heavy.

"We've it all said. Normally, as you know, it would be straight to the ward with her – but with all these changes taking place, we have to be sure."

The phone on the desk rang.

"Yes," was all the matron said then laid the receiver down. She looked at James. "It's best you leave now – we'll give her something to help her settle."

James stood up quicker than he might have.

"Oh, one last thing," he said. "When I met her at the station, she was holding on to the sleeve of her cardigan. Some old flower thing – she wouldn't let go of it. She was at it again on the way down in the car. Peggy said to mention it."

He left without looking back. Relieved to be finally free of the burden.

It would be the last time that he saw his sister.

Walking slowly down the steps towards the waiting hackney cab, he felt the heaviness in his heart. He would return home to Peggy with the news that he knew would please her. How he wished it could have been different! But it wasn't different.

He could do it no longer – Peggy couldn't cope with her and she was his life now. Best to get on with it and put it out of his mind. He had little choice if he was to have any sort of a life himself. Ignoring the tears building up in his eyes, he got into the back seat of the car.

"Off we go. Hope that wasn't too long of a wait. She's all settled in the best place."

"God, it looks like rain."

Seeing the driver roll his eyes up towards the sky and reading the look correctly, James felt ignored, even by the hackney driver. He shut up. Tears came easily, remembering a day long ago when he had sat in the back of another car, sobbing, because he had been cruelly separated from his twin. Today the anguish had returned to distress him.

* * *

The matron accepted what she had suspected. James Payton had given up on Molly. She disliked being judgmental, but life could be so unfair for vulnerable women. James might be lacking, in one sense. But at least he had someone at home waiting for him.

Too many times had she seen families relieved beyond all to have their relatives committed – social outcasts – mostly never seeing them again. People sitting in her office, all but begging her to take their family members. In many cases dumping them there.

In fairness, she had noticed the tears in James Payton's eyes. But what could he have offered Molly?

Matron opened Molly's file to add to the notes. Taking a few moments to refresh her knowledge of her background, she concluded that Molly was no different to any of the other long-termers. Her fate had been more or less sealed in two paragraphs.

It stated under her history that she had been born as a twin in 1935 in the local workhouse. Their mother had died of TB. The twins were sent together to the children's home. When they were eight years old the boy had been boarded out with the Bates family, a childless couple.

The file read that Molly had screamed uncontrollably when she received the news that her brother was boarded out. She had isolated herself, stripped, cut her arms and legs and smeared both herself and the space around her in her own excrement.

From that day forward, Molly had scarcely cried another tear, or raised her voice. She had become sullen and subdued.

The file noted that Molly's responses to life events had never been those of a normal child. She had been first admitted to Ultan's at the age of seventeen when she had lost all control of her mind, after being reunited with her twin, having spent nine years apart.

Matron closed the file. Sometimes her job was the hardest in the world. It was seldom she allowed her own feelings to creep in, but today had been one of those days. It would not happen again any time soon.

Chapter 7

The Widow and Her Child

After a year and a month had passed, Rose O'Neill could hardly contain herself as she signed the adoption papers. Daisy Jean O'Neill was legally hers. She celebrated by inviting Father Mac and Nurse O'Dwyer for tea and Victoria sponge.

Sitting in the warm kitchen where it had all begun a year before, the three marvelled at the joy the child had brought into Rose's home.

The chatter about the baby in the bag had died down with no one being the wiser – a nine days' wonder.

The nurse had called in to Rose every month at the beginning, then less regularly as time passed, happy with the way things were going for the child. Father Mac was a frequent visitor.

There hadn't been a word on Daisy's birth family. Nothing. It was as if her mother had vanished into thin air.

There would be no other babies arriving to be taken care of. Rose's life was complete. The child became the very core of the widow's existence.

Her daily trips to the graveyard were no longer essential. Daily Mass became weekly Mass.

As her priorities shifted, she felt a love for this child that she'd never known could exist. Daisy in turn reciprocated the love, looking up at her mother with nothing short of adoration in her eyes. The child was a gift, soaking up all the love and attention that Rose could give her.

The townspeople didn't question the fact that one of the widow's babies was actually growing up. The sight of the tall straight woman pushing her pram around Ballygore was no longer a given – instead they got used to seeing the woman walking hand in hand with the growing child. Even though she looked more like a posh old governess than a mother. They kept their distance.

Rose had a half-sister in the home place in Galway, who visited a couple of times a year. The visits would be planned well in advance, by letter. Rose would make sure there was nothing out of place. Daisy would be presented in her best frock, gifts would be exchanged, conversations kept light and non-invasive. Never close, the sisters were nevertheless careful in preserving the sibling relationship between them.

Each day became more of a blessing for Rose, who demonstrated from the outset that she was more fulfilled than she had ever been in her life.

She tended to her garden with her daughter at her side – filling small plastic pots, growing seeds, cutting flowers from spring to first frost. The sweet scent of lilac, blossoms swaying in the wind. The strong scent of geraniums. Honeysuckle creeping along the back wall – waiting to surprise them with cheeky flowers of yellow tinged with red. Bringing weary bulbs indoors for winter warmth. Feeding stray cats with three legs or missing ears, or eyes that sported yellow puss – they were all God's creatures, according to Rose – but they were not allowed in the house. Chasing away the bigger birds – allowing the smaller ones to feed – wondering if that was the right thing to do. Feeding the pretty ones didn't seem right, Rose said. But that's just what they did. Picking up dead baby birds when their mothers discarded them from their nests. Irony, Rose said.

Putting her good black suit away for church occasions, Rose's style of dress became less formal as the realities of daily life took hold. Her greying hair was no longer pinned up in a tight bun, becoming softer, less orderly. She introduced a splash of colour to her normally plain wardrobe, starting with a pale-lavender turban, wearing it with pride – later a multi-coloured brooch. She smiled more, much more.

It hadn't gone unnoticed with the locals that her demeanour had become less rigid, less stuck-up as she took Daisy over and back to school. She was by then relaxed enough to salute the other mothers on her way, but never comfortable enough to address them by their Christian names. Or they her. Sometimes she wished that she could open up and chat away with them, but it just wasn't in her. When she had tried to, it seemed false, forced even, and Rose decided that she would be the person that she had always been. Just herself. And if they didn't like it, they could lump it.

"Good morning, Mrs. Norton."

"Good morning, Mrs. O'Neill."

"Lovely day, Mrs. Conway."

"It is indeed, Mrs. O'Neill."

"Warmer today, Mrs. Hunt."

"Lovely cardigan, Mrs. O'Neill."

Too personal a comment for Rose – no need to reply.

Rose was never going to be one of the local women – she had no wish to be.

While being more relaxed in herself on the street, she maintained her standards when it came to tutoring Daisy. She raised her daughter the only way she knew how – old school to a fault. Having been brought up in a household where children should be seen and not heard, she brought Daisy up accordingly.

"You don't speak to grown-ups until you're spoken to and, when referring to the neighbours, or speaking to them, use their title."

"But, Mam, everyone on the road calls the neighbours by their first names – why can't I?"

"Because you are a child."

"But how will I know what title to give them?"

Rose couldn't help but smile. "Well, if the person wears trousers and looks like a man, refer to him by the title 'Mister'. If the lady has a wedding ring and has children, well, that's usually 'Missus'. It's 'Miss' for all the others. But if she wears a habit, then she's a nun, so it'll be 'Sister'."

There was a certain humour in the banter between the older mother and her child.

"And what about the priest? The new one. Just John, is it?"

The older woman would pretend to be shocked at Daisy's childish impudence – but she could never be too serious with her.

"Ah, Mam, I'm only joking – shur, I know that already."

When she had asked about her father and why there was only the two of them in the family, Rose would distract her, skilfully changing the subject.

When the time came for Daisy to start secondary school, she found it both intimidating and exciting. It had been the scariest day of her life, moving from the familiar classes of the small primary school where she had known everyone and they her, to a much bigger school where new pupils from the country schools now joined the town children.

So many changes, she was afraid that she wouldn't remember them all – fearing that she'd get lost trying to find her way around.

As she progressed in the first year, things calmed down for her as she made new friends. She liked the country children, who seemed to be calmer, less giddy than the town children.

But it wasn't long before she came up against her first real clash with her mother.

Rose had insisted on walking her to school each day. After school, she would be in the same spot, on her own, where she had left her off that morning.

Daisy would walk to the school gate with her friends, leaving them at the railing to go to her mother. She found herself becoming increasingly embarrassed and began to cringe when she'd see her there, afterwards feeling guilty for doing so.

She begged her mother to let her walk home on her own – it wasn't that far.

After constant objections from Daisy, Rose had relented by the beginning of second year.

Daisy recognised that her mother hadn't found it easy

to give her the independence that she craved – she would have preferred their uncomplicated lives to remain as they were. When Daisy asked if she could hang out around the town with the girls at the weekend, Rose refused, using the country girls as an excuse, saying that they had no choice but to go straight home on the school bus and they weren't trawling around the town at the weekends.

"You can walk home with the girls, now that you're over the first year, but no dilly-dallying, Daisy. No hanging around that town, loitering, like the crowd at Duffy's corner."

Daisy was fourteen, enjoying her new sense of freedom. Liking it, testing the boundaries – it would be enough for now. But she knew that some of the town girls were laughing at her behind her back – she had heard the comments. Her mother had become the joke of the school.

Rose's choice of preferred reading material for her daughter was far from what her friends were buying.

They had laughed in her face. "My God, Daisy, what are you reading that yoke for? That's for old wans and old lads, a matchmaker's guide for the over-forties!"

Daisy had felt like a complete fool in front of them. Nothing new there.

The girls would stop at Daisy's gate for a chat before they headed on home, knowing well that the widow was behind the net curtains – but as long as she didn't appear at the door to order Daisy in, all was fine.

It wasn't usual for them to go beyond the gate, nor was it usual for Daisy to go to their houses. They had been well warned by their parents. Rose O'Neill was as odd as two left shoes – and a snob who mollycoddled her daughter.

As she got older, Daisy began to question her mother's

logic more and more. And the girls seemed to know an awful lot more about the world than she did. Much more. She grew more embarrassed.

When it was time for Rose to instruct her on what she referred to as "the birds and the bees", it had been done in a "round-the-garden" type of manner. That's what her friends had called it. No straight facts or figures – just Rose's own take on the whole business. She said that she didn't need to read up on these matters in the modern books – human nature didn't change.

She told Daisy that she remembered her own mother passing on the same wise words to her and they hadn't let her down.

"Daisy, love, decent men may think that they are the strong ones but when it comes to it, believe me, it's the woman who holds the upper hand. A man will plough ahead – the woman can stop. If the woman says no, and he cares enough for her, he will stop. Most are decent, but there are those who are no different to animals in the jungle, no sense of control – just animal instinct."

Rose had visibly shuddered. It was more uncomfortable than she could manage all at once.

One of her distraction techniques would be to press the button on the small brown cassette player. Then the older woman and the girl would move around the kitchen to the music, as the atmosphere in the room softened.

Daisy knew that she'd be a laughing-stock at school, if her friends could see her dancing around the kitchen table with her mother, to silly old songs that they probably had never even heard of.

Rose continued to offer snippets from the past, which she remembered hearing as a girl. "I once heard a rumour that

82

a girl got pregnant when a fella put ashes in her drink."

When Daisy shared Rose's this latest piece of information with the girls they had laughed straight into her face, calling her Crazy Daisy.

One day Bernie and Anne took her aside.

"Daisy, don't be an eejit, for God's sake. Listen to us. We're trying to save you from being the laughing-stock of the whole school."

Daisy nodded in acceptance.

"For feck sake, a fella and a girl have sex – and how do you think they do it? Ashes, is it? Jesus, what a laugh! Your mam must have been born in the Dark Ages, to be coming out with all that shite!"

"He sticks his up hers, and that's that!" Anne said.

And Bernie and Anne had taken off down the road, laughing their heads off, leaving Daisy standing there.

The vision in her head as she walked home was one of confusion.

Rose was standing on a stool in the kitchen with a duster in her hand.

"Mam, you'd never guess what Bernie and Anne are after telling me about getting pregnant. Bernie said 'he sticks his up hers'. What does he stick? And where does he stick it?"

Rose stumbled off the stool, before regaining her composure.

Then, excusing herself, she left the room, leaving Daisy not just confused but disturbed at her reaction.

Soon, Daisy received a packet in the post. It contained a book: *My Dear Daughter* by Angela MacNamara.

Rose looked at Daisy, having decided to add no more than was necessary. She would leave it to the experts and would no longer be passing on her knowledge of the birds and the bees to her daughter.

"I heard her on the radio," she said. "Read it in your own time. There's more in it than I can ever teach you."

Daisy flicked through the book, finding out all she wanted to know about the female and male anatomy. She wasn't sure if she'd been ready for the detailed drawings in the book – not sure how she felt seeing it all there in front of her.

She would never forget her first introduction into the ways of the world from Bernie and Anne, and neither would Rose.

By the time Daisy celebrated her fifteenth birthday, she had become less inclined towards telling her mother everything. Sick of being the gullible, naive girl, she had become more secretive. She had to.

She loved being one of the girls at last – fitting in – no longer relying on Rose to advise her. No longer trusting her mother's words of wisdom, she learned how to sidestep, how to take risks that she knew would upset her mother – if she ever found out about them.

It hadn't taken her long to figure out that a walk down the town with the girls did not mean that she was loitering. She was just a teenager having fun.

Daisy loved her mam – but, all the same, she had learned how to cod Rose, pretending to listen and take heed, leaving Rose right where she was happiest, stuck in the past. After all, prayer had cured all, in Rose's day.

As Daisy prepared for her Leaving Certificate, they had little reason to be drawn into uncomfortable conversations. At last, Daisy thought she had it sussed.

Until the day she mentioned meeting Tom Arnold in

town. Ten years older than herself, self-assured, and most handsome. Walking around with an air about him. Tom Arnold's name was in the top three of fine things in the town. Daisy knew enough about him to want to know more.

Rose's usually pale cheeks had turned crimson. She warned her to steer clear of him, making it clear that she didn't want to hear his name mentioned in the house again. Then she walked out of the room.

It was obvious to Daisy that, whatever her mother felt about Tom, it was all nonsense. More rumours. When he asked her out on a date, she thought she was going to faint. He'd asked her out to dinner. She couldn't believe it. It was her first real date. And with Tom Arnold!

Borrowing clothes from Anne, she got ready in her house.

The dinner date was wonderful and Daisy fell in love.

She wouldn't be fool enough to mention his name at home again any time soon. But she was doing as she wished and there was nothing her mother could say or do, to make her give him up. She would soon be eighteen and could do as she liked.

Tom had changed her life, offering her a taste of his adult world. She saw him every chance that she got, in the process becoming a master at sneaking around. She could tell from her mother's attitude towards her that she knew that she was up to something. She just couldn't prove it and Daisy didn't care whether she knew now or not.

Daisy felt proud to be seen with Tom who was more of a man than any of the boys around the town of her own age. She had fallen head over heels for him. There would be no one laughing at her now. She had Tom Arnold looking out for her. He was in a different league to any of her friends and she knew it and so did they.

Going to meet Tom in the pubs in town became second nature to her. It was easier to meet him there, than have to come up with excuses as to where she was going and who she was going with. Continuing to borrow clothes from the girls whenever she felt like it, she was becoming a familiar face around the town. The locals supposed that whatever stock the girl had come from was certainly a world apart from that of the Widow Nail.

Life became much more fun as Daisy adjusted to the world outside of Rose. She was questioning many aspects of her life at home with her mam, asking Tom's opinion when she felt unsure. He didn't laugh at her. She resented her mother more and more, continuing to see Tom on the quiet.

She gradually became more defiant towards Rose, boldly dropping Tom's name here and there when she was in earshot.

Finally, no longer caring about the impact his name had on her mother, she blurted out the truth.

"Yes, I'm going out with Tom Arnold. So bloody what? And I don't care what you think, because it won't make any difference. All you've ever done is smother me, making me look like a right dope. Walking me to school by the hand and all of them laughing at us. Telling me lies and ignoring me when I asked you about my father. Remember, I'm eighteen now and ready to stand on my own two feet."

Rose could not have been more hurt. Not so much in hearing that her daughter was seeing Arnold – she had guessed as much – but Daisy had just attacked her best efforts to rear her in the only way she knew how.

The relationship between the two became more tense over the coming months.

Daisy's Leaving Cert results when they came out were a disappointment to Rose, who had hoped to steer Daisy towards a nursing course in Dublin, away from the influence of Arnold.

Daisy herself didn't care. She told Rose that she was staying in town to be near Tom and that was that. She had plenty of time to apply for a job.

Rose could see that Daisy was on a path to destruction when she came downstairs one morning to find her precious cassette recorder in pieces on the kitchen floor. It had belonged to John P and Daisy knew that. She felt deeply wounded.

Too proud to discuss her fears with another soul, too hurt to have her troubles on display, she at last hinted about her difficulties to her sister.

Her words had shocked Rose.

"Sure, you haven't a clue where she came from. She could have come from anywhere. That'll be the breeding coming out in her now. Leave her off to her own devices and get on with your life."

Rose guessed that Arnold would take the very best from Daisy before leaving her to pick up the pieces.

At last, despairing, she tackled Daisy head on.

"No class, no respect, he's a gambler and an alcoholic who treats women like dirt. Stay clear of him. I can't live your life for you, but I can tell you now that he's no good."

Daisy gave her back as good as she got. "Shur you haven't a clue. Who may I ask would be telling you anything? You haven't a soul to talk to!"

"I have eyes and ears of my own, Daisy."

Whenever she could, Daisy took the opportunity to lash out at her mother.

"You're giving out that Tom is far too old for me. So how old are you exactly? The girls are saying that you're about the same age as their grandmothers. And they said you look pure stupid – going around like the Queen of Sheeba with the turban on top of your head."

She reminded Rose of the many times that she had distracted her when she asked questions that Rose was not prepared to answer.

"You made me out to be stupid, with your 'don't be bothering your little head about adult stuff now, Daisy. Let's think about what we'll have for tea, Daisy'."

Daisy's voice became animated as she taunted her mother.

"All my friends had summer jobs – except me, of course. Because you wouldn't let me, in case I'd get in with the wrong crowd or get pregnant."

Rose continued to have her say – her daughter's relationship with Arnold would lead to nothing but pain and regret.

Daisy replied by saying that she had certainly learned the hard way, finding out that most of the stuff she had been taught at home from Rose had been fiction and lies.

She continued to wound her mother with as many jibes as she could think of.

"You do know what the girls call you – or do you? They say that you're way too old to be my mother. An old hag."

Rose hid her hurt and still tried to reach Daisy with the hard facts. "You'll have nothing only trouble at your door, with the likes of that one. His father and grandmother before him were alcoholics, drinking in doorways, and he's no different. I've seen them in their day, falling out of the pubs in broad daylight."

All to no avail.

***

Two years had passed since she had met Tom. She was nineteen, confiding in Tom, repeating back to him what her mother was saying about him. Telling him that Rose didn't want her to have anything to do with him. Feeling smart as she repeated to him more than she thought she should. Saying things about her mother to him was making her feel good – in control – making her feel that he understood her position.

Chapter 8

Mind Games

Tom Arnold worked as a sales representative for a company that produced work coats. Workcoat Ltd. There since the start, he had been asked by the director to take a reduction in pay, to get the company off its feet.

He had agreed. Having worked hard in the early years, Tom was promoted along with four others, to Middle Management.

While it felt good at the time, it was more of a copout as far as he was concerned. He would have much preferred a title of his own, such as senior executive. He deserved it above anyone else, but he knew that senior management were just being clever. Trying to make the men feel important. Promoting them. To nothing. There had been no pay rise – no status. Just Middle Management. A weekly meeting with the bosses on a Friday evening and off to the pub straight afterwards. Where they felt like real men, standing around in their business suits, full of their own importance.

The company had surpassed all expectations.

Workcoat Ltd. had become the leading supplier of work clothing. Orders were coming in at a pace much faster than they could deliver on. They were refusing orders, demand far greater than supply.

Recognising the opportunity, Tom seized the chance to set up his own sideline business. He would be his own senior executive. Hadn't he worked his backside off? And to what end?

He would produce and sell the same work coats under his own company brand. *Coats by Thomas*. Perfect. Sourcing the material wasn't difficult – he had the contacts already on his books. Being on the road every day, he would use the company car. The petrol was paid for – lunch receipts covered. All expenses paid. Best of all – fake invoices. A win-win situation and people trusted him.

Two of the machinists at the factory were more than willing to work from home until he found a suitable workshop. Sorting out a couple of industrial machines from the storehouse wouldn't be difficult.

Daisy had turned out to be an expert at producing small print in black ink. Giving her a few of Workcoat's invoices to use as templates, she had practised until she had perfected the art. Often he had to look twice himself, to see which ones were which. She was only happy to be helping him out and pleased to be earning a few pounds for herself.

What was there not to like about being Tom Arnold, he'd ask himself. Hadn't he a steady job and his own business on the side, a best friend and a girl that would bend over backwards for him?

Before persuading Daisy to move in with him, he had

to ensure that she had cut all ties with her mother. If the widow wasn't having anything to do with him, then she wouldn't be having anything to do with Daisy either. The Widow Nail would rue the day she had badmouthed him. Anyway, he didn't want that old witch thinking that she could turn up at the flat, whenever it took her fancy.

Coaxing Daisy to stay a few nights in the flat with him had been easier than he had expected. One thing Tom knew how to do was turn on the charm when it suited him. He sent Daisy back home, having spiked her drink with just enough vodka to make her merry. No smell. A tried and tested trick that he'd used many a time, when a bird might need the edges knocked off her. It had served him well enough.

Daisy had mentioned that the widow would be waiting up for her. Tom sniggered at the thought of the old woman accusing her daughter of drinking alcohol – Daisy denying it of course, insisting that all she'd had was a couple of soft drinks.

The result was a huge row. Rose had accused her daughter of deliberately lying to her, being underhanded, insisting that Daisy had drink on her. While Daisy continued to swear on all their lives that she hadn't touched a drop.

The damage was done. Not long afterwards Daisy began to drink in earnest and returned home on the following morning after spending the night at the flat with Tom, aggravating her mother, knowing that she didn't look like she'd had a good night's sleep, dishevelled, smelling of alcohol … and with a colourful love bite on the side of her neck. Secretly proud of the stamp, she had intended to hide it from Rose, and then forgot. Rose clearly noticed it but said nothing.

After that, her mam seemed to finally accept that things had changed between them and carried on, going about her business as usual, her head held high. She gave up on phoning Daisy at the flat when she didn't arrive home. Knowing Rose as well as she did, Daisy figured her pride prevented her from picking up the phone. 'Pride suffers pain' was one of Rose's many sayings – well, now let her feel the pain.

On a good day, Daisy was well aware of how much she was loved by Rose. But in her heart she knew that Tom would never be accepted by her. It had been a hard choice, but one that she felt she had to make.

Finally, Rose gave her an ultimatum. Daisy knew that she had done so out of sheer frustration, that she hadn't known what else to do.

She had said that it was too late for Daisy. Saying that she was the talk of the town as it stood. And no self-respecting girl would move in with a man, any man, without having a wedding band on her finger. Living in sin with the likes of Tom, in Rose's eyes, was as low as she could go.

"I will tell you now, Daisy O'Neill, that so-and-so will never be welcome in this house … and neither will you if you marry him. If you end up as his wife, you'll be sorry. You'll have made your bed and you can lie on it, because you'll no longer be welcome here. *There*, I've said it."

Their relationship had become so strained it was easier on them both to stop talking altogether. Daisy believed that Rose meant everything she said. She had no reason to think otherwise.

She simply adored Tom. She was so proud of him. He was established, distinguished-looking, mature. When he scolded her, for one reason or another, she saw no harm in it – it was just for her own good. Like telling her to take her foot off the side of the stool – saying that it was bad manners.

But when he asked her why she hadn't changed her clothes before going out, she was surprised and said she had. In fact, she had made an extra effort and was feeling that she looked good.

No. Denim jeans were not for going out in, according to Tom. They were for workmen.

She changed. Compliant.

She was Tom's girl now. She would do anything for him.

Pretending to support Rose, Tom subtly persisted in leading Daisy to resent her mother's attitude towards their relationship.

He was anything but pleased as Daisy continued to tell him about the arguments at home. But he wasn't upset for her. Tom Arnold was fuming that the widow was still going on about him. She was relentless. So, she wanted her daughter to have nothing to do with him? Nobody treated Tom Arnold like dirt and got away with it. *Nobody.* And no woman was going to stop Tom Arnold from getting what he wanted.

By keeping the mother and daughter apart, he would conquer them both. He soon had Daisy exactly where he wanted her.

Once Tom was sure that he had loosened the grip that the widow had on Daisy, he began to add his own few words to the mix, knowing that Daisy listened to him, heeded his words. She had no idea of the lengths that he was prepared to go to destroy her relationship with her mother.

After a night in the pub, he listened as Daisy told him about the latest threat to come from her mother. Once again he pretended to defend Rose, reminding Daisy that she was probably just looking out for her. The woman was no fool – he would keep on her side in front of Daisy. For now.

Away from his girlfriend, he had a different tale to tell. No "bitch of a woman" was going to keep Tom Arnold from doing as he wanted. The cheek of that one, to say that he wasn't welcome in her house! He had her now, where he wanted her, on the outside.

He assured Daisy that he loved her and would take care of her, no matter what was said about him.

He said he could afford to look for a house for them. Between his job and the profits from his little company, they would manage. And there was plenty more where that came from.

He then said that he was not going to be left waiting for months for cheques to arrive in the post. Daisy could travel with him on the days the payments were due. Hand-delivering the invoices, showing her face, collecting the checks. Finally no longer depending on Rose. He would pay her for each check collected. It worked. Even she herself admitted she was amazed at how good she was at collecting what was due.

Shopping more often, buying new clothes, she couldn't remember a time she'd felt as good about herself. After spending three years going out with Tom, Daisy was having the time of her life.

Buying the monthly issue of *Cosmopolitan*, which kept

her up to speed on fashion and topics of interest to women, the stylish girl walked through the town with her head held high, no longer the innocent daughter of the Widow O'Neill. She'd laugh when she read articles in the magazine that she knew would make Rose blush – blushing herself, realising that she still had a lot to learn.

The word *sex* was mentioned several times in each issue. Abortion, contraception, pre-menstrual tension – it was all in there. And explained. Subjects that she would never have dreamt of, never mind asking Rose about them. Rose would never have tolerated such magazines in her home. She would have seen them as trashy and sinful, just another bad influence. There was even a list of abortion clinics in England on the inside of the back page. Termination was the word used. When she saw it first she'd thought it sounded like a train journey.

It was her turn to enjoy the look of shock on her friends' faces, when she brought up subjects that even they weren't comfortable discussing.

Her past had been shrouded in avoidance and ignorance and she was done with that.

Chapter 9

The Trap

When she began to feel queasy in the mornings, she couldn't bring herself to tell her mam. Too much had happened between them. Ignoring the thought that she might be pregnant was not difficult. The arguments had reached breaking point. It made it easier for her to agree to moving into a new house with Tom. The flat was too small for the two of them.

"Eight weeks gone," the doctor told her, as he worked out her due date.

There was no delight – she didn't know what to do.

Anxious, her heart pounding, she told Tom.

He hadn't flinched.

"We'd better get married so, I suppose."

With Rose out of the picture, Daisy knew that she had little choice. The shame attached to being single with a baby was not an option she could consider. People in a small town were all too quick to judge. She would be stared at and talked about. The baby illegitimate.

And she wouldn't give it to say to Rose that she had been right all along. Pride before a fall, as Rose would say.

The following day, they drove to the city where Daisy picked out a small cluster of diamonds. The couple were engaged.

Daisy was hugely relieved but knew that she should have been happier than she was. Something inside was holding her back. She ignored it.

Tom said he had to tell his mother and introduce Daisy to her before word got out. They drove to the house at dusk – he had suggested that it would be best if it wasn't in broad daylight. The plan had been to tell her once they were settled with a cup of tea in the kitchen.

But, as the car pulled into the driveway he changed his mind, deciding that the news would be best coming from Daisy herself. She was too shocked to reply.

"I can't tell my mother that you're pregnant – I just can't," he said. "You tell her. I'd feel awful weird talking about that stuff. Here she is – do it quick. I'll go on in."

He got out of the car and walked quickly towards the house.

"Ma, this is Daisy. Sit in there for a minute, she wants to have a word with you."

Daisy looked at the low-sized woman who was about to sit into the car beside her – her thin thighs were the first thing she noticed. Wearing a short red miniskirt, pulling her bright-yellow cardigan across her ample chest with one hand, she held the top of the door open with the other. Mutton dressed as lamb, as Rose would have said.

Tom's mother smiled at her, fixing the clips on her jet-black hair as she spoke.

"Oh! All right. Pleased to meet you, Daisy. My God, what an introduction! And the hair like a bush on top of my head. Tom has kept you well hidden. He told me about you on the phone. You're the Widow Nail – Mrs. O'Neill's daughter then. What do you want to talk to me about, love?"

As she waited to hear what Daisy had to say, she shouted after her son, who was already at the front door of the house.

"Tom! Put the kettle on! There's a packet of biscuits in the press!"

She sat into the driver's seat.

"Well, what's up? A fine introduction, I must say … that's my lad for you. I'd heard all right that you were in the flat with him."

Daisy could hardly hear what the woman was saying. The smell of her perfume made her want to gag. She just wanted to hurry up and get it out, into the open. Here she was sitting in the car, with a woman she had just met, about to confide in her a secret that would affect their whole lives.

"I'm pregnant, Mrs. Arnold." She could feel the sweat springing out on her forehead. She lowered her head.

Tom's mother looked straight out of the front window.

"I see," she said. Any warmth that may have been in her voice before now had gone. She had the door opened and was halfway out of the car when she looked back at Daisy. "I take it there's no doubt that it's Tom's? Right?"

Daisy didn't answer. She felt humiliated and more uncomfortable than ever in her life before. Rose's face came into her mind.

"You'd better come in, I suppose," Tom's mother said.

As the two women entered the kitchen, Tom was taking mugs out of the cupboard.

"Tea, Ma? Tea, Daisy?"

Putting the milk carton down on the table, his mother sat and spoke to the room. "Well, this is some shock, isn't it now?"

She stared at Daisy, who felt as if she were on trial. The woman probably thought that she had snared her innocent son into this situation.

Tom held up Daisy's left hand, showing his mother her engagement ring.

"A bit small for an engagement ring, isn't it? I suppose ye'll have to get married straight away. How far are you gone?

"Two months. Just."

"So the wedding will be sooner rather than later."

The look on Sally Arnold's face said it all.

"Remember, there's decent people living around us. There'll be no wedding anniversary celebrations in the future. It'll be anniversary, or the child's birthday, not both –"

She paused mid-sentence, lost in thought, making a familiar speech that she herself had heard somewhere in the past.

She poured the tea, without making eye contact with the couple in front of her.

"More shame for the family. We're bad enough as it is, trying to hold our own after your father went. We'll just have to get on with it." She looked at Daisy. "And what has your own mother to say about all this? Tom tells me ye don't talk anymore. I believe she was always causing trouble, badmouthing my family. The very nerve of her! And is she expecting my Tom to fund you? Have you even got a job?"

Daisy kept her head down – how much had he told her? She couldn't reply.

"That's enough about it now, have the tea. We'll get on with it and keep our heads held high." The frustration in her voice was clear. Looking across at Tom, she said, "I haven't seen very much of you either. A few bob here and there wouldn't go astray. Now that your lady here is in the family way, don't forget who reared you!"

Daisy felt like she had committed the greatest crime. Demeaned and embarrassed, she didn't know what to say. She felt at the mercy of this woman whom she had just met. How she missed her own mother! Even though it would be a bigger shock for Rose, she doubted that she would make her feel the shame and humiliation that Mrs. Arnold just had.

She was also trying her best to ignore the cowardice in Tom, who had left her to face his mother.

She didn't know him as well as she had thought. He had let her down.

Chapter 10

The Happy Couple

Everything happened quickly after that. The following week the parish priest had given the couple a date to get married, three weeks later. There was no pre-marriage course – there was no time.

Emmet Roche would be Tom's best man. Emmet had been Tom's friend since they were boys.

Daisy's bridesmaids would be her two best friends, Anne and Bernie. The other guests were to be made up of Tom's family and friends.

Rose was excluded, as were others. Tom had been successful in cutting them out of their lives.

"We'll be grand, Daisy. Small wedding, sure what the hell? Unless you've the cash to cover a bigger one, that is. Would your mother like to chip in, I wonder?"

Daisy was sick most of the days as she prepared for her wedding. Tom didn't concern himself. She felt that she was annoying him.

The couple were married in the small chapel in town

and the reception was held in the hotel dining room. Twenty people had received invitations.

Daisy would have liked to invite people that she had known since her childhood but she couldn't, as her mother had been excluded. It was easier in the end to let Tom organise the wedding.

"We have a mortgage to secure if I'm to buy a place. I'm not made of money – if we invite one outsider, we'll have to invite them all. Anyway, you've the two girls there, so you can't say they're all from my side."

Bernie and Anne were quieter than ever she had known them to be.

They had guessed that she was pregnant. They called her to one side before the ceremony.

"Daisy, look, we know you love Tom," Bernie said. "But are you sure in your heart that you want to marry him?"

"We'll help you in whatever way we can, but please don't go through with this … if you've any doubts at all," Anne pleaded. "It's not too late to change your mind."

Daisy didn't answer, even though she knew that she should be defending her husband-to-be. The girls were just jealous, she decided. She loved Tom and, even if she *was* rushing into things, Rose didn't deserve the shame of having an unmarried daughter with a child. Of course she would marry Tom. The niggling doubts that were surfacing inside her were just pre-marriage nerves. But there was no real excitement in her – no pleasure to be had in standing there, pregnant, in a lace wedding dress that had been bought in a hurry.

The smell of whiskey from his breath as they made their vows made her want to throw up.

Tom's mother left straight after the ceremony.

***

Daisy had been eleven weeks pregnant on her wedding day.

A week later, she lost the baby.

Brokenhearted, pining for her baby, left with a longing for what might have been, the dreadful sense of loss that she felt she carried alone. She was confused with the way things had turned out for her. Had she let him down? Let herself down? Tricked him into marrying her, just as Sally Arnold had implied? She was lonely, sad, in need of comfort. It was not coming from her husband. Too ashamed to call her friends, after the advice that they had given her on her wedding day, Daisy felt truly alone.

Rose's voice was echoing in her ears: she had made her bed and now she must lie on it.

Moving out of town had been Tom's plan all along. When he spoke about buying a house, it was always going to be in the country. He had plans and that included expanding his mini-company.

A house with a large work shed would be ideal. He would expand his business at the back of the house – nobody would be the wiser. It was safer in the longer term than continuing to work from town.

Daisy had come to believe that she too wanted the move. It wasn't as if she was leaving her family and friends behind her. Being in Ballygore was just a constant reminder that her mother was within walking distance of her at any given time. But out of bounds.

Taking driving lessons was the next step, once she had recovered from her miscarriage. Tom told her that it would keep her mind occupied. He had his eye on a property on the outskirts of Ballygore. He would buy her a runabout when she had passed her driving test.

They moved into their new home four miles out from town at the end of April. Daisy had just turned twenty-one. Tom joked that it was her birthday present. Key to the door. It had been a straight deal, made over a bar counter. There had been no auctioneers involved and the bank approved the mortgage.

Daisy saw the inside of the house for the first time the day after Tom had made the deal. She couldn't believe her eyes. Standing with her arm on the windowsill of her new home, she breathed in the air, with a sense of pride that was new to her. Finally, something to look forward to. She was excited. Tom told her to take it easy.

"Once we're settled, you can see what's out there. No wife of mine needs be depending on anyone so we'd better get you your own set of wheels to get around as soon as you pass that test."

She had mentioned to him that the girls wouldn't have a problem giving her a lift in and out of town when she needed one. She was secretly hoping that they would get in touch with her and had every intention of calling them once she'd settled in. But the idea put Tom in bad humour so eventually she gave up.

Instead he mentioned her friends a few times, particularly when he was drunk. He was becoming more vulgar and demeaning towards her.

"Guess who I bumped into in town – the Healy one and her mate. Jesus! They're two right tramps! And no allegiance to you, I might add."

"Why, what did they say?" Unsure if she wanted the answer.

He laughed. "Say? Well, does trying to get off with your husband count? You stupid bitch!"

She didn't know whether to believe him but, in any case, she was wounded that he was using it as a stick to beat her with.

Now that Rose was out of the picture, having full control over his wife, Tom intended to keep it that way. He had been getting tired of listening to Daisy go on about missing her two friends, whom she hadn't heard from since the wedding in February. They had been cooling off for some time before that. And it was now September. He had told her that they were just jealous. Two old maids, he'd called them. Adding that they would more than likely end up on the shelf. Tramps, the two of them, he'd said.

By making the girls feel uneasy in his presence, it didn't take long for them to step away. He had seen them at the wedding, whispering to Daisy – he didn't trust either of them around her. She could meet whom she liked in town but neither of the two of them were welcome in his home.

Brushing the back of his hand over the curve of Bernie's rear end a few times had done the trick for him. The first time he apologised, the second time it was she who apologised. The third time she had stalked away. Gone.

Anne, who had remained in touch longer than Bernie, had drifted away as well. One night, in the pub, he had overheard her saying that Tom Arnold gave her the creeps. He'd winked at her with a look on his face which he knew unsettled her. Eyeing her up and down. Fixing his gaze on her breasts for a few seconds and then her privates. Then giving her the eye.

Yes, it had been easy, He'd had such a laugh as he taunted them separately. No need to open his mouth. He had enjoyed making them feel uncomfortable. Better still, Daisy hadn't an idea of what was going on. Neither of them would have the guts to go to her – they would be half afraid of him to do so. And what could they say anyway? That he had made a pass at them? Looked at them crooked? Given them the eye? Daisy had been so blinded by him that she would never believe either of them, over her husband. Daisy told him everything anyway.

He had them cleared out of the picture in no time. He had got to them. Each in her own way intimidated by him, their relationship with Daisy had become strained – the desired effect. It had been nothing more than a game to him.

Daisy was eager to keep the peace.

"I might look for a proper job, something part-time – I can still do the invoices in the evenings," she said, trying to impress her husband, letting him know that she wasn't just using him. Nervous in a sense, knowing that her career prospects were limited. "Maybe I'll do a course – go back to education."

No response to that ever so she stopped saying it.

But, true to his word, he bought her a used car within weeks of her passing the test. Delighted that he had gone to the trouble, she wouldn't complain, but she would have preferred to have picked the car herself – she wouldn't have chosen bright red.

Tom hadn't given it a second thought – he had paid cash for the small red car. He said that he wouldn't have to be under pressure, bringing her here or there, or collecting her from town. He'd have more freedom and wouldn't be at her beck and call. Joking with her that he would easily spot the car if she were in town, checking up on him.

Having the car was her joy. She got used to its colour and called it by name: Red. She loved it – taking off when she felt like it, talking to it while driving, singing along with the radio. Sad songs, songs that made her cry. Or happy songs, songs that made her want to dance. All depending on her mood. Stopping for coffee if she bumped into someone she knew. Light conversation. Always home around six o clock, knowing that if her car wasn't back in the yard Tom would head back in to the pub ... but only if he had come home himself in the first place.

The house had been bought so quickly that she hadn't had time to think before they'd moved in. There had been no discussion about the interior, or indeed any part of the house.

Initially delighted, she began to see its flaws – many flaws.

Tom saw nothing wrong with it. "Jesus, are you at it again? Are you ever satisfied? I put a roof over your head. Here am I trying to sort out my business plan and all you do is complain!"

He ignored her decorating ideas – and, much worse, insisted on pouring cement on much of the lawn at the front – no need for grass – too much time needed to look after it. Resisting, she couldn't believe that he would destroy the garden, where he knew she would be happy. But he did.

The house had an old feel to it. The decor was old-fashioned – large patterned carpets, yellow and green rubber tiles in the hallway, black spots on some of the walls. The bathroom walls wouldn't hold the new wallpaper – it had peeled off within weeks. The smell of mildew never seemed to leave her nostrils.

Daisy never felt at home. It felt like someone else's house. Tom said it was perfect.

Rose's house, even though it was old, had always been a warm, bright spacious house with high coved ceilings and lots of light. Daisy tried hard not to compare. How she wished that she could turn the clock back!

Tom Arnold couldn't relax in his own home – he said he couldn't anyway. He rarely took his jacket off when he came in, unless he was going to bed. She hadn't really noticed as he was always on the move. Coming in or going out, seldom home. Daisy would joke that it was a bed and breakfast that she was running.

She was feeling very lonely within a few months of her marriage. Weary. She had not contemplated just how miserable her life would become.

It had begun slowly and sporadically. Slow enough to give her time between episodes to forgive him. Had she overreacted? Space enough to give him time enough not to feel remorse. Dismissing her. Throwing food at her. The odd push. A light slap across the side of her head.

Getting more serious. Holding her head under the tap. Punching her. Lifting her straight off the floor with his two hands around her neck. Justification enough to make it all seem like it was her fault. She had believed him in the beginning.

The newly married couple were moving from one serious argument to the next. Tom Arnold was beating his wife. The chase was well over for him.

Rarely needing an excuse to humiliate her, all she had

to do was look crooked at him at the wrong moment. Demeaning her, constantly calling her names – *an insecure fucking parasite – an ugly bitch – a whore*. Reminding her that she had no qualifications. No money. Nothing.

Rose's words came flooding back to Daisy.

She held on to a flicker of hope that he would come home one day, and all would be fine. It was a dream that returned to comfort her. Knowing that as long as she had that dream, she wouldn't be going anywhere.

Tom's drinking was getting worse. Sometimes she thought that it hadn't changed at all – that she was just seeing him for what he was.

The work shed at the back of the house remained locked up. He said he was too busy to do anything about it for now. He continued to ramble on about his great plan, his drinking getting out of hand.

Sometimes on good days when her husband was sober, she was living with the best part of him. When he showed any kindness towards her, she would be so relieved that she gave him the very best of herself without question. But she seldom saw that part of him anymore.

Allowing him to get away with insulting her, pushing her about, she realised that she wasn't doing herself any favours. The beatings and aggressive behaviour towards her became more frequent. She knew what was coming most of the time.

To give out about her life with him would be futile – she had been so adamant that she wanted to be with him. Naively believing that Tom was highly regarded, there would be nothing to be achieved by telling anyone that he was beating her. There would be no saviours. It would be she who would look bad.

Over time she learned how to hide her feelings, recalling her mother's words – "You've made your bed, now you can lie on it" – refusing to show him the face of the victim that she knew she was.

"Well, little Miss Fucking Know-all, so tell me where your whoring friends are now?"

Coming so close to her face – his eyes an inch from hers. The brown stains around his lips stale and dry. His breath stinking of stale booze. She hated him.

"I will tell you where, will I? They're fucking miles away from you, that's where. They're not bothered to keep in touch with you, cos they see you for the whining bitch that you are."

There would be no stopping him now.

"You're lucky, so you are. I'm the only one who cares about you in the world and that's growing thin, I can tell you. Mama Rose gave up on you, didn't she? I said, *didn't she*? Are you deaf now as well as everything else?"

He pushed her into the corner where she fell sideways to the floor.

Kicking her in the back as she tried to get up, he drew his foot up the second time to repeat the act.

But the look in her eyes made him hesitate.

She had taken enough from him. She stared at him with more contempt in her eyes than she had ever shown anyone. Eyes that bore right through him. There was no fear there.

Seeing that, he was unsure how to react.

She spoke in a slow measured voice. Beyond fear.

"Have you finished for today?" she sneered at him, holding his gaze. "Oh! There's another one coming?"

The look on his face was enough.

Taking the kick, she would never let him see fear in her eyes again.

He turned, then spat back on her.

Spittle trickling down the side of her face, she feigned a smile, but not with her eyes.

He walked out and started the car. She hoped that he would never come back.

In the earlier days she would have done anything to protect her relationship, believing against all the odds that it was Tom and her against the world. She had been too young and naive. She had adored him. Now everything looked different – thinking about the last few years with him, the constant battles and humiliations. The times when she had been stupid enough to believe in him. The time when she had followed him into town begging him to come home with her, being humiliated without even realising it. Times when the best that could happen would be that he wouldn't come home for a few days.

Living in the flat in town had been easier – she wasn't so isolated. There had been fun times, laughter. Looking back, she realised that the signs had been there, she just hadn't seen them.

She had kept pots on the small balcony to the back of the flat, filled with geraniums, one of her mam's favourite plants in the summer. He said they smelt like cats' piss, emptying the pots out over the railing. There had been no sign of them on the lane the next day. She'd hoped they had gone to a good home.

Chapter 11

Torture Chamber

Two miscarriages since moving to the house, both as a direct result of the beatings. The first not long after they'd moved. Suggesting to him that they get a new bed had been enough to set him off. Lifting the mattress off, he caught her without warning, shoving her across the base of the bed. Quickly lifting the mattress up again, he replaced it, down on top of her.

She couldn't move, the weight of the mattress holding her pregnant body in place. Her head sticking out the side, face down. She thought that she would suffocate. She couldn't catch her breath. She was lying on her front.

"The baby!" she cried. *"The baby ... mind the baby!"* She was shouting now with all her might. Struggling. Screaming.

She had sworn that she would never allow him to see fear in her eyes again. This time the terror she felt through every fibre of her being was not for herself – it was for her unborn child.

He had lain on top of it, picking up the nearest thing

he could find on the nightstand. He wanted to shut her up. Her voice was getting on his nerves. A bottle of fizzy orange. He poured it into her ears as she wiggled to free herself. It had been the worst torture. The noise of the bubbling liquid in her ears was beyond all. She couldn't move. She was going to die.

She lost her second baby. Putting her favourite maternity dress back on its hanger, she was devastated.

Six months later she was cleaning out the linen cupboard. He came in behind her. Turning, she told him that she had been invited to a birthday party in town, but he said it was too short notice. There was no reason given. Answering him back, she told him that she was going whether he liked it or not. He reached in behind her and, with one jolt, removed a narrow length of wood from its position in the cupboard.

He raised it to hit her. She was too quick for him. Off out the front door and down the road. Running at speed with him after her. But not fast enough.

Twice was enough to hit her – she lost the baby the day after.

Cars had driven past, the drivers minding their own business. People who didn't want to get involved.

He had collected her from the hospital, insisting that if she signed herself out on the day they "cleared her womb" – he would take her out for a nice meal in the hotel. On one condition: the miscarriage would never be mentioned again. She gave him her word, before hanging her favourite blue maternity dress back in the wardrobe once again.

Then there was the night she went to the hotel looking for him, thinking that she had upset him. Some awkward words had passed between them that morning. She'd wondered if he was up to something but maybe not. He'd stormed out of the house, banging the door hard. She'd heard the car rattling over the cattle grid. Feeling sad and anxious, she wondered what she had done this time. She decided that if he didn't arrive home she would find him and try talking to him.

At one o'clock she went into town. His car was parked outside the River Hotel. Ringing the bell, she waited for the night porter to let her in, believing that Tom was drinking in the late bar.

It took more than a few minutes for the man in the black jacket to appear. Red in the face, spluttering and muttering to himself, no eye contact. She explained that she was there to meet her husband, Tom Arnold.

He said, "I'll show you where he is," and led her up the stairs.

Tom had booked a room for the night. He'd had no notion of coming home.

Feeling bad, she followed the man towards the white door at the end of the corridor.

He knocked on the door, before gently pushing it open.

"All right, Tom? It's the missus!" said the man with the red face in the black jacket.

Daisy couldn't see inside very well. The familiar smell of heavy stale booze hanging in the air. She saw him in the bed, her instinct being for a second to get in beside him. She didn't.

Her eyes became used to the darkened room as she looked around.

Bedclothes strewn over the bed and floor.

He sat up, clearing his throat.

"What the hell are you doing here, Daisy?" he asked.

Not in a harsh voice. In a voice that had her fooled into thinking he wasn't cross with her.

She lay down beside him. It smelled. But she was used to the smell of stale stout from him – it didn't matter. She was almost grateful. She made an attempt to hug him, but he was having none of it.

"You shouldn't have come here," he said, turning his back to her. "Get up now, out of here!"

"Tom, look, I'm sorry. I just wanted to make an effort to make things right between us."

He kept insisting that she go home.

Eventually, she persuaded him to come home with her, relieved that she didn't have to suffer the embarrassment of walking out without him.

The man in the black jacket nodded at Daisy's husband as he opened the heavy black door to let the couple out. Tom nodded back, winking, pressing a ten-pound note into his hand.

The man put the crumpled tenner in his trouser pocket as he headed back up the side stairs towards Room 22. If only he had a tenner for all the times he'd helped a man out of a messy situation in the hotel.

He could hear the banging well before he opened the door. He turned the key in the wardrobe and she scrambled out.

Kicking a stray pillow out of her way, her face was as red as his. Her straw-coloured hair stuck to her face with the sweat that she had found herself in. Her fleshy arms were bare and exposed – as was the rest of her.

He thought that she must be twenty stone. Too big for the wardrobe. Small wonder she hadn't brought it crashing down on top of her.

Karen Boland cursed at the man in the black jacket.

"Tramp," he muttered under his breath.

She was too busy talking to hear him.

"The other fucker is well gone, I suppose – shower of bastards – the minute that one comes along, Karen is fucked into the wardrobe!"

The man in the black jacket stood there, as she picked up the clothes that had been thrown into the wardrobe after her. Bra around her neck, she tried to cover herself with the pillow – too late, it didn't hide very much. Retrieving her black pants from the wardrobe floor, she looked as if she didn't know whether to scream or to cry. She tugged and pulled at her trousers which were inside out, caught up in her underwear.

Making a gesture with her hand, she shooed the man in the black jacket out of the room. "Get out of here now, you pervert! I'll sort myself out. I hope you've had a good fucking gawk for yourself."

She banged the door shut behind him.

"Ignorant bitch!" he said. She could find her own way down to the lobby.

Karen dressed herself. Having separated her tights from her trouser legs, she stuffed them into her trenchcoat pocket. The quicker she got out of there now, the better.

She was seething. Furious. The minute that Tom's wife came along, she had become surplus to requirements – fucked into the wardrobe like a rag doll.

The bastard wouldn't even let her hide in the

bathroom – in case Daisy decided she needed to use it.

"*Daisy!* What a stupid fucking name anyway – *Daisy*. Daisy, my arse!"

Karen had known Tom Arnold for years – they had often hooked up for a few hours together. It used to be the front of his car, down a side road – hard to manoeuvre but they always seem to manage. Tom was no lightweight, neither was she. Later, when they could afford to book a room to spend a few hours, that's what they did.

The only time she got to be with him was when he was well oiled. Half of the time he seemed to be more interested in looking into a half glass of brandy than at her. But she knew how to handle a man. A whisper in his ear at the top end of the bar was usually all it took. He'd go to the phone on the counter to book a room. Promises, promises, she thought. 'Twas more in the mind than anything else with Tom.

Karen was getting a bit fed up of his company anyway. It wasn't as if he was a stud – she'd had better, and a lot better, but he was a well above what was on offer at home.

Giving herself a few minutes to compose herself, she was hoping that there wouldn't be anyone left in the bar.

Well, that was the last time that she would be shuttled to the fucking wardrobe at the River Hotel. Wife or no wife. Karen Boland thought more of herself than to be treated like a common whore.

The man in the black jacket looked relieved as he opened the heavy door to let her out. She guessed that there would be no checking up and down the street, as he had probably done for Arnold and his missus not fifteen minutes before – no doubt he was thinking she was in the right frame of mind to puck anyone that might try to accost her as she walked to her car.

Off home with her and no one would be the wiser.

Tonight had been a close shave, there was no doubt. She'd had barely two minutes to get into the wardrobe after the night porter had banged at the door to warn Tom. Just in the nick of time.

Tom went off to work on the following morning, Daisy remaining at home. The good wife. She could collect her car later.

There were times when she wished that she had a real job to go to, but she knew Tom expected her to stay put and look after the house. He paid the bills – she looked after the house.

He had told her that his father had left for England when he was seven, to find work on the building-sites, leaving himself and his mother on their own. That was the last they'd heard from him.

Tom made out his mother was entirely to blame. If she had been at home for them when he came home in the evenings, his father wouldn't have fecked off. He said that she was always on the road – mad for the high life – they never knew where she was half of the time. No way, he told her, was he having his wife gallivanting around the town whenever it suited her.

Daisy thought about what a fool she'd been, thinking that she could in some way make up for the loss of his father. Staying at home. Trying to be the exact opposite of his mother. When he himself was nearly a carbon copy of her.

On occasions when she had gone out with him, it was seldom without issue. She seemed to be always covering up something – or someone else was covering up for him. The men he drank with protected each other. And then there were the many whose wives covered for them, wives around long enough to get the measure of husbands who didn't respect them enough to put them first, wives who hung on to their marriages in name only, carrying their load. Wives who chose to ignore the behaviour of husbands, protecting their households at any cost. Just for the sake of the children.

She was close to joining their ranks.

Nobody called to the house – except Tom's mother the odd time. Unannounced. Usually looking for a handout from her son.

While there, she would take ample opportunity to undermine Daisy, usually commenting on whatever dinner was drying up in the oven. Advising that a plate on a pot of hot water would do a far better job – keeping the dinner from drying out.

Daisy began to leave the dinners there – in the oven. Drying out. Stockpiled. Some unrecognisable. Sally Arnold was anything but impressed. Daisy had sniggered to herself.

Anything to break the monotony.

When someone rang the doorbell, Daisy would nearly jump out of her skin.

One day the Public Health Nurse called, asking about one of her neighbours. Daisy told her that she didn't know anyone in the area. She invited her in for tea. The woman was surprised. She accepted.

"So you're here in the country, in the house most days, and you don't know anyone around you. Have you any friends?"

"Of course. I go to town to meet them – I'm no recluse. I just don't come from a big family. Tom's mother Sally calls, or we go to see her. But my husband makes up for me – he's the social one."

Daisy's attempts at humour weren't working. Her visitor seemed to be giving her the strangest of looks – openly displaying her dismay.

When she'd left, Daisy felt uncomfortable. The way the woman had looked at her. She'd felt the need to defend herself.

And she had no bruises visible that she knew of. She checked just in case. No.

Unless the woman was strange herself. Maybe she was. Her eyes gaping at her, head forward, mouth half-open.

She let it go for now.

Daisy never wanted to evoke that look of pity in anyone ever again.

Chapter 12

The Winds of Change

She had taken to sleeping at the edge of the bed. Making sure that there wasn't an inch of bare skin under the blanket that might tempt him during the night.

Nightdress, dressing gown, all secured tightly around her body – there'd be small chance of a successful fumble, if he did wake up.

When his leg touched off hers, keeping her bottom in the bed she would slide her two legs over the side, careful not to rouse him. Her well-covered body remaining in position from her bottom up.

She slept lightly, making sure that she didn't slip back over to his side of the bed, giving him any vibes. While he might not insist or force her anymore, he had gone too far on more than one occasion.

Reaching for her in the bed.

"Jaysus, where are you there? You're like a bloody nun, all covered up."

No need to answer. Usually drunk, chances were he

would fall back asleep before any damage was done.

His constant uttering of other women's names had strengthened her resistance. Denying the scent of perfume on his clothes and insisting that the lipstick on his shirt collar was the stain of a red-paper napkin where he'd wiped it.

Beatings when she dared to breathe a word about such things.

Arguments about money when he couldn't think of another reason to have a go at her. The job not going as well as it had. His sideline gone to ground.

"Money is getting tight, don't you get it? I'm working my ass off here to provide for you – and all you do is complain. Why is it, of all the people in my life, you are the only one that aggravates me? That's the rearing you got – or maybe 'tis just in you."

After an episode, he would produce a bunch of red roses for her. Hiding them behind his back, all sheepish and mushy, depending on his mood.

"Many a man's wife would give her eye teeth to get a dozen red roses."

Even her eye teeth weren't safe from him.

"Roses for blood," Daisy would say every time he turned up with the red flowers.

Red roses, always red roses.

An argument, red roses.

A kick or a slap, more red roses.

Blood dripping down her face, red roses.

It was always sorry.

"Sorry, you annoyed me so much."

"Sorry, I get so annoyed when you just keep on and on,"

Forever reminding her how lucky she was to have

such a thoughtful husband. Asking her not be aggravating him.

Bruises, ranging in colour, depending on the overlap from the last beating. Never hitting her in the face, just everywhere else. Tom Arnold had beaten the feelings out of her. No matter what he did to her now she would never let herself be afraid of him again.

It was well past midnight on a stormy night in December when Daisy knew that there was no going back. It was over. No more excuses. Thinking of all the times at night alone in the house when she had thought about leaving him, planning her escape. But, as morning dawned, the terrors of the night would be left behind.

But now she was tired of the constant struggle. It was wearing her down. He had inflicted too much hardship on her. This time it had to be for real.

There was no great plan as to where she'd would go, or how she would manage. But the spaces between the bad times had become too narrow. The impact of the bruises that she had endured on the surface were deep and permanent. How wrong she had been, in thinking that she could ever change him.

She no longer wanted him. After being with him for nearly five years, the thought of his body, reeking of alcohol, coming near her, made her feel sick.

It had been an easier transition than she'd thought. She used to cringe at the thought of him being with another woman. Now he could touch whoever he liked. One thing was for sure, he would no longer be touching her.

What would her mother say, if she could see her now? Just as well that she couldn't.

She would plan carefully and wait for the right time to get out. One thing was for certain, she was going.

Poking the fire to stoke up the remaining embers, she wondered should she wait up for him or not. It didn't matter. Going to bed didn't mean that she was safe. If he was going to start, he would do so regardless.

The television programmes had ended for the night, the coloured test-circle displayed on the screen – the high-pitched sound. She turned it off, thinking that she mightn't hear him at the door. Not that it mattered – he had forced the front door open so many times now one quick push with his shoulder was all it took. The architrave was splintered and unstable around the lock where it had been fixed time and time again. Tom, the person who had caused the damage, would make a big fuss of fixing it, until the next time.

She was used to being on high alert, alone at night, listening carefully for all sounds outside – identifying the sounds as she recognised them. Listening, as the old tin bucket was blown across the yard. She recognised the sound of loose felt flapping against the roof, where it hadn't been cut away.

The wind howled through the trees, branches scraping and tapping at the windows, then silence. It was two o'clock. None of the neighbouring house lights were visible.

Darkness, loud sounds, then silence. Daisy was uncomfortable with all three.

As she stoked up the fire again, the storm was well under way. She imagined the windows coming in on top of her.

Trying not to think about the stories the neighbours had told her, she went to check on the window at the far end of the bungalow, as she did each night now from force of habit.

The old couple that had lived in the small stone cottage facing the back end of the house were long since gone. But the stories had remained.

The old man had died, and his wife, refusing to bury him, had kept him with her at the cottage. Throwing his body over the donkey, leading the animal around the yard. Nobody knew how she managed to lift him – but she had. The woman had put a curse on the land, when discovered.

Some believed the tale, more didn't. But neighbours did refuse to walk past the land. Past their house. Soon after, the woman had died and strange things had begun to happen. A child in the nearest house had died suddenly. Lights had appeared at night on the child's pillow.

On her own at night, Daisy believed every word.

Some had sold up and moved on, selling their houses at prices well below the market value, stories well hidden until the houses were sold. Tom had got a right bargain – and he didn't believe a word of the stories.

The noise of the wind startled Daisy as she returned to the sitting room.

A minute seemed like ten. She checked the time on the wooden carriage clock on the mantelpiece. It was now ten to three in the morning and no sign of Tom.

Feeling resentment building up inside her, she couldn't let go of the thought that he was as usual suiting himself, with no thought for her. She had become like a piece of furniture in the house, a possession. She despised him.

She reached behind the mantel clock, taking the plastic pen from behind it, then sat back on the armchair by the fire. Absentmindedly she took a writing pad from the box by the fire and began to write, slowly at first then at a quickened pace, digging the pen hard on the paper. Going over each word many times, excited with the relief it was giving her.

Bastard.

Creep.

Fucker.

Coward.

Bully.

Repeating every expletive she could think of again and again – lines and lines of the same. Words came out of her mouth that she had never uttered, but words that she had become more than familiar with, having been called them many times. As she wrote, she spoke each one aloud.

Revenge.

Clenching her teeth. Pressing the pen deeper into the page. Feeling powerful and stronger the more she wrote.

Daisy felt a surge of power against Tom that she had never felt before. Torturing him, using the paper and the pen as her weapon.

Sitting closer to the fire, ready at the same time to burn the paper if she heard him at the door.

The wind outside was so loud it was hard to distinguish between the sounds.

Then all of a sudden she heard the door being forced open. He was home.

Quickly crumpling the pages, she threw them in the fire. The paper started to smoulder immediately. The pen dropped to the floor. She didn't pick it up.

As he came into the sitting room, she recognised the look.

"Why the fuck didn't you open the door?"

He was drunk – nothing new. The dry brown stains at either side of his mouth were enough to show it.

Daisy passed him at the sitting-room door and walked down towards the bedroom. She felt relieved that he was home. She could go to bed now. The night no longer frightened her.

Just as she got into bed the door of the bedroom burst open and the light came on. Tom was white in the face, except for the blood running down his nose.

"*What happened to you?*" she said as she got out of the bed.

She ushered him up towards the kitchen, grabbing a towel on her way past the bathroom and handing it to him. There was blood gushing out of his nose. A dark deep ugly gash. Was that a small thin bone sticking straight out from his nose?

"*Jesus!* What happened to you?"

"I fell in the sitting room," he said.

She thought he looked like a child.

"How did you fall? How did you hit your face?"

"I went to follow you – 'tis all your fucking fault – I slid on a pen on the floor by the fire. It rolled under my shoe and I went with it. My arm must have knocked your bloody clock before it hit me. All dizzy now, with the shock of it. Wonder I didn't end up in the grate."

Were those tears in his eyes? Surely not? *The baby. The coward.*

She felt nothing, nothing at all, apart from amusement and feeling sick at the sight of the dark blood dripping from the gash at the side of his nose. He could look after it himself.

Smiling inside, she went to the sitting room – he stayed where he was.

She looked for the pen on the floor. She couldn't find it.

Finding herself at first quietly sniggering, then louder – rising – she couldn't stop. Putting her hand over her mouth, she tried to muffle the sound. Not caring whether it was nerves or sheer satisfaction – she couldn't help it. Let him hear her. The satisfaction she felt in seeing him suffer was indescribable. He definitely was in no shape to start anything now. It had been the one and only time that she had seen his vulnerability.

Placing the clock back on the mantelpiece, she noticed it had a chip missing, the clean wood of the break obvious against the dark stain.

Going back to him to make sure. Yes, it wasn't a small bone sticking out of his nose after all. It was the thick splinter of wood from her precious carriage clock.

Once again, feeling the urge to giggle. She went to the bathroom for the tweezers to remove the chip of wood from his nose. It came clean out.

A quiet Tom went off to bed. Tomorrow, when he was gone to work, she would fix her clock.

She felt a sense of peace. The shoe had been on the other foot.

Tom was the victim, she apparently the perpetrator, albeit not intentionally. She felt good about it. It might not be too difficult to get away from him after all.

Chapter 13

Birds of a Feather

Emmet Roche had been Tom Arnold's best friend for as long as he could remember. He had been brought up in the town, not too far away from Tom's. Except that his house had a history. Or so they said.

Tenants had been put off their lands years before, when they'd refused to pay rates to the landowners. Money had been raised in America to rehouse them. The result was a row of fine stone houses. The only three-storey houses in Ballygore. A certain pride had always been attached to the buildings.

But Emmet reckoned that he wouldn't be too proud if he was thrown off his own land. Growing up, he couldn't figure out what they were all so proud about. Pride in ancestors that would rather have nothing than pay rents to the landlords.

His parents were teachers, who seemed more interested in the academic abilities of their offspring than anything else.

His mother, Mary, was a small thin woman with fair hair cut straight across the nape of her neck. His father Michael was tall and thin with snow-white hair, big eyes. They were so alike in nature that they looked alike. Both teaching in the national school in Bally. They were seldom apart – every evening out for their walk, arms linked.

There had been little manual work in the town as the boys were growing up. It was not unusual for his classmates to have fathers working in England, sending the money home. Tom Arnold had been one such boy. Emmet had often wished that his own father would head off for England, to work on the building sites. It might have loosened him up a bit.

All his parents talked about, apart from education, was the serious stuff about the history of the Irish – and how it was the hard work of the Irish that built many a town in England.

When America was mentioned it was always in a softer tone – the sadness for all those who'd left and never returned. Families losing every one of their children to foreign shores. The love for the Irish in America.

Emmet couldn't understand it. His parents were odd people. They hadn't a notion about life outside of themselves and their history books. He would make excuses to leave the house, whenever he could.

Tom's mother, Sally Arnold, never talked about anything like that. She never mentioned history or school. He often wished he could close his eyes, wake up and be Tom Arnold.

Emmet didn't want to hear any more about history. He couldn't have cared less. His only dream was to be confident and popular – just like his best mate Tom.

And Tom's mother was the exact opposite of his own, always laughing and making jokes. And always smelling nice. She insisted on being called Sally. Even Tom called her Sally sometimes.

"Now lads, none of this 'missus' business. Call me by my first name – Sally."

Emmet had never felt comfortable calling a grown woman by her Christian name, so he avoided it as best he could.

Sally Arnold made the best dinners for her children – whatever they wanted. Tom's mother cooked burgers and chips every day if they wanted them. Chipper food if she had the money. No sitting at the table – eat it in your lap. Never a fuss.

Emmet had grown up resenting his parents, embarrassed easily by them, especially when Sally Arnold got going.

"Well, Emmet, how's the mammy keeping? Is she waving that stick – I bet she gives your father the odd tap of it. Come on, Emmet, you can tell me!"

A big laugh would follow as she threw her head back, opening her mouth wide to show a mouthful of gaps and black fillings. By that point, there would be no talking to her.

"Emmet, do your parents have any life at all, outside of that school? Are you sure they live at home at all?"

The laughing would continue, Emmet squirming inside, pretending to laugh along with them.

"I wonder would your mother come down with me to the local, for a game of darts. I'd say we'd get on great? Will you ask her?"

He became a master at playing the fool, when the need arose.

Sally Arnold never mentioned school, except when she found herself up with the headmaster defending her children. Fighting. Threatening the teachers. Tom's mother answered to no one.

She liked to party – going out a few nights of the week with friends. Once she left the house, it was a free-for-all. They could smoke and drink cans. There was nothing said. Emmet had thought this was surely the best type of home there was.

Reaching seventeen, he was no longer sure this was the case. When he was younger, he would have gladly swapped his parents in a heartbeat if there was such an option but he changed his mind as he got older, when Sally Arnold began to embarrass him even more than his parents. Tickling him, which had made him laugh as a child, but cringe as a teenager.

"There's a few cans there in the fridge, work away, I'm off. Not a word at home, Emmet."

His mother wouldn't be seen dead in a pub. The one time she had gone in for a cup of coffee she said that she felt out of place. She wouldn't be making a habit out of it.

Emmet used to block his ears when his mother started on Sally Arnold.

"Stop right there, Mother, I don't want to hear it. At least Tom has a mother who's not always on his case. I could get the stuffing beaten out of me at school and you'd end up blaming me. Tom's mother defends her son."

As Emmet got older he saw the two sides of Sally Arnold. He began to see through her. As long as she was all right, she let her children have the reins.

As the boys turned into men, he realised that apart from the booze and the cigarettes, there was little else going on for her. She was selfish. No advice for her boy when he was accused of bullying in school. No advice when he was suspended for smoking in the toilets. No discussion when a drunken Tom had been fighting in town. No encouragement towards his education.

She did what she was best at, she fought back. Emmet began to feel sorry for Tom.

Chapter 14

The Affair

Emmet Roche continued to be Tom's best friend as they grew into men. Excusing behaviour, letting things go, putting it all down to the loose rearing he'd had from Sally. The two were inseparable.

Tom could find himself aggressively on the wrong side of an argument very quickly. Emmet had been the mediator, often the alibi.

Little had changed over the years, except that Tom the man believed he could hold his own in any disagreement – his fists were often the only ally he needed. Still, Emmet liked to be there for his pal. The big fella, whom everyone seemed to respect or fear, he didn't know which it was half of the time.

Emmet didn't consider himself to be anything special. He saw himself as Mister Average, who worked in accounting, in the office of the County Council in town. But having Tom Arnold as a best friend made him stand out. There was nothing average about Tom.

They looked alike and were often mistaken for brothers,

if not each other. Both men were well built, almost six foot, with fair wavy hair. They dressed alike, preferring to wear smart formal clothes as opposed to casual wear. Their likeness ended with their looks. Emmet was the go-for – Tom the go-to. And no mistake there.

Since Tom and Daisy had bought the house outside of town, Tom had become more dependent on him than ever. Emmet had thought he was joking when he said he was buying a place a few miles out.

"Are you mad, Arnold? How the hell do you think you're going to get to the pub? Or home at that rate?"

Emmet had ended up driving his pal home at all hours of the morning, just as he'd expected. All Tom had to do was ask. And ask he did. Calling on Emmet to take him home after a hard night – but the hard nights seemed to be becoming a regular occurrence. It was all the same what night of the week it was – Tom would be up and out to work the following morning.

Emmet liked to have early nights during the week when he had work the following morning but Tom would ignore his friend's complaints, saying that he shouldn't be answering the phone in the first place if he didn't feel like driving in for him.

Emmet knew that Tom saw him as good for a loan. Small loans – not enough to worry about – here and there – never repaid. The habit began to annoy him.

"Emmet, throw us a fiver there, will you?"

"Have you a tenner on you, Emmet?"

"Emmet, fix up for that there."

Emmet could see that Daisy was not cut from the same cloth as her husband. And the way Tom treated her. Walking all over her.

He began to feel irritated about things that he wouldn't have dwelled on in the past. Feeling used.

Tom's familiar voice. "Hey, Roche, any chance of a lift home?"

"No problem, Boss – I'll be outside in twenty minutes."

Being Tom's friend did have benefits over the years and Emmet hadn't been shy in that department. He'd been more than willing to accept the nod from Tom, when he had encouraged women his way. Tom certainly knew how to lay on the charm, when it came to chatting up the ladies. Wherever Tom Arnold was, there were women.

Tom could sure cut a dash but the drink seemed to be the only dash that Tom was interested in lately. Emmet, there by his side, ready to pick up the pieces.

He was seeing a different side of his pal, a side that he didn't much like. Daisy was being treated like a doormat. He had seen Tom spit into her drink in the pub before handing it to her. Just because she asked for the same as he was having and not her usual half pint of Guinness. He'd made no comment. No point at the time.

Emmet had chosen to ignore Tom's treatment of Daisy when they were living in town. Getting to know her better, he realised she was nothing like the others – certainly no match for Tom.

It just didn't seem right. The girl was stuck in a house, miles outside of the town. He knew that she was twenty-three, but it was hard to tell her age – she seemed much older than her years. Too settled for her age.

His parents had said that she was much too good for the likes of Tom. But, from the beginning, Daisy had been completely enamoured of him – hadn't he himself been blinded for years? Well, it was time to take off the blinkers.

Tom had gone ahead and bought the house without giving any thought to how Daisy would cope. He had isolated her. When they had lived in the flat in town, at least she could walk out the door and meet people – go for a drink with her friends if she felt like it.

Emmet had tried to broach the subject, without getting too close to the bone.

"Hey, how's Daisy handling life in the sticks. Is she missing the town?"

"Oh, for fuck's sake, Emmet! Give over. Daisy this and Daisy that. I paid for the blasted driving lessons, with that twat in town. I bought her the bloody car. What more can a man do? Cost me three hundred quid. What else could she want for, for fuck's sake? Oh, and isn't she married to the greatest stud in Ballygore?"

Tom chuckled at what he had just said. Emmet joined in, bravely contemplating his next question while they were on the subject.

"How's her mother doing at all, Tom? Any sign of them making up?"

"Right, sham, go to hell now and don't mention that Rose bitch again. That's a closed shop. That's if she was her real mother in the first place. Doesn't add up. The mother said there was talk about the Rose one years ago, taking in babies. I couldn't give a hoot. The farther away she keeps from us, the better."

Trouble was that Emmet had seen her leg blackened from her knee up her thigh. He had seen both of her arms black and blue. He had got used to seeing the marks on this girl whom he had become so fond of. But no matter how sickened he was by his friend's behaviour, he felt helpless. Wishing that he had the courage to challenge him. He didn't.

"Daisy is fine with me, she has my crowd to watch her back. And that's that, Emmet. Right, are you on for a pint?"

Emmet was getting fed up with Tom's demeaning comments about Daisy. It was becoming clear to him that the man he had looked up to since they were boys was nothing short of a bully. A man who beat women.

He found himself thinking more and more about Daisy – more than he thought he should. He found that when he spoke with her she looked for nothing back from him. Daisy listened to him without dispute. He got to finish what he had to say. There was no need to be cracking jokes all the time to get a response – he felt at ease. He had never met anyone like her. Relaxed in her company, he didn't need to pretend. He was fine just as he was. Important. Just as important as Tom.

Loyalty had always been Emmet's code. He wouldn't be one for stabbing his friend in the back. Yes, Tom treated Daisy like dirt. But interfering in his marriage was a scary thought. Not an option.

Every time he brought Tom home, or called to the house for whatever reason, he saw a look in Daisy's eyes that made him feel ashamed to be Tom's friend.

If Tom ever had suspicions of himself and his wife spending all that time together in his own home, the consequences were outside of Emmet's thinking. Tom would make it his business to destroy him, after bashing the daylights out of him first. Nobody crossed Tom Arnold and got away with it.

It crossed Emmet's mind that he would have asked her out himself, if he'd got there in time. Maybe. But he hadn't. He would have looked after her and treated her with respect. Given her the very best of himself. But too late now, to be dreaming about what might have been.

Emmet lingered on at Daisy's when he called.

His excuses were trivial – he knew she didn't mind him calling.

She had been living there for four years when it happened gradually. Neither of them had a plan, each just enjoying the secrecy.

He would make excuses to call, whether Tom was at home or not. Sensing the awkwardness which had developed between them – it wasn't a bad awkwardness – it was just there in the room with them, when they were on their own.

It was exciting. Better still Tom had no part in it.

As the two became close, Emmet knew that the awkwardness became a thrill.

He would sit and have a cup of coffee with her, particularly late at night, after he had helped a drunken Tom to bed. They would wait in the kitchen, listening for the snoring to start. Daisy had said it sounded like a chainsaw. Or a combine harvester.

Neither would say a bad word against Tom in the beginning, using head and eye signs instead, to communicate about him. It was easier for them to laugh and snigger, than malign him outright.

But as time passed they became outspoken.

They referred to Tom as if he were a child.

"Is that him up again?"

"*Shhh* … did I hear him getting out of the bed?"

"God, Daisy, do you know, we're like the fecking babysitters here, except there's no money changing hands for minding the brat. And he snores."

Bursts of laughter would follow.

When she confided in Emmet about the violence perpetrated by Tom, he had to face what he had previously chosen to ignore. He admitted seeing the marks from the beginning. He told her that he had always known Tom to be hardcore but beating a woman brought him to a new low.

Daisy had confirmed it for him, showing him the bruises as they happened.

There was an innocence about her that made him look out for her.

Emmet gave her his full attention as she relayed to him how Tom blamed her for upsetting him so much. He listened. She told him about the beatings, losing the babies, the night in the hotel after which she had realised all was not as it seemed. She mentioned the freak accident with the pen and clock when Tom had slid across the floor. Telling him how she had giggled when she saw him standing there, with a chunk of her good clock stuck in his nose.

When he heard about Daisy's ordeal underneath the mattress, he had heard enough. She'd been four months pregnant. Any man that would hit a defenceless woman was nothing short of a coward. But a pregnant one! The stuff he had put Daisy through was barbaric. Holding her head under the bath tap to shut her up. *The bastard.*

Emmet knew enough to fill in the missing pieces. Tom had told him about Daisy appearing at the hotel. He had booked into the hotel with that whore, Karen Boland. When Daisy had turned up, the night porter had warned him in time and Karen had hidden in the wardrobe. Tom had said it was the best tenner he had ever spent.

Emmet had known about her losing the babies, but he had believed that she had miscarried naturally, like she had the first one.

141

The one thing that he knew for certain was that his first mate, his life buddy, had been knocked off his pedestal. And there was no getting back up on it.

Emmet felt ashamed. Ashamed that he had given his good years to a man who wasn't worth a single day of him. Ashamed that he wasn't man enough to have it out with him.

Remembering how Tom had bragged with drink on him.

"The only way to keep a bird in check is to show them who's boss. Otherwise, they'll walk all over you. It's either them or you."

Emmet had never taken his pal seriously when he had thrown such a comment at him.

"I'd love to give that bitch a good puck in the mouth, or something else to shut her up."

He had laughed with his pal. But no more.

He had feelings for Daisy that he had never felt before in his life. Call it lust, love, pity, shame – Emmet wasn't sure, except that he felt a kind of joy when he was around her. He liked her as a person, as a woman.

What he was prepared to do was the best option. He would slowly lose Tom Arnold from his life. He no longer deserved consideration. It suited Emmet to dismiss him more and more – he thought better of himself for doing so. What a complete fool he had been, admiring a man with less morals than a wild animal.

Emmet had always known that Tom had married Daisy to save face. She was pregnant and too late to go for an abortion, according to Tom, who would never give it to say to the Widow Neill that he wasn't man enough to take on his responsibilities.

Daisy hadn't been the first girl that he had got pregnant,

Emmet knew – because Tom had confided in him. Emmet also knew that Tom was not suddenly going to act like a married man – he would continue to mess around.

The marks on Daisy were getting more serious. He could see why she tried her best to cover them up.

Daisy knew that Emmet felt sorry for her, she could see it in his eyes. She said nothing. It wasn't pity that she was interested in. She remembered the look of pity that she had seen in the District Nurse's eyes a few years before. Daisy had given up on pity.

Seeing that Emmet's allegiance to her husband was growing thin pleased her. Tom treated him like more of a possession than an equal, just like he treated her.

Sometimes, the look in Emmet's eyes showed much more than pity. She would feel herself blushing at the way he held her eyes, lingering, unmoving just for a few seconds, especially when he was saying goodbye to her. She liked the feeling, believing that possibilities must have entered his mind, but were never mentioned. The anticipation was enough.

There was no real deceit in him being there. Nor any chance of scandal. There would be no heed paid to his car in the yard – it looked like Tom's.

Tom had knocked the innocence out of her. Now she was a woman who would no longer take people at face value – a woman who would find a way to make Tom Arnold sorry that he had ever laid eyes on her. What better way to start than to sleep with his best friend?

The affair was inevitable – it was going to happen – any respect that either of them had felt for Tom was now a distant memory. The attraction between the two was stronger than either could deny. It was only ever going to be a matter of time.

It began with a hug, on the spur of the moment. A hug that left the two of them clinging to each other.

Whether Tom was there or not, they hugged when Emmet was leaving. Simple and benign when he was there. Nothing special. When Emmet and Daisy were alone, the hugs would leave them a little breathless, as they breathed in the scent of each other.

She found herself checking her reflection in the hall mirror when he was there. He in turn would linger a little longer than was necessary at the front door before leaving. They began to whisper little things to each other. Flirtatious things. Making eye signals behind his back. The two had become as close as they needed to be.

Tom didn't notice. If he did, he never said a word. Daisy reckoned it wouldn't even dawn on him – didn't he own the two of them? They laughed.

Emmet told her that Tom had said she seemed in great form lately – no longer moaning about everything. He'd said that she was less needy – more positive and light-hearted. They'd laughed again.

Daisy loved the attention. Knowing that she looked better. She was being noticed, taking up her own space again – not just as Tom Arnold's wife. She felt real, excited, alive. Looking in the mirror she saw a happy face looking back at her, no longer that sad, depressed face. It was perfect, and all confined to the same space – her home. There were no suspicious eyes on them.

Chapter 15

Love or Lust

Daisy was thinking about Emmet in a way that had been previously reserved for Tom. Daydreaming, wondering what it would be like to seduce him – to take control for a change. She had never controlled anything in her life. Maybe it wasn't for her.

But she liked him, the way he flicked his head from side to side when he laughed. Admiring his well-rounded bottom as he walked by – wondering what it would be like to lie with him – to wake up beside him. She wasn't quite certain what she was feeling, but whatever it was it felt good.

Being intimate with Emmet was on her mind – she wanted it to happen. She had seen the pleading look in his eyes.

Having sex with Tom, no matter how clean and sober he was, was now out of the question for her. He could sleep with whoever took his fancy. He made her sick. They were over.

* * *

The night the two got together, Emmet had called to the house to tell her that Tom would be away for the night. He told her that Tom had telephoned him earlier, asking him to let her know. He didn't tell her what Tom was up to. Hadn't she enough to contend with?

"Don't let me down now, mate. Just tell her I stayed at your place. Tell her the cops were pulling, and you'd a skinful yourself. I can't call her – the blasted phone is out of action. Don't let me down now, mind."

Before making any promises he might as well make sure that there was no chance of him appearing back unannounced. Just to be on the safe side.

"Where are you, Tom, just in case like?"

"In Tilly Ronan's in Clonleen. The car is in the carpark all closed up – I"ll be back well before she gets up in the morning. Bit of business to attend to. If you get my drift."

Emmet could hear the dirty, grainy laugh as he hung up the phone.

Dialling Daisy's number, it rang out. He wondered if Tom had pulled his usual stunt – yanking the wire from the wall, throwing the lot out across the yard. He had seen it for himself sitting there, in under the hedge. Daisy had told him that Tom could bring it back in himself.

It was payback time. Feck Tom, he was sick of being at his beck and call – sick of him doing the dirt on Daisy and getting away with it.

Wearing his dark suit, he knew that if his car was seen parked at the house, it wouldn't be that big a deal. And it was unlikely that any of the neighbours would be walking by in the dark. The only other person likely to call was Sally Arnold and she was away. The timing was perfect.

He drove to the house, excited yet nervous. The chance to be alone with Daisy for a few hours, perhaps even the night, was all he could think of. He would be well gone by the time that Tom came home.

Daisy he hoped would be equally up for it, once she knew that Tom was out of the picture. The anticipation of finally making love to her had taken over from everything else.

Parking his car in the yard, he could feel the anxiety in his stomach. He was more than ready. They had spent long enough dancing around each other, taunting each other.

Half afraid at the same time, in case Tom would appear back.

It wasn't worth thinking about. Not now.

Checking his watch, he saw it was just nine o'clock.

He shook his head to shake off any panic that might be setting in.

Taking the two steps in one, he was at the door.

Daisy stood there, holding the door open for him. She said she had heard the car. She looked pleased to see him. Very pleased. Asking him what he was doing there, telling him that she hadn't heard from Tom. Saying that the phone was gone again.

He told her that Tom had asked him to pass the message on to her. She didn't ask for details – she said that Tom could stay away for good, for all she cared.

He knew now she was as pleased as he was. He could see it in her eyes. Glinting, smiling back at him. A knowing look. Tilting her head to one side, almost closing her grey eyes. She was pouting at him – her mouth open just enough, holding her tongue in place between her lips, before gliding it softly across her mouth.

Almost at the point of no return.

There was no need for warming up. No need for a drink to get them in the mood. No conversation about Tom and what to do if he were to suddenly arrive home unannounced.

Taking the initiative, offering him her hand, she led him down to the bedroom she shared with her husband.

She undressed herself clumsily – then reached out to him – tugging at his shirt – steering him towards the bed. Almost tripping over him. Responding to his kisses. Kissing him. Fumbling with his clothes. Seeing him undress, clothes strewn around the room, her breathing rapid and erratic – inhibitions abandoned – there was no holding back.

She guided him onto the bed and lay down beside him. Watching him, fuelled by the sight of his naked body taking up space – Tom's space. Kissing his face, as his head pressed its shape deeper onto Tom's pillow. *Fuck Tom.*

Lying there, needing him – touching him with wild abandon like she had never experienced before, her passion raw and unguided. Frenzied. There was no time for foreplay – no expectation of gentle caresses or grand gestures of love.

The sense of exhilaration was heightened for her by an unspoken need for revenge on the man who had led them there.

Savouring the thrill, knowing that the greatest mark of pleasure in this encounter would be in destroying the control that Tom Arnold had over her. No more.

And what a better place to punish him, than in his own bed?

It was over before they knew it. Before either of the two would have liked.

Emmet had turned on his back, sweating, arms raised over his head. Daisy, trying to regain her breath, lay also on her back. Side by side, they stared at the ceiling in silence.

Lost in the moment – she had but one thought in her mind.

She had finally got the better of Tom Arnold.

Emmet would have smoked a cigarette if he'd had one. Suddenly jumping out of the bed, he headed towards the bathroom where he grabbed a towel – once he had finished with it he took another and threw it to Daisy. *Catch.*

He lay back on the bed. He was disgusted with his performance. At a loss. He hadn't expected this – it was way too fast. He couldn't believe what had just happened. *Jesus.* Daisy had certainly flummoxed him. No way would he have believed that she had it in her. What he had expecting was a far different experience. He was a giver. But she had taken complete control over him – he felt used. Like his input didn't count. He had certainly seen a side to her that he hadn't expected in a million years. She had taken the reins and run with them.

Disappointed – suddenly exhausted – he wanted to turn his back on her to get some sleep. Then decided against it.

Wondering if by chance he had a loose cigarette in the car – even a butt in the ashtray would do – he dismissed the thought. Jesus, why was he thinking of a bloody cigarette? He rarely smoked.

But he needed one. He needed something. Daisy didn't smoke and neither did Tom.

He lay with his arm around her for a few minutes, not knowing what else to do.

There was no conversation. No promises of love, no endearments – both realising that the rawness of what had just happened had been the core of their wanting each other.

When he sat up and swung his legs over the side of the bed she sensed that he was running scared and was about to leave.

She didn't mind – she hoped that he would leave. She needed time to saviour the pleasure she had just had. The pleasure of knowing that she was no longer at the mercy of her husband.

He was looking back at her.

"Daisy, that was amazing. You never said. Was it all right for you?"

"Oh, Emmet, the best."

There was little more to be said.

Sitting up, using the towel to cover her nakedness, she slid her legs out over the other side of the bed.

She went to the bathroom, mouthing to herself as she went: *Now, Mr. Big Fucking Tom Arnold, what are you going to do about that, eh?*

She folded the used towel back over the side of the bath.

Back in the bedroom, she saw a red-faced Emmet was jumping around on one leg, trying to get his trousers on. She recognised the humour in it. He had his shirt and loosened tie on already.

He must have been rushing to get dressed before she reappeared.

When they had both dressed, Daisy asked him would he like a drink, or a coffee, seeing as Tom wouldn't be around. She didn't expect that he would. She asked anyway.

"Jeekers, no, Daisy, I'd better be out of here, just in case, like."

"Yes, you're right. Of course."

"That was really something, Daisy."

He kissed her once on the lips before picking up his keys from the hall table and hurriedly heading towards the door. It was nine forty-five.

Daisy didn't mind – she had enjoyed the wildness of the encounter. She was feeling exhilarated.

Daisy O'Neill had her very own lover. Who'd have thought it?

She would linger over the brief time they had spent together in Tom's bed. The sheer excitement of what had taken place there. Savouring the urgency of it.

The scent of him remained on her. Feeling more at ease with herself than she had for a long time, she felt empowered. And satisfied. And not expecting anything more of Emmet, apart from his friendship and a repeat of what they had just done. It suited her. She guessed it would be the same for Emmet who seemed to have got quite a shock at her performance.

Daisy poured herself a single malt from the decanter on the sideboard. Tom's precious whiskey. Taking a sip, she immediately felt the good of the warm, soothing liquid. She picked up her magazine from the armchair in the corner of the bedroom and got back in to bed.

She read for only a few minutes. And then slept better than she had in a long time.

Their affair was short-lived. It lasted no more than six weeks. Almost over before it had really begun. During that time they had continued their rush of clandestine excitement at the house, in Tom's bed. But it wasn't to last, once she had got over the initial passion. It was all very good – but she wanted more than a few minutes of pleasure.

Her need for company, her need to be held, was greater than what Emmet had to offer her. Or what she had to give him in return. Once the thrill was gone, there was little left for either of them.

They had outrun their affair. The hugs had changed. They were no longer hugs of anticipation, hugs where two lovers breathed in the deep scent of the other. No more now than two friends could offer each other.

The biggest thrill for her had been making love in Tom Arnold's bed – with his best friend. She sensed that it was the same for Emmet.

It ended as it had started – no plan, no discussion, it just happened.

Emmet had called to the house. Tom happened to be at home.

Behaving as if he had was part of a comedy act, Emmet cracked stupid jokes which Daisy and Tom laughed at – becoming more animated as the evening passed.

Daisy had played her part well, treating him as her husband's best pal, nothing more. There were no side glances, no looks, no awkwardness.

They respected each other enough to accept what was happening.

What she had felt for Emmet was not love, not in the way that she had loved Tom in the past, with her heart, her soul, her body. Tom just hadn't been capable of loving her back. But she had adored him, given him every part of herself – believing that he had been sent to her to take care of her. Convinced that he knew it all. Love had made a right fool of her.

She would never give away so much of herself to any man again.

Emmet and herself never had, or would have, any sort of meaningful love.

They were friends and probably would be in the future. She hoped that the sex hadn't damaged that.

Emmet was more than ready to cut all ties with Tom. Enough was enough.

He would always have a special fondness for Daisy – but it would never be anything but tainted.

Tom Arnold would always be in there, between them. Even if Daisy were to leave him, the history between the three would be there. He had to check himself at times – was he going soft? Had she not in her own way manipulated him?

Without doubt she was no longer the quiet, innocent girl that Tom had married. Sometimes, he had thought he saw traits in her that he had seen in Tom – having seen the look in her eye – a look that frightened him sometimes – a look that said: "I'm playing you."

But only for her he would be still dancing to Arnold's tune.

It was time to find a girl of his own, someone he could have a future with. And without baggage. He was done with carrying someone else's load. No longer was he interested in listening to woes from Tom, or about Tom – he had his own life to live.

Tom Arnold was a fool. His mother had been right about the Arnolds all along.

There would be no more drunken nights, putting him to bed like a big child – no more listening to bullshit. Most of all there would be no more secrets – no skulking around. He would keep his distance.

It was easier than he imagined to break loose. He figured that Tom was gone too far anyway. He had no connection with anyone anymore, aside from a pint glass.

He hadn't batted an eyelid when Emmet began to turn down his requests for a favour. The calls became less frequent as Emmet came up with the lamest of excuses.

"Hiya, Emmet, any chance of lift? I'm a bit under the weather, I'm here in Philly's."

"No, Tom, I'm a bit under the weather myself this evening."

"No problem, mate, sure I'll call a hackney so."

"OK, Tom, that's fine. I was thinking, would it be easier for you if you were to get a regular hackney driver to pick you up? At least you'd be guaranteed a way home."

"'Twould be handier all right – if a fella can't depend on his mate, he can always pay for a bloody taxi." Tom laughed – the usual couldn't-care-less laugh.

Tom thought nothing about the wedge that his friend was trying to forge between them. It never dawned on him. Tom Arnold just got on with things.

Emmet continued to call to the house, but much less often. He always rang ahead first, pleased in the end when he got no reply. At least if he phoned, he felt less awkward.

He knew that Daisy was getting ready to leave Tom. She was at last standing up for herself. He had watched her grow in confidence as she distanced herself from Tom – life had become easier for her. That was for sure. He knew that she was there half of the time when he rang – ignoring his calls. He didn't mind – it suited him in the end.

Chapter 16

The Journey

Daisy needed to confirm what she already knew. She made an appointment to see the doctor in town. As a young married woman, it wouldn't be unusual to bring a urine sample in to have it checked. No shame. She'd been here before.

She already knew what the result was. Feeling the same as she had done on the other occasions. Nauseous. She was pregnant. The young doctor took out the cardboard disc, to check her due date.

She was seven weeks pregnant – baby due the beginning of October.

He told her that they would have to keep a close eye on her – given her history. She felt like telling him the truth. Wondering what information he had on her, she took no notice of his advice.

Going straight home, she sat at the kitchen table. It was familiar to her, hers to lean on, hers to cry on. She lay her head in her arms and cried her tears.

Having felt the first flutter of a baby growing inside her, the joy of planning for the future, the excitement of talking lovingly to the baby forming inside her. Then nothing. The dreadful sense of loss. No baby. And no baby this time either.

Letting her deep sadness take hold, she allowed herself the time to accept it.

Finally, as her head began to clear she weighed up her options.

Forcing Tom to have sex with her, pretending the baby was his? Out of the question. No. The idea of him coming near her was the worst option. He was already responsible for two of her miscarriages. She would not be pregnant again while living with him.

Returning to Rose wasn't an option. Far too complicated and even if she pretended that the baby was Tom's, Rose would want nothing to do with it. Her mother's words echoed in her ears. *"You've made your bed, now you can lie in it."*

Telling Emmet might be her best option. After all, he was the father.

Picturing the scenario in her head – Emmet might tell her he loved her – they would live together and have the baby.

Knowing Emmet as well as she did, this was not an option.

There would be no Happy Ever After. She trusted him as a friend, but as a relationship it was out of the question. A pipe dream. Bullshit.

At least he wouldn't open his mouth, her secret would be safe with him.

She picked up the receiver. Dialled his number. He answered straight away, joking with her that he had been waiting all day for her call.

"Emmet, can you call to me please, before he gets out of work? There's something I want to discuss with you. Can you or can't you?"

She could hear her voice faltering as she spoke.

"No problem, Daisy. Are you OK? Has something happened? Look, never mind telling me now. I'll be over around five."

When she heard Emmet's car pull up, she checked herself in the mirror before opening the door. Seeking courage from her image for what she was about to tell him.

"Daisy, what's up? It sounded urgent on the phone. Is everything OK? Jesus, what has that halfwit done to you now?"

"Emmet, come in – we need to talk."

The two walked towards the kitchen. Emmet sat at the table. Daisy stood at the cooker, not daring to look at him, keeping her eyes on the kettle.

"I'm pregnant, Emmet – I'm seven weeks pregnant."

She thought for one split second it was all going to be all right.

Emmet stood up and walked over to her. "What are you telling me, Daisy? Are you sure? It's Tom's, right?"

"No, it's yours, you fool! I haven't done anything with him for ages – you know full well I haven't."

"Surely you're not saying it's mine? It can't be. We only did it a handful of times."

"What? Are you that ignorant? You think it depends on the number of times?"

But she recognised the denial in him. Bowing out.

"Emmet ..." She was crying now, crying with frustration. Crying with the shock of realising that he was not going to take control. He would take no responsibility

– he would leave it all to her. "Oh, just leave, Emmet, just go. *Get out!*"

She lay her head on her arms on the table.

"Sorry, I'm sorry," he said. "Just let it sink in … of course I believe you." He was pacing now. "Don't be crying. We'll sort it out. Apart from anything else, your man will kill us both if he finds out. No question about that."

Daisy wiped her eyes as he continued.

"Let me think … Jesus, it's an awful shock to get. I know it's the same for you. We need a bit of time – just to think this through. Telling Tom isn't an option, is it? No, it's not! You ll have to get rid of it. You'll have to … I see no choices here … nothing is right about this … nothing …"

Daisy sat there, staring at the man that she had trusted as her confidant and friend. She had just been shown how gullible she had been, yet again.

The man pacing around the room was denying her, denying the baby in her womb. Wanting her to get rid of it – she couldn't look at him – he made her sick. He was in many respects little different from the man that she had married.

This time, it was weakness and shallowness that did the hurting. He was showing himself for what he was, a weak pathetic excuse for a man. *Birds of a feather flock together.* Another of her mother's well-used sayings.

She remained silent – gazing at him.

"Look, don't worry … just get the name of an abortion clinic in England. I'll pay for everything. That magazine you read, *Cosmo*, is it? I saw a list of clinics in England when I was flicking through it. I thought 'twas disgraceful at the time."

He sat down, looking like a man who had come up with a well-thought-out plan.

"It's the only way, Daisy, I'll take you to the airport in Dublin and collect you … that way no one will see us. You can't have a baby. We need to sort this out, before it's too late."

She no longer paid any heed to what he was saying. Her options had just whittled down to one.

She nodded her head but not in agreement.

Before leaving, he picked up a copy of *Cosmo*, opening it from the back page. He folded the page over and handed it to her.

"Not a word to anyone, Daisy. Have a look through those and see what you can come up with."

She dropped the magazine to the floor. Looking at him – almost pleading.

"Emmet, just think about it first. We don't need to make a decision today. Call me tomorrow – promise me you will sleep on it."

"Daisy, I'll call but there is no other option."

There was nothing more to be said between them.

Emmet was gone out of the yard a minute later. He said that he might as well call to the bank on his way home. He would get enough money to sort it out.

Daisy waited for him to call, knowing inside what he was going to say. Hoping that he would change his mind – they could find a way.

Distancing herself from the foetus inside her was not going to be easy. Recalling how sickened she had been when a female doctor had referred to the last baby she'd lost as a foetus. A clinical term. She had been devastated.

Emmet wouldn't be calling her to tell her what she wanted to hear – she knew that his mind was made up.

* * *

By the following morning, she had chosen the clinic in London. Dialling the number, the soft English voice at the other end of the phone gave her the information that she asked for.

Feeling supported, she had little choice other than to trust what this lady was saying to her. Writing down the instructions, she no longer felt hopelessly lost. She would follow the directions given to her. Emmet was out of the picture. He could help her in practical ways.

There was a counselling session to be booked in Dublin before travelling. This, she was told, was to ensure that she was ready to go ahead with it.

Later in the evening the phone rang.

"Daisy, it's me, can you talk?"

Deciding to hear what he had to say, she said yes. She was holding on to a glimmer of hope.

"Look, Daisy, I've hashed it round in my head. It has to be an abortion. That's my answer. There's far too much at stake here and –"

"Emmet, I didn't expect anything else but remember it's on your head. Your decision and not mine. We could have worked it out some way between us. But I've looked up the clinics in the magazine as you said. I made an appointment in Dublin earlier, through them. I have to have a consultation before travelling. It's in some Well Woman place. If that goes OK, it can all be over in four days."

Emmet remained silent. She guessed he was relieved – afraid in case she changed her mind. She wouldn't – not now.

"Emmet, are you listening?"

"To be honest, Daisy, I'm just relieved you're making the right decision. I'll take you wherever you want. I got the money to cover the cost."

At that moment, she despised him as much as she had ever despised Tom. He hadn't asked once how she was feeling. He had his mind made up.

Rose's words – how true they had been. Avoidance – masquerading as strength – in reality, weakness.

In between making arrangements and being sick, Daisy considered again the fleeting thought of leaving Tom and going home to Rose, pregnant.

No matter how it was sugarcoated, the scandal would be unimaginable. And Tom would make their lives a misery. She had put her mother through enough. it definitely could not be an option.

At least she didn't have to worry about Tom, who'd been drinking heavily over the past days. On the missing list most of the time. If she'd ever wondered whether her husband was an alcoholic, she now knew for sure he was.

Deciding to leave it to Emmet to figure out what he was going to say to Tom in her absence, she told him to say whatever he liked. She was beyond caring.

The worst that could happen would be that he'd beat her up. In a way she hoped that he would. She would take her punishment for getting rid of the baby. Either way, it didn't matter anymore. If he did beat her up, she'd probably lose it anyway.

Emmet said he would tell Tom she'd gone to stay with Rose's sister in Galway for a few days, to clear her head. He wouldn't be in the least put out by her absence. It wouldn't change anything for him and he certainly wouldn't bother trying to reach her.

Emmet told her that he'd taken the day off work. They left early in the morning for Dublin, they'd be home by evening.

The consultation with the counsellor was booked for

161

ten o'clock. Daisy went in alone. The session started at ten fifteen and ended shortly after that.

Daisy had been worried that they wouldn't sign the forms recommending the termination. Not understanding the process, she soon realised that she was just one of many more women, in the same situation.

She told her story to a girl who seemed to be about her own age, impersonal and clinical. She listened, before asking Daisy if she was sure this was what she wanted.

"Yes, it cannot be any other way." Daisy had explained her situation, in as few words as she could, the tears flowing freely down her face as the counsellor made notes. The session ended when she stood up, offering her hand to Daisy.

Daisy was to call the clinic in England back, to make the final arrangements, later in the day.

The booking was confirmed from a phone kiosk in the street. The smell in there made her feel nauseous. Emmet had handed her coins to make the call.

There was no going back, decision made.

She would be admitted three days later, spend one overnight and back the next day. She wished she could close her eyes and it would all be over.

The music on the way home from Dublin made up for the lack of communication in the car.

When they'd been travelling for an hour or so, he reached to take her hand. She slapped it back at him. Emmet would do whatever he needed to, as long as she went ahead with the plan. That didn't mean she had to talk to him.

Once home, there was no contact between the two, until the evening before her trip to England. She kept herself busy making the final arrangements.

The clinic had been great, helping her in a way that she had not expected. They had made her feel connected, not alone in her misery. Being women themselves, they understood.

Emmet made the call to Tom at work – Daisy had gone away for a couple of days. It had unsettled him. Daisy didn't seem to care what he told Tom. He knew how he felt himself. He was certainly no match for Tom Arnold – if the truth ever came out, Tom would flatten him.

As he suspected, Tom showed no great interest.

He said, "Why the hell didn't she call me herself?"

If he was put out, he didn't show it.

Chapter 17

The Clinic

Daisy boarded the plane, relieved to feel the gust of fresh spring air against her face, as she stepped on the tarmac. She felt numb, sweaty and nauseous.

She was terrified in case anyone from home would see her. Fearful that she wouldn't make it back, or even to the clinic in the first place. London seemed very far away from what she was familiar with.

It was her first time out of the country. The hardest part of her journey would be to keep herself from passing out. The smell of cigarette smoke coming from the back end of the plane sickened her stomach – she wanted to vomit. She didn't.

Making no conversation during the journey, she couldn't believe that they'd landed so soon after taking off.

Heathrow. Terrified, in unfamiliar surroundings, she found her way to the Tube, going straight to Oxford Street. She hailed a black cab and the driver brought her straight to the door of the clinic. The knowing look on his face was enough to convince her that he was well used to making this trip.

She was shaking as she entered the place, avoiding the few banner-holders who stood outside, parading their signs like good Christian beings, proud and full of condemnation for the female murderers about to defy their God.

Sitting in the waiting room with the other women, she no longer felt alone. She recognised the familiar look of loss and sadness in their eyes. The women looked at each other knowingly, with a certain sense of respect and understanding.

The environment was calming, all-accepting. No blame here, just women like herself who had come here because they saw no other way out. Not a man in sight. Apart for the one she had seen outside – waving his placard in her face. *Killers of the Unborn*.

Women from other countries, women who recognised the empathy in the other. It was a comfort of sorts.

One of the women left in tears – she couldn't go through with it. The others looked at each other – they remained seated.

Daisy was afraid to speak at first – they might recognise her accent. The last thing she wanted to do was chat to another Irishwoman. She was fearful of being found out and traced back to Ballygore.

Women sharing a confined space – each focused on the reality of their own situation. All in the same boat. Like mothers after giving birth on the maternity ward. Protectiveness. At the same time, estranged, a clear understanding that none of these women would be meeting to catch up, pushing their buggies into coffee shops. There would be no birthday cards. No marking of baby's developmental stages. No talk of C-sections and bladder control after giving birth. No need for pelvic-floor exercises. And no babies to love.

Daisy exchanged small talk with mothers who sat beside their nervous daughters who looked much too young to be pregnant. Older married women, who'd found themselves pregnant, too many children already. Women who had been there before. Women who would return again. Women who would never find themselves in the same position again. Ordinary women.

There were no judgements. It felt like the safest place to be – no room for condemnation. Those outside on the street holding their banners were only too willing to condemn.

There was one payback. Being her fourth pregnancy and nothing to show for it – she swore to herself that she would never be pregnant again.

As the day went on, the atmosphere was one of quiet anticipation. The women spoke softly with each other, some explaining the predicament they found themselves in. Most often boyfriends having taken flight once the word 'pregnant' was mentioned.

Daisy's termination was on the list for later that evening. Those who were travelling home later in the same day were treated first.

The nurse remarked on the newness of the rings on her wedding finger.

"They're not on that finger too long. Are they, love?"

Daisy didn't expand.

It was all over surprisingly quickly. Relief. She opened her eyes, realising that she was back in the bed. No longer pregnant.

The sense of relief she felt was as obvious as the ache in her groin. She felt lighter than she had for some time.

The doctor came round. Everything had gone well. She had been seven to eight weeks pregnant. The relief remained with her, as she prepared herself to face the journey home.

Emmet picked her up at the airport in Dublin, sheepish and detached. He said very little on the journey back to Ballygore.

They stopped for coffee on the way. The conversation was limited.

Daisy knew that he had taken himself out of the picture. He acted as if he was helping her out with a problem, nothing in the world to do with him.

"So it's done. It's over. Are you OK?"

"Yes, Emmet, it's done and I'm fine – relieved, to be honest. What did Tom say?"

"He said nothing much at all. In fact, I'm sure he didn't take any notice. Have you much pain?"

"Not really, just a warm cramp, not really pain. They said it's normal. It'll be gone in a few days. Home to bed, to the end room. Ring him and tell him that I caught a bug in Galway. He'll stay clear of me – he'll be too afraid he'll catch it."

She was giving him orders. If she sounded harsh, she didn't care. Sitting with the man whose only offering had been for her to get rid of the baby. The man who would not have a finger pointed at him – who would never have to answer for his actions. What actions, she asked herself. It was all on her head. He was without conscience. Free from responsibility.

During the journey home, Daisy found herself consumed with thoughts of her mam, making her mind up to go to see her as soon as she felt better.

Her mind was clearer than it had been for some time. It was time to put things right between them.

For now it was enough for her to be alone, after which she would leave Mr. Arnold for good.

Chapter 18

Karma

Daisy woke up the following day in the end room. It was half past six. There was no sign of Tom. Getting out of the bed slowly, she felt the familiar cramp in her abdomen. It was nothing like she'd expected. No different to her monthly cramps. Taking two pills from the packet that she'd been given, she swallowed them down with water. She slept, on and off – woke, aware of a faraway noise. Sleep taking over once again.

She woke again. There wasn't a sound in the house. She found it hard to tell what day it was, counting on her fingers to work it out – she'd left the house three days ago for England.

Feeling well enough after her rest, she walked around. Where was Tom? Going from room to room, everything was as she'd left it. He wouldn't have cooked, or even made a cup of tea for himself. There was little chance of anything being out of place in the kitchen. Walking around slowly, half expecting him to jump out at her.

His car wasn't in the yard, just her own small car, parked around the back.

Stopping outside their bedroom, she felt uneasy, putting it down to being the after-effects of the anaesthetic.

She tried to open the door but it wouldn't budge more than a few inches.

Something was blocking it. She pushed against it with all the strength she could muster. It was useless, the door wouldn't move.

Her heart pounded in her chest. The door was blocked by something heavy. Not being able to fit her head around it, she pressed her face through the open space. She could see the side of his foot sticking out.

His body was blocking the door.

"Tom, Tom, can you hear me? Tom!"

No answer.

"Jesus! Is he dead?"

In a panic she closed the door shut and ran to the bathroom, thinking she was going to be sick, but nothing came.

Her mind racing.

Pacing up and down the hallway.

She would call Emmet.

No, she wouldn't – he would call the gardaí.

Would she call the doctor?

Would she call Rose?

No, she couldn't, not now.

She sat down on the chair beside the hall table.

The house was eerily silent.

With one quick motion, she yanked the phone line away from the wall. She opened the front door and threw it out, over his precious cemented lawn, towards the hedge – just as she had seen him do many a time.

He had even taken the bloody grass away from her.

She would call nobody.

Walking back towards the room, she listened again for sound. Nothing.

Maybe she could hear him breathing, she wasn't sure. Pushing her body against the door again, it didn't budge.

A cold sweat broke out all over her. She couldn't ignore the feeling that came with it. She felt a sense of excitement, exhilaration.

He could stay where he was – on the floor. She despised him.

"Oh Jesus, help me!"

She walked away.

Panicking, not knowing what to do.

Maybe she should act as if she'd never gone near the bedroom door? Hadn't she become an expert at ignoring things, pretending that they didn't happen?

She hurriedly dressed, grabbed her handbag and went outside.

Walking around towards her car, she stepped back a few paces, kicking the cream phone set from where it lay, right in under the hedge and out of sight.

"Now, Tom, back at you! It's your turn."

Speeding out of the yard, the car rattled over the grid and set off towards town.

She would disappear for a couple of hours. The picture was clear in her head. What had she seen? She hadn't seen a thing. Tom must have come home at some unearthly hour and gone to bed, without her knowing. Emmet could vouch for her – she would make sure of it.

By the time she got back, it could all be over. She

desperately hoped it would. He didn't deserve anything more. It dawned on her that had she still been pregnant, it could have worked – a pregnant widow. *Hmmm.* She dismissed the thought. Dreaming again.

Wondering would he vomit and choke – he was lying on his back. Maybe he had a heart attack or stroke. Maybe he was already dead.

If he wasn't dead on the floor when she got back, she was leaving him anyway. If he was dead, she would deal with that too. The old Daisy was also dead.

Tom Arnold had taken enough from her. Emmet Roche had too, in his own way. There was no going back.

The blue sky over her head served as an omen – things were looking brighter.

Since when had she become so calculating? Who would have believed it? Daisy O'Neill – lover – abortion – dead husband and all in the space of a few weeks.

She would have her hair done.

Nobody would guess that she had a termination days before. Nothing about her suggested that she felt a wild sense of relief at the thought of finding her husband, dead on the floor, behind the bedroom door.

Sitting under the hair dryer, she had plenty of time to get her story straight.

Serves him right. She had a picture in her head – there was no panic in her. She would face whatever it was once she got home. She'd had too many beatings from him to be scared now.

She asked the girl on the till for the time before she left. She had watched enough crime movies to know that an alibi would be handy.

The girl smiled at her. "Just after three, my love."

Driving home – anticipating the scene.

Turning the key in the front door, trying her best to remain calm.

No sound.

Walking down the hallway, passing the kitchen door on her right.

All quiet.

She tip-toed towards the bedroom.

"Oh, Jesus help me!" she said aloud, turning the doorknob slowly, ready to feel the resistance pushing against her.

No resistance. The door opened freely.

The room was empty. But she could smell him.

She couldn't believe it. She'd allowed herself no thought other than her finding him dead on the bedroom floor.

Panic took over. Back to the present. What if he knew all along that she'd left him there?

Or maybe someone had come to the house and ...

His voice when it came made her jump.

"Daisy. In here. Now!"

It was coming from the end room. Her heart was pounding – the blood drained from her face. She was stuck to the spot.

She forced herself to move.

He was sitting there on the edge of the bed.

"What is it, Tom? I was in town having my hair done. You all right? Are you off out?"

She was hoping it would be the latter.

She would be well gone by the time he came home.

"Emmet said you went off to Galway to visit your aunt. What was that all about? You couldn't tell me yourself?"

How she despised him. More than despised him. He made her sick, just looking at him.

"I just decided the last minute. Thought it might be a good idea to have a few days, before I get back in touch with my mother. Yes, Tom, you heard correctly. My mother."

"Just make the bloody tea. You off gallivanting around the country. Ye're all the bloody same. And me here – passed out. One minute I'm in the bathroom having a leak, next thing I'm on the ground, trying to get up. I'm up now. I won't be venturing out again – so bring the tea down here. And I'm not going back into that bloody room again tonight – 'tis jinxed."

She wondered if she'd heard right. Had he said he wasn't going out?

That was a first.

"Do you want me to call the doctor?" she asked, feigning concern.

"Do not. I'm not paying that quack to tell me I have concussion. Maybe the curse of that oul' one up the back is on me now."

No need to answer – she was trying to hide her disappointment.

"Don't sound too concerned, whatever you do."

On her way past the hall table, she noticed that the phone was back in place. Had he thought he'd thrown it outside himself?

Having almost convinced herself that she had endured the last of him, here she was cooking his bloody tea. She hoped that he wouldn't notice the tainted taste on the meat – a week out of date. Just perfect.

And he hadn't even noticed her hair.

She might not be the grieving widow – but she

wouldn't be at his beck and call for much longer. Of that she was sure.

Two days later, Daisy got the news. Emmet called to the door. She knew by his face something wasn't right.

When he told her that he'd had a call from the hospital at work, she thought it was about Tom.

Standing in the hall, Emmet told her that Rose was very ill and wanted to see her. Rose had asked the nurse to contact him – she knew that he would get to Daisy.

"It's not looking good, Daisy – it seems that your mother has some sort of cancer."

Daisy could feel her legs weaken under her. Emmet led her to a chair.

"Paula Rafferty is the nurse, I know her from school. She told me that she'd contacted Tom on two occasions some weeks ago and when they hadn't heard back from you they were suspicious. Rose got them to contact me instead. I don't know how she even knew to contact me, but there you go – she must have had her eyes on you, all along. Your mother has been in a nursing home for some time. It seems that she wrote to you as well, a while back. She gave up hope, when she heard nothing back. She thought that you wanted no more to do with her."

"*Oh, no – no!*" Tears began to flow down her face.

"There's more, Daisy. Tom has definitely known for some time about your mam. Paula the nurse told me she herself called your house phone a few times. When she couldn't get a reply she called Tom's work number. Rose did get to speak with him. She begged him to tell you that she wanted to see you. So he knew all along."

"Oh my God, that bastard never told me! Poor Mam!

175

Unless she was desperate she would never have begged Tom in a month of Sundays. How humiliating for her. That's it. He can go to hell now!"

"I can take you to the hospital, love, if you're up to it. You can leave a note for him, if you want. Or I can ring the office to tell them."

"There'll be no note and no call. I'm done playing the fool. Will you take me there, now, right away?"

"Sure, love. Look, here's the hospital number – maybe you should call them to say you are coming?"

"Thanks, Emmet."

Daisy picked up the receiver and called the phone number. They put her straight through to the Ward Sister who explained the situation to her.

"Please tell my mother I'm on the way. I should be there in half an hour."

While Daisy rushed upstairs to get her coat and handbag, Emmet quickly dialled Tom's office, telling the work secretary what had happened. He wasn't going to risk Tom taking it out on him.

Rose lay in the bed, her face pale and drawn. When she saw Daisy appear in the room, she sat up with her arms outstretched.

"My Daisy, you came, you came!"

Daisy swiftly went to her and sat on the bed, cradling her in her arms.

Then, drained with the shock of seeing her daughter, Rose lay back on her pillows.

She looked pale and thinner than she had ever been. The once perfectly groomed proud woman looked frail and worn. Her hair white and wispy. A coloured crochet shawl was around her boney shoulders.

"I didn't know, Mam, I never knew. If I had known!"

"I know, pet. I spoke to him and he told me you were his now – to forget about you. The nurse had to make enquiries. She knew to contact Emmet Roche."

Daisy was inconsolable.

"*Shush*, Daisy, you're here now. There's so much to say, child. I prayed for more time and here you are. The Lord and John P have answered my prayers."

Daisy's tears flowed freely down her cheeks – she did her best to regain her composure.

"Mam, of course there'll be time. Mam, I'm so sorry. You were right all along. My stubbornness got the better of me. I listened to him, above you. I got pregnant – I saw no way out. I lost the baby. No excuse, that's what happened. I'm sorry, Mam. But I learned the hard way. It's over. I'm finished with him now, it's over."

Daisy was saying more than she needed to. She couldn't help herself. She was back with her mother.

"Mam, we won't let this happen again."

"Daisy, we've both been stubborn. We need to let it go. There's not much time."

"Mam, you'll get better and I'll come home to mind you, I promise. The weather's getting better – it's March – soon we can sit in the garden and plant our flowers just like old times. Wallflowers – remember how I used to love the smell of them? And geraniums, your favourites."

Rose stopped to breathe deeply, before she spoke again.

"You will tend the garden, love. But it'll be your garden. Your life with him was never going to be easy. From what I heard, it hasn't been. Arnold will get his comeuppance some day. But as long as you're safe and away from him for good, that'll do for me."

The two embraced, safe in knowing that they were reunited, despite Tom's best efforts to keep them apart.

Rose drifted off to sleep then woke again.

"My Daisy! You're here ... Believe me, I have loved you as my own, from the first day I set eyes on you. You are my very own heart, Daisy O'Neill. Don't you ever forget it. The day will come when you'll wonder, but remember my words, dearest daughter. Promise me?"

Rose was breathing quickly as she stopped talking.

Daisy could barely speak – her throat would not allow her. Nodding her head in reply, she leant in to embrace her mother. "Mam, I promise."

Rose slipped into sleep easily, feeling the comfort of her daughter's presence.

While she slept, her words played in Daisy's head. "*I have loved you as my own.*" I have loved you as my own? What? Had she heard her right?

"*The day will come when you'll wonder.*" What did she mean?

Maybe she was just raving. Not knowing what she was saying.

She put it to the back of her mind for now.

Holding hands was enough for the two, as they reconnected. Rose didn't need an apology. She'd heard the words from her daughter mouth. She had waited for almost five years to hear those words, since the day when she had first heard the mention of his name. Daisy had told her it was over.

Three days passed in the hospital room, the two women happy to be together. But Rose's condition deteriorated rapidly.

They chatted when Rose was able – her sentences

becoming shorter as her breathing deteriorated.

"Go home, Daisy. The place is yours. The money too. You don't need him. You'll have no worries. Let no one tell you otherwise. Talk to Thornton. Go to Thornton. My will is there."

"Don't talk about wills, Mam. I can't bear to think of my world without you. Even though we'd fallen out I knew you were there."

"Child, you have to listen to me now. Not much time. I've written it all down."

Daisy attended to her mother's needs as best she could. She held the water to her lips, dipped cotton wool in the glass – letting it drip gently into her mouth when she became too weak.

She wiped the stray tears from Rose's eyes, not knowing if she was crying or not. The nurses came in and out, attending to Rose's pain and discomfort, making her as comfortable and pain-free as they could.

The two women had become as close as ever they'd been.

Daisy barely left her side, eating a little in the hospital canteen, sleeping at night by Rose's bed.

Emmet called each day. He'd wait at reception while the nurse would tell Daisy that he was there. He brought her to town, to get whatever she needed, while Rose slept.

Tom stayed away. He'd called the hospital, leaving a message for Daisy to call him. She didn't.

She had no thoughts of him. She was where she needed to be. Her mam faded with each day. When visitors came, Daisy would excuse herself and go to the canteen. She had nothing to say – avoiding anyone that might have listened.

Emmet told her Tom had hit the drink bad. He had

asked Emmet to keep an eye on things and let him know.

Daisy figured he would stay well away. It shouldn't take him long to figure out his marriage was gone. Tom Arnold didn't do regret.

Daisy was with her mother when she slipped away in her sleep. She died as she'd lived, calm and dignified. She had lingered on to spend time with her daughter – the only human being that she'd ever truly adored, after John P.

Daisy called Emmet, warning him to tell Tom to keep away. He told her he had already done so.

He told her, "Tom is well up to speed on all that's going on."

The reality hit her. Rose was dead.

After a few hours, two orderlies came to the room with a trolley. Covering Rose with a white sheet, they rolled her away. She wanted to ask where they were taking her – she couldn't.

She looked out the hospital window. Standing in disbelief. How dare the trees sway so furiously when the world had stopped. Daisy sat and cried until she could cry no more. She cried for her mam who had tried to warn her about him.

Crying for the innocence in herself – long since gone.

She cried for the times she had hurt Rose, allowing Tom to get his way. The pain pierced right through her. Daisy knew that life would never be the same again.

The funeral was a blur. She knew the townspeople would talk. She didn't care, they could say what they liked. She owed them nothing.

Rose had always kept herself to herself. Apart from

relatives and neighbours, it was a small funeral. She could see Thornton standing at the back of the grave, looking at her.

Tom stood beside her. Sally Arnold was with him. The smell of whiskey from his breath was undeniable. His clothes smelt. He looked as if he hadn't washed for days. His tie had beer stains down the front. It didn't faze her.

Sally was dressed as if she were going to a party. Black patent handbag – hair jet-black – too dark. Red mac to her knees – red-patent high heels.

Tom had tried to put his arm around Daisy – she brushed it away before it landed.

Emmet was there at the other side of Tom, nodding to Daisy, to let her know he was there. Looking sheepish. Rose's words seemed fitting: *Running with the hare and hunting with the hounds.*

There was no going back. She would do as her mam had wished – move back home, at least until she was straight in her head about the future.

For the first time in ages, Daisy felt safe.

Straight after the funeral, she returned to the house she'd shared with Tom. It was her birthday. But she was in no mood to celebrate. Holding no sentiment for the house, the decision to go back one last time hadn't been difficult.

It was all the one to her whether he appeared or not. He wouldn't touch her now.

She lifted the carpet in the bedroom where she had hidden her "bus money", as Rose liked to call it: "Daisy, put aside your own few bob. Never tell another soul about it. It'll be your bus money, when you might need to take a trip. John P would laugh at me, but I've always had my own few bob. What they don't know won't trouble them."

She had three hundred pounds, made up of the money from her old bank book, topped up with the cash that she'd slipped off her weekly housekeeping money. It had taken her over two years to prepare for this day.

It had been a simple exercise. He liked the best cuts of meat, fillet steak, lion of pork. She'd buy the cheaper cuts, hammering them until they were tender enough. So many dinners had been binned. Dinners thrown at her. Or at the wall. And the wall didn't mind which cuts of meat were thrown at it. There were no questions asked. She saved.

The clothes she chose to take with her fitted into one bag. Everything else she left behind. Including her blue maternity dress, which she left trailing over the bin in the kitchen. He would get the message.

It was raining when she left the house for the last time. Knowing that she would never set foot in it again, she whispered to the wind.

"Goodbye, house, and good riddance! Goodbye curses and all that's bad around here! Goodbye to your bloody red roses! *Good riddance, you bastard, Tom Arnold!*"

She had opened the window wide at the end of the hall before leaving.

"No more ghosts for me!" she had said aloud.

Walking away from the house for the last time.

Driving back to her real home.

She was free at last.

The feeling that came over her was one of calmness, her mind no longer fixated on Tom. She felt at peace. It was finally over.

Chapter 19

Going Home

Embracing the new life that had come to claim her, she settled back into her childhood home. The house had been let out, through Thornton, managed through David Keogh. It had been Rose's intention to keep the property aired and maintained. The tenants had moved out just a month before her death, leaving the place in a decent state. Thornton had handed Daisy an envelope with the accumulated rent, plus a sum of five hundred pounds which would see her through until things were sorted. Any of the bigger bills were to be sent directly to him for payment. Rose had known exactly what she was doing. Taking no chances, she had thought everything through.

The house was more or less as Daisy remembered it, not that she'd be making any changes for a long time – there had been more than enough changes in her life of late.

The will was simple and concise, a one-page document. Daisy was to be the main beneficiary of the estate. A small sum of money had been left to Rose's sister and a few others on John P's side.

Thornton told her that there would be no contesting the will. Any relatives who were likely to contest it had been mentioned in it.

A sum had been left aside, to cover Rose's funeral and legal expenses.

Thornton was to ensure Rose's wishes were followed. Being the executor, he would organise everything. He had more to say.

"Daisy, I'm asking you to follow my lead on what I'm about to tell you. You may have to read between the lines. We've been dealing with the O'Neill family for many years. It's a delicate matter. One that is best kept off the page, so I ask you to trust in my legal expertise to protect your inheritance. Do you understand me?"

She nodded, not knowing what was coming but guessing it had something to do with Tom.

"There is a codicil to the will. I have a letter to be given to you once all matters relating to the will are sorted. And not before. There is no hidden agenda. In a nutshell, you will receive your full inheritance – but only if your husband has no claim on it."

She understood perfectly. There was a sum of twenty thousand pounds, payable only in the event of a legal separation from Tom.

He advised her that should her husband attempt to go after Rose's money, he would divide the lump sum into weekly payments for her for the rest of her life. In that instance there would be no worthwhile one-off gain for Arnold – if it came to that.

There would be a holding period of six months

without claim on either side – or a legal notice stating that Daisy had a legal separation. Whichever came first. Thornton would start proceedings immediately for a separation agreement.

Tom had made sure that Daisy had no hold on their house, making sure that she had removed her name from the deeds. Thornton had agreed that it was in her best interest in the longer term. As long as she wanted nothing from Tom, it was straightforward – without complication. He would know that the widow's place would be hers. She figured that he wouldn't have too much to say, as long as he remained in the dark about the rest of her legacy. Tom Arnold wouldn't be seen going after Rose's house – he'd be too afraid in case Daisy went looking for a share in his own estate. And he'd be too busy protecting his own corner to worry about her.

The agreement, once signed, would state that from that date forward each had no claim on property or money accumulated by the other party after the fact.

Thornton had not let Rose down – the will had been well thought out.

She had the house and more than plenty to keep her going until it was all sorted.

Daisy told Thornton that she would follow his instructions to the letter. She had waited long enough to leave Tom – she could wait some more.

Back in her childhood home, little had changed. The neighbours were much the same and once the initial gossip had calmed, the net curtains no longer parted as she came and went. Daisy got on with her life.

She offered pleasantries – but no information on her

return back to the road. Being polite, smiling when she felt like it, was the most she would offer. It had nothing to do with neighbours, Tom Arnold or anyone else.

Everything was much the same as it had been when she walked out nearly five years before.

Daisy felt secure in the familiar surroundings where she had grown up. While she missed Rose, she knew in time that she'd be all right – going about her business, feeling more comfortable, going into town – her head still edgy, in case she would bump into Tom or worse still his mother Sally. It hadn't happened or else they themselves were keeping a low profile. Highly unlikely.

And she was no longer fearful of being on her own at night – realising that there was no one to fear. As for ghosts – she'd left them all behind.

After five months a call came from Thornton, asking her to make an appointment to see him. Daisy would now legally inherit the sum of twenty thousand pounds along with the house and whatever shares John P had left. Once the six-month mark was up in September she would receive the letter finalising the remainder of the will.

Having access to her inheritance, she was finally independent.

Rose's memory would always be a huge part of her life but, at twenty-five, it was time to start living her life.

Thornton said he wasn't convinced that Tom wouldn't try to come after a share of her inheritance. Over her dead body, she told him – she would burn it first. Anyway, he wasn't going to find out, was he? Tom Arnold would never let it be said that he relied on any woman's money, let alone the widow's. Keeping the exact terms of the inheritance to herself wouldn't be a problem – no one need be the wiser.

Once Daisy felt the time was right to come out of mourning, she went to town to the best boutique, spending more money than she'd ever spent.

She bought expensive stylish clothes, colourful and modern. Two pairs of high heels completed her buying splurge for now. Her new clothes made her feel confident and glamorous. She had her hair highlighted and styled.

She was at her best and she knew it. People admired her. They told her how well she looked. She liked the feeling. There would be no more "Poor Daisy Arnold". Tom Arnold's property. The victim of domestic abuse. Presenting herself as a confident, stylish young woman, there wasn't a trace visible of the tired defeated young woman of the past. It was buried deep inside. She was ready to take on the world.

Tom had called to the house twice – late at night when he was drunk.

She hadn't answered. The one time he did call to her in daylight was to give her the number of a marriage counsellor. He could stick it. There was no going back.

There were times when she thought that she recognised the sound of his car driving slowly up and down the street, when she was in bed. Eventually she learned to ignore it.

Daisy guessed that he was so messed up he would imagine all sorts. She knew that he would continue to pester her for some time – not because he loved her or missed her but because he had lost control over her.

A call to an irritated Sally Arnold, telling her that if her son didn't stop harassing her she would send the Guards over, had been enough. Sally did not want the gardaí at her door again. Daisy had chuckled to herself when the call was finished.

The tables had turned.

When the doorbell rang on a cool night in September, Daisy couldn't believe that he was up to his old tricks again. It was well after eleven. Careful in case she was seen, she peeped through the lace curtain. She could see who was standing there, under the porch light. Well, he could stay there until he got tired of it and fecked off home.

It was Davie Keogh. Davie Keogh from the garage. What on earth did he want?

Thornton had told her that he had rented out the house while Rose was in the hospital – other than that, he had no business here. And at this hour?

Well in his fifties, a notorious womaniser, Keogh figured he was above most of the people in the town. He wasn't, he was just a Jumped-up Johnny, as Rose used to say. A mushroom that grew up overnight. She had no fear of him. Greasy grey hair, huge ears, grey sports jacket, bright green tie.

He looked like he had no intention of leaving, persistent as he rang the bell for the third time. Cruising around the town in his silver Jag – the girls laughing at him – he thought himself to be stud material. But when his wife was around he was no more than a lapdog. The eejit.

Daisy pulled herself together before answering the door.

Leaving the door chain on, she opened the door a few inches.

"Yes. What do you want?"

"Apologies for calling so late in the evening. I think I might have damaged your car."

Daisy took the chain off the bolt. She opened the door.

"What?" was all she could say.

"Oh, sorry to bother you so late, love. I was just passing up the road. I think I might have tipped the side of your car. The mirror. I didn't want to leave it, so I said I'd call now."

"What do you mean?" said Daisy as she tried to put together what this man was saying to her. She could feel her patience slipping. "What do you mean you *think* you tipped my car? Didn't you look to check it?"

Daisy took her house keys and went out, closing the door behind her. She went down the steps, Davie stepping quickly in front of her. The streetlights were enough to reassure her. The car looked the same as she'd left it. She checked the side mirror. It was perfect.

Remaining silent, she walked quickly back up the steps towards the front door, Davie behind her.

She folded her arms, facing him, once safely back inside her door.

"I don't know what the hell you're doing here. You didn't hit my car, David Keogh. Yes, I know well who you are – and you know well who I am. Goodnight." She made to close the door.

"Oh, don't be like that now, Daisy … isn't it? I thought I had touched the mirror. Listen – come on down for a drink with me to the hotel to make up for disturbing you. Come on, I'll buy you a vodka – brandy – Bacardi, whatever you want. Come on. Just to make it up to you."

"I certainly will not do any such thing!"

She tried to make sense of what this creep was about.

He stood there, rubbing the sides of his greasy hair.

Then it dawned on her. Tom must have put him up to it. After the call to Sally, he couldn't have been too pleased. They probably had a bet on in the pub to see if he could lure her down.

"Do you take me for a complete fool?" she said. "How dare you show up at my home, this hour of the night! Don't you or any of your bloody cronies come near my house again, or I will call the Guards. Better still, I will call your wife!"

"Don't be like that, love. I came to the door only because I thought I had scraped your car."

"Look. Maybe this is closer to the language you understand. *Fuck off, Davie Keogh!*"

She shut the door in his face.

She was shaking.

Later on, she was sure it was Tom's car she heard, turning at the bottom of the road, passing up by her house again.

It was six months since Rose had passed. The legal separation had been stamped and Daisy had received her inheritance. She was now on her way to get Rose's letter from Thornton.

She had a feeling that the letter would have answers to questions that she had bombarded Rose with as a child, as any questions to do with family history had been a no-go area for Rose. She knew that her mother hadn't lied to her but the effects of her avoidance technique had tormented Daisy. She might as well have lied through her teeth.

Thornton was sitting behind his desk, full head of white

hair – gold-rimmed glasses on his long thin nose. He wore a navy, wide-pinstripe suit. His usual bright tie. Pink. In front of him on the desk was a white envelope with Daisy's name printed in black marker.

After the usual formalities, he wasted no time in handing it over and completing formalities.

Daisy had nothing to say, anxious to get out of there to read her letter, to touch the print, to feel close to Rose. She thanked him and left. Why hadn't he just posted the letter out to her?

She stopped the car and pulled over. She couldn't wait a minute longer. She opened the envelope and recognised her mam's familiar handwriting on the pages before her. It was easily the most beautiful handwriting she had ever seen. She wondered why the writing on the envelope hadn't been Rose's.

She began to read.

St. Mary's Nursing Home
Laltywood
Ballygore
24th June, 1988

My Darling Daisy Jean O'Neill,

I am writing this letter to you, having spent some weeks in the Nursing Home. I am here for a little while but hope to be home soon. They take me in for a rest, when they feel that I need the care.

I really hope, Daisy, from the bottom of my heart, that we have reconciled by the time you get this letter in your hand. Mr. Thornton will be in touch with me to the end, and after I have gone will ensure that my wishes have been adhered to and that it is safe for you to receive this letter.

You know I was never one to express myself comfortably when it comes to emotions. However, I have to disregard that for now, as I know I owe it to you to explain to you about your life.

Firstly, I have to tell you that you are my life and have been since the day I set eyes on you. I love you as my own, even though I have never had a birth-child.

Daisy gasped at what she had just read. Had she seen things? Was she imagining it?

No, it was there in black and white. Her heart was pounding in her chest, in her head, she could hear it thumping all over. She couldn't believe it. It had all been a lie. One big fat lie.

Rereading the last paragraph she continued – afraid of what might come next.

I know it is quite a shock to get. I never had the heart to tell you as I didn't want you to be hurt. I have little choice now but to tell you the truth, as I have been ailing for some time.

This is what happened. I was coming from Mass one Sunday on the 4th of April, 1965, when I saw some commotion around a blue canvas bag which was sitting at the railing of the house next door to the church. You were in the bag, Daisy, yes you, left by some poor soul who couldn't look after you. You were only a few days old. You were all wrapped up in blue baby-boy's clothes, so the people that were around thought it was a baby boy in the bag. This last fact was to be a miracle in disguise, Daisy. It later led to the townspeople never realising that you, my little girl, were the baby found in the bag. You see, I had been fostering babies for years so the townspeople were accustomed to seeing me pushing a succession of babies in my pram.

Word went out that a little boy was left near the church gates and Father Mac and the Nurse did all they could to find your birth mother, but nobody came forward.

So I reared you as my own, Daisy. You had been well dressed in the blue crochet outfit, with a yellow holy badge pinned to your matinee coat. There was no note, just a beautiful baby that was you. There was a daisy patch stitched to the sleeve of your cardigan. So, Father Mac baptised you that first day right there in my kitchen. I named you Daisy Jean. Daisy because of the daisy patch and Jean as you know after my John P – Jean being the feminine form. I was allowed to adopt you a year after you were born, and you legally became Daisy Jean O'Neill. DOB 01/04/1965.

I became your mother, my Daisy. You came home with me, love, on that day and never left until that day that we fell out. I hope that you can forgive my weakness. I was afraid to tell you for fear of losing you. If I am to be honest, I feared most of all that you would be taken from me.

The bag, blanket, baby clothes and some other items are all in the attic of the house, Daisy. They are hidden behind the wooden panel to the right of the far wall. John P made it years ago – he was a master in making sure that what was hidden was safe. The panel below can be opened by pressing down hard on the ledge, right on the corner.

The bag is wrapped in plastic, deep at the back of the cavity.

Mr. Thornton will keep a copy of this letter on file, just to be doubly sure that you receive it.

I cannot say more, Daisy, except that I am sorry, but not for loving you. I trust that you will go out and look for your own answers. Remember, none of this is your fault – the faults lie in the mistakes of others. Be self-assured and remember that I carry my love for you with me here and beyond.

I finish this letter to you, my darling, hoping beyond all hope that we will have time to spend together before you have to receive this. Even though I am doing very well at the moment, I am no longer at the early stage of my illness. They don't hold out great hope for me. Do well in your life and let nobody make you their victim again. You are a strong young woman and must build on that strength in the years ahead.

My love and my life

Rose

The tears flowed down Daisy's cheeks. She had ignored the feeling over the years when she'd felt her mam was keeping things from her.

Now, placing her hand over her heart to soothe the hurt inside her, she spoke aloud. "Oh, Mam, why didn't you tell me this years ago, when you could have helped me to deal with it all? So was it all a dream, Mam – Rose – your dream?"

She needed time to adjust. If her mam wasn't her birth mother, then who was? And who was her father then?

She was angry. Angry with Rose. Surely, if she'd loved her as much as she insisted, she'd have told her the truth long ago. Angry with herself, for not listening to her gut years before. She had sometimes wondered and now she knew. Angry with the woman who had given birth to her – whoever she was.

She had the raw truth, and Rose was no longer around to have it out with her.

She called Emmet the following morning – she needed to tell someone. He was the only person right now that she knew would hold her secret. There was no point in calling

Anne or Bernie until she accepted the truth herself.

One thing was for sure, Emmet would never betray her confidence.

She told him she'd had some upsetting news, asking if he'd meet her as she needed a friend.

"Of course, Daisy, but look – it's better if I don't call to the house to see you – not because I'm afraid of what Tom might think – I couldn't give a shite what he'd say. I'm just thinking about you, and all the tongues wagging. Meet me wherever you want – we can chat then."

"Swear on your life that you won't tell a soul, Emmet. This is much bigger than me. I don't know what to do."

"Daisy Arno – O'Neill, what do you take me for? We are friends as you yourself have often said. That's that. I don't have a lot, but I do have honour."

Daisy let out a nervous chuckle. "I know you wouldn't tell."

"Look, meet me tomorrow – say, two o'clock at the New House Inn. It'll be quiet. I was there with Susan last week. And there wasn't a sinner in it."

"Susan? Susan who?" She didn't know anyone called Susan, did she?

"Oh! I didn't see you to tell you. Her name is Susan Doyle – I've been seeing her on and off now for a couple of months, nothing serious. Yet." He laughed. "But I don't want to mess it up."

"It's OK, Emmet – you have no explaining to do to me. We're adults, remember?"

She was sitting at the table waiting for him. Watching him come towards her, she couldn't help but admire how handsome he looked. Navy sports jacket, white shirt, black shoes polished to the last. Emmet was always well groomed. She had liked that about him from the beginning. Unlike Tom, who wasn't always the best in the hygiene department.

Now that she knew he was dating Susan Doyle, he looked even more dapper in her eyes. She was surprised that she was feeling more than a little put out. She didn't own him after all. Breathing in the familiar scent in the air around him, she was glad to see him.

"Look at you, Emmet Roche! She must be special all right."

"And look at you, Daisy Arnold – O'Neill."

"I know, I'll have to get used to the O'Neill bit myself, but I will ... in time. Though I may have to get used to another name altogether. Once I find out what it is, of course."

Her eyes filled with tears.

"What in the name of ... What do you mean, Daisy? Have you met someone too? Jeekers, it's a bit soon, isn't it?"

"You ape, Emmet – did you seriously think I'd be fool enough to get involved with a man again? Any time soon?"

She felt her face redden, as did Emmet's.

She leaned over to her left, taking the letter from her handbag. She passed it across the table to him.

He read in silence.

Once finished, he folded the letter neatly, sighed heavily and passed it back to her.

He stood up and beckoned her towards the door.

"Let's get out of here, back to your place. I'll be there straight after you. There was me worried about the neighbours! I couldn't give a damn right now. Let's go. I'm parked around the back, beside yours."

The waitress was on her way over to take their order as the stylish couple stood up and walked out.

Once inside the house, Emmet hugged her to him.

"Come here, you! How long have you known?"

"Just yesterday," she whispered, taking full advantage of the embrace. It felt good to be held, familiar.

"I don't know what to say."

They sat at the table in the kitchen.

She looked across at him, her hand over her mouth. Waiting for some kind of reassurance.

"Oh Daisy, what a shock to get! Look at the positive side. What could your mother have done, Rose I mean, after saying nothing all the years? Then recently, given all the stuff with Tom and then her being so sick. You heard the nurse yourself – she did try to get in touch with you."

Daisy knew that he was at a loss – trying to say the right thing.

"You know that Tom wanted Rose well away from you," Emmet went on. "Looks like she was trying to get in touch for some time. That bollocks blocked her every time. No point in blaming the woman for anything. She must have had serious guilt after you left. For your own sake you'd better forgive her and move on. I'll help you whatever you decide to do. Jeekers – you might have family around the place, did you think of that at all? Whoever had you is probably still around. You could have brothers and sisters, aunts …"

"Stop right there, Emmet. I hadn't even thought about having another mother, not to mind anyone else. It's all too much. My God, I can't get my head around it. I was left in a bloody blue canvas bag. Imagine – and dressed as a boy. Jesus, can you believe it? Can you bloody believe it?"

He sat there, shaking his head.

"Rose will always be my mam. Nobody can take that from me. But I need to truly believe that her reasons for keeping me in the dark were because she loved me. I need to let it sink in."

"You do."

"And her last words were to tell me how sorry she was. And me, the fool, wondering for what. Well, now I know, don't I?"

"You mustn't let it overwhelm you. You're strong now, Daisy, a damn sight stronger than ever you were. You toughened up and that's for sure – living with himself for the past five years. You got rid of him. Don't take one step forward and two steps back. You were everything to Rose. She proved that with her will. Hasn't she left you well off? You need to be careful about that. There's a lot of grabbers out there."

She knew that he was fishing – he didn't need to know – she didn't trust him that much.

"Emmet, will you stick to the point! What do I do now?"

"Well … you have two options, I guess … You can accept things as they are and go on with your life. Or … you can try to search for your birth mother."

"You're right. It's as simple as that."

"Well, take it from there then. Give yourself time to get over the shock and make that decision."

He stood up to leave.

"I'm here for you. When you're ready to talk again, give me a shout. And if you want to, we can make a start on the search. Whatever you want – at your own pace."

"Well, I do know one thing. I can't face going up to the attic any time soon."

"Take your time. Until you're ready. Do you know, I'm just remembering Tom rambling one night about Rose. He said his mother had said something to him about Rose fostering kids years ago. I didn't take any notice." He sighed.

Daisy stood and put her hand on his arm. "If there was talk – someone might know something. Though Rose said nothing was ever found out."

"We could start there?"

"Emmet … I think I have to find out who I am."

"Think about it, love. You may not like what you find." He held her in his arms before releasing his hold quickly.

Daisy felt better in herself after confiding in Emmet. It was a short straw but she couldn't trust anyone else right now.

Chapter 20

The Journalist

George Doyle had landed on his feet all right – he was now a fully fledged journalist with the *Daily News*. He didn't mind life in the city – although he hardly spent a weekend in it, preferring to travel back to Ballygore, to work behind the bar with **Philly Manson's Hotel** in big gold letters above the front door.

He was almost thirty-seven and unmarried. Not that he was bothered about the married piece – he left all that to his mother, who spent many an hour on her knees praying that he'd meet someone nice. He'd met quite a few, but never a girl that stopped him in his tracks. And that's what he wanted. He could wait – as long as he could put up with his mother's endless questions about his love life. Or lack of it. All the same, he appreciated the sacrifices that she'd made, to get him through college, ending up in a career that he knew was mapped out for him.

He had done his own bit, helping Philly keep the bar running for what seemed like forever. He couldn't believe it himself but he had been there on and off for over twenty years, confused as to why it was ever called a hotel in the first place. There were other small hotels in the town that kept people overnight and served food. Philly only sold crisps and peanuts – telling people to move off somewhere else if they weren't satisfied with what he had to offer. For as long as George could remember, it had been the same.

As he got older – and odder – Philly Manson opened the bar when he felt like it, and that had whittled mainly down to the weekends. Likewise, he closed when it suited him. No matter who was there at the time. He was well known to be an oddball. Eccentric. But as long as George came back at the weekends, the bar would remain open. The older man trusted him above anyone else.

Having learned the trade through Philly, George had no interest in alcohol. He could take it or leave it.

"Stay clear of it, lad. I make a living out of the bloody stuff but I've seen it destroy too many fine people."

Working in Philly's had been an education in itself for George. There since he was fourteen, starting with the glasses and cleaning the toilets which had been an eye opener. Especially the men's toilet, where the bar of soap might be in the same spot for the night. Unused. While the hand towel might be on the floor. People's antics never failed to intrigue him, seeing customers come in as decent people – leaving or being told to leave as loudmouthed uninhibited fools. Most people were decent enough. It was the same few all the time.

Philly had always been peculiar. Five foot three inches tall, with more than a slight hump on his back and a tongue well capable of downing a man of any height. In his day, if he took a notion, he could order a customer off the premises before anyone knew what for. A regular occurrence. He had thrown many a patron out. Good or bad depended on how he was feeling. If they had put their dirty feet on his covered stool, they'd be out the door before they knew it. Or stamped a cigarette out on his flagstone floor. When Philly copped that a spit had hit the floor, they were thrown out straight away. Yes, Philly Manson was well known for keeping a clean house. And the punters kept coming back. Feeling almost grateful when Philly made conversation with them. The regulars knew him well enough not to take much notice. They accepted him for the oddball that he was. As he was pushing on, he had lost some of his gusto – but he could turn quick enough. The punters respected him – George could tell. If he gave them any time at all, they'd order another drink. It was just the way it was. Philly didn't suffer fools gladly, no matter how fast he was pushing on. They knew what was coming by the look he'd give them, especially if he was rubbing away at a glass with his tea towel, his eyes squinting and he staring straight at them. Giving them the look – and he barely visible over the high bar.

Over the years, Philly had given George more hours than he needed to. He knew that times were hard on the family. George's mother had cleaned and ironed for him when they were young. George had seen Philly drooling over his mother in the early years, his tongue half out of his mouth. He'd copped it a few times, after which Philly must have given up. He might have been hopeful – maybe. But Kitty Doyle hadn't the slightest interest in him. Or any other man. It was out of the question. Her kids were her life and that was it.

She told George that Philly was nice man and all that, but she wouldn't touch him with a forty-foot pole. He had paid her well and it suited her as she was out of sight of the customers. In and out again before the bar opened. Philly had been a lifeline for the family.

George loved working in the bar though he hadn't much to offer in the line of conversation outside of what interested him. Refusing to get stuck in idle gossip, he'd heard it all, without having to engage. George hated the way the men talked about women, especially when they were well on. Their own wives exempt from their lewd comments. Any such comment there, would be seen as a slur on themselves.

George was not exempt from bar gossip, particularly when Philly had gone up for the night. The slagging would start.

"Look at you, Doyle. In for a bloody fortune when Manson kicks the bucket. You thought that one out all right!"

"The cute hoor, waiting around to take over the place!"

"'Tis the likes of him that'll get the place! A Doyle from the Hill Road!"

George knew that some of them were only waiting to bring him down. Particularly those who saw his education as more of a threat than anything else. He was well able for them.

After a busy night working in the bar, he would wind down as he had always done – lying on his bed at home – working on his diaries. His hobby. He found it relaxing. And all in the name of good investigative journalism.

He reckoned over the years he'd heard enough to fill a thousand newspapers without ever having to leave the bar.

* * *

The hotel bar was a long L-shaped bar. The regulars had their spots. If a regular wasn't in his spot drinking then more than likely he wasn't there. David Keogh was one such man, as was Tom Arnold and a few others who held up the corner of the bar until the small hours. Simon Harris was well in his sixties but still making lewd comments to every female as they passed.

"Look at the pins on that one! Hey, love, do they go the whole way up to your arse?"

A guffaw would follow.

George wondered if Harris realised that the type of women he attracted saw his wallet before they saw him. Simon didn't care as long as he was getting a bit of attention.

And Keogh wasn't much better. He lived in the big house further along the Hill Road. Married to Grace with her nose up in the air. Full of shit they were. He was a pathetic excuse for a man but a cute hoor at the same time. Not much escaped Davie Keogh when it came to making a few quid. George had seen him many a time plotting a deal at the bar. Drunk or sober, he had a head for figures.

Tom Arnold was the messer, more so with drink in him. One minute charming and polite, the next a proper thug. He'd cause a fight as quick as anything and leave it twice as quick. Often told to leave, it had no effect on him – swallowing his pint back in one go, moving on to the next pub.

George was well pleased that his mother no longer worked in the pub. His sister Susan wasn't one to drink at Philly's either, preferring the more modern bars in the town.

He worried about Susan, who seemed to light up of late when she mentioned Emmet Roche's name. And his mother had told him that she had been out on a few dates with him. Before adding that he came from good stock, the parents being two teachers.

George didn't have to ask who Emmet was – he knew well who he was. Tom Arnold's sidekick. Over the years where one appeared, the other wasn't far behind. George would keep his eyes and ears open. The last thing he wanted was for Susan to be getting mixed up in that crowd. If he thought that Roche was up to no good with his sister, he would level him. His saving grace, as far as George was concerned, was that he hadn't seen him around Arnold as much of late. Maybe he was keeping well away. And he had noticed Emmet ordering bottled water for himself when it came to ordering his own round. Asking for ice and lemon – maybe he was just tight – or most likely pretending it was gin. But it didn't stop him from holding up the bar with Arnold, Keogh and the others when it suited him.

George cocked his ears on hearing Roche's name mentioned.

"Look at the other bollocks – Roche. *Hah!* Best friend, my arse – and he bonking Arnold's wife, all the way to the races," said Simon Harris.

"She's some detail all right, that one. No wonder poor Tom is in the state he is."

"Who could blame him?"

"I might give her a go myself!"

"Didn't she try it on with you, Keogh?"

George said nothing but took heed. He was fuming.

Susan was not going to be made a fool of, right under his nose.

Was Roche having an affair with Tom Arnold's ex? If he was, he would make sure that he never laid eyes on his sister again.

Susan wasn't stupid. He needed some more proof before warning her. There was no point in causing upset until he had his homework done.

He'd remembered his mother saying that Arnold's wife had left him and was back living in the home place. She seemed to think the girl was a decent sort who just got mixed up with the wrong man.

George began to watch out as he drove past the Widow Neill's house at the weekends. Not a sign of Emmet's car.

The slagging continued late at night on and off. When George got to a point where he'd heard enough he decided to face Emmet with what he had heard. The opportunity came faster than he'd expected.

Emmet was parking in their yard on the following Friday evening, just as George came out of the house.

George walked over to Emmet who rolled down his window.

Before he could open his mouth, George began. "Emmet, can I sit in with you for a minute. There's something I want to run by you."

"No problem, sit in," said Emmet as he leant across to open the passenger door.

"Straight to the point, Roche. You can take what I have to say any way you want. But I'm hoping you'll take it seriously – as in, that's my young sister you're seeing."

Emmet looked alarmed.

"You see," George continued. "I'm hearing constant rumours for a while now, from the corner end of the bar. About you." He paused as he drew a deep breath before continuing. His speech was slow and measured. "Now, you'll understand that I'm saying this to you, on the understanding that you care for my sister. That your intentions towards her are decent."

Emmet nodded.

"Now, man, is there any truth in the scurrilous rumour that yourself and Tom Arnold's wife are, shall we say, more than friends?"

Emmet attempted to answer but couldn't seem to get the words out. His face was white with shock.

George raised his hand, making a gesture to Emmet not to speak. "Let me finish now. I know the lads like to mess about and all that, and I'm certainly not one for idle gossip. But obviously Susan means more to me than anyone in that bar, including and especially you. Like I said, I'm hearing rumours. If you have anything to say, now is not the time. Think carefully, man. Are we OK with that?"

Emmet nodded his head again – he didn't feel he had a choice.

George continued. "As I see it, you have a few options here."

He was trying his best to stay calm. He took a few breaths before speaking as he did when doing an interview for the paper. He was used to getting information from difficult people in difficult situations. This was the one time he was having difficulty. He hoped it did not show.

"Firstly, if you are having an affair with Arnold's wife, it's none of my business. Except to say, you will do the

207

decent thing now and tell Susan yourself. Before I do, that is. Secondly, if it's all lies and gossip, then you'll still tell her about the gossip. Before I do, that is. The third option is that you fuck off out of this yard before Susan comes out and I will explain the lot to her. Trust me, if I give you a fourth option, you will not like it."

George opened the car door and looked back at Emmet.

"You have one week, man, before the shit hits the fan."

George got out, leaving Emmet shaken in his seat.

He had just got into his own car when Susan appeared. She ran towards Emmet's car but then noticed George. She waved. "See you later, Georgie."

He gave her a wave and drove out of the yard.

Susan got in beside Emmet. "What's the matter? Jesus, you look like you've seen a ghost!"

Clearing his throat, he started up the engine. "Nothing's wrong, love. Just having a chat there with George. We were just talking about Philly and the crack in the bar."

Chapter 21

Rumours

Daisy woke up the following morning to the sound of the phone ringing in her ear.

"Daisy, he knows! George Doyle fucking knows!"

"Emmet, I'm in bed, barely awake – slow down – what are you on about? George *Who* knows what?"

"George Doyle. About us, he knows about our fling, and he's threatening to tell Susan if I don't tell her."

"Emmet Roche, will you calm down and tell me what has happened?"

"I said I'd call you first thing – I can't be seen at your place. I can't lose her, Daisy, I just can't. She's the best thing that's ever happened to me. I've plans for the future. Oh, you know what I mean!"

"Emmet, calm down! Stop babbling and tell me what happened with George Doyle!"

"Susan – my Susan – she's George Doyle's sister. You know him, from the Hill Road. He drives a white Ford. He's a journalist, comes back to Bally every weekend to work in

Philly Manson's. Big fella. Kind of rugged-looking. He's Manson's right-hand man. He caught up with me when I was picking Susan up yesterday. He said the rumours are flying, that you and I are having a secret affair."

"Stop right there, Emmet, and catch your breath. Tell me *exactly* what he said to you."

Daisy suddenly felt wide awake and alert.

"Well, I don't know exactly where he heard it – but he said it was all around the bar. He said that if I don't tell Susan he will. He gave me three choices. And a fourth which doesn't sound like an option. Basically, he said if it's true I better tell Susan, and even if it's not true I have to tell her anyway about the rumours. I have one week. He was bloody serious, Daisy, and If Tom finds out – I'm a dead man."

"OK, let me think about it. Call me back at lunchtime when you've calmed down."

She hung up.

Lying awake she thought how cowardly and childish he'd sounded. He was more afraid that Tom would go after him than anything else. Well, he did care about losing that girl too.

From her point of view, who cared if word got out – she'd lost enough already.

Pulling the covers over her head, she went straight back to sleep.

Emmet rang at one o'clock sharp.

"Well, what do you think? I'm going out of my mind here."

"Listen to me. You're blowing this out of all proportion. Whatever the rumours, no one really knows about 'our little fling', as you call it – unless you said something yourself, that is?"

"Of course I didn't, I'd never say a word. I have too much to lose. But, I was thinking after that, I haven't really cheated on Susan and it's never going to happen again. It's all in the past. So why am I so worried?"

Because you're scared of a beating, she thought, or too embarrassed to give it to say that you'd had an affair with a married woman.

"Right then, as far as anyone is concerned – the only times we were seen together was around the time my mam died, in the hospital, or in the café. You were there for me during all that – but as a friend. They know nothing. Tom knows you're his mate. He trusts you – so no worries there. *Deny, deny, deny.* But you will have to tell Susan about the rumours. And tell George that we're just friends."

"Of course, of course. You're a genius. Sure, wasn't I always at your house with Tom anyway? There's not a single person can prove anything. They're only guessing. But Susan can't find out the truth – I don't want to lose her."

"Too much time has passed, Emmet – even if someone copped you there with me. Anyway your old car was the same as Tom's and ye do look alike. It was foolproof. Just forget about it, will you? If you deny it to yourself, it'll be easier with others."

"So what will I tell her?"

"Tell her about your friendship with Tom since ye were boys. How you brought him home at night. How you liked his wife so much you slept with her."

"Are you stark raving mad, Daisy?"

"Jesus, take a joke, will you? So George knows that you and Tom were friends from working in Manson's. If you're convincing enough, Susan will be fine. She has no other reason to doubt you, has she?"

211

"No, no, you're right. Deny, deny and forget about it. We're friends, that's all. It was all a huge mistake. I'll talk to her over the next few days. Should I ring him, I wonder, or leave well enough alone?"

"Ring nobody. Wait the week. You can do nothing about the gossip. The last thing you want is cause suspicion with your reaction. Offer him nothing. As far as you are concerned those dopes at the bar are talking horseshit. Can a man and woman not be friends? Of course they can. If you bump into George, which you won't, look him straight in the eye. Tell him he's got his story wrong this time. You're the one here with a lot to lose. I really couldn't care less anymore. I'm done with this victim crap. But I can do without the drama. I have a plan to shut him up if it comes to it – well, more to deflect him. He's a reporter with the *Daily News*, you say?"

"Yes, he is. What plan?"

"Never mind for now. You can bring Susan over to meet me properly some evening – that would be a good move. She'll see for herself that we're just friends."

As the conversation ended, she felt as used as ever she'd felt. She would never again allow herself to be traded like that. He had made her feel next to worthless. He had the cheek to say it was "a huge mistake". Emmet didn't even know Susan until well after their affair. A decent man wouldn't have reacted as he did. He was ashamed and weak.

Emmet Roche and Tom Arnold were well matched all right.

Emmet was on the phone again before the week was out. He was still stressing about George finding out about the affair. He asked her was it OK if he brought Susan over to meet her.

"I've thought about it and you're right. I should make it as normal as possible. Like you said, she'll see we're just friends. That I'm only interested in her."

God, he was so insensitive! "No problem. Come over for a cuppa on Thursday evening. But you need to relax or she'll sense something is wrong."

"God, anyone would think we have something to hide!"

She laughed at his comment – understanding.

"It was all messed up between us, Daisy. All to do with the shite going on the last few years with Tom."

Suddenly Daisy was seething. He continued to demean her at every turn. She was remembering not too long before when those emotions had been reserved solely for her. How easily it had all turned around!

"Absolutely," she said. "But, Emmet, are you going to tell her about the rumours before you bring her here?"

"Yes, I must. Though I'm afraid I'll chicken out."

"Don't. And, Emmet, I'm getting fed up with all this drama. Just deal with it."

"After all the shite with George Doyle – I'm just on edge – on my guard. You know, Daisy, I'd have done time for you."

"Emmet, enough. You've been there for me over the last few years, in more ways than one."

She hoped he didn't hear her snigger.

"We are friends – nothing has changed in that respect."

"I'll see ye both on Thursday then."

Chapter 22

The Introduction

Susan Doyle walked in the door a few steps ahead of Emmet, who seemed intent on wiping his feet vigorously on the mat.

"Hi, Susan, come on in! Emmet, come on, your shoes are lovely."

Rubbing his hands together, he followed.

"Susan, this is Daisy." He looked nervous. "Daisy – Susan."

Daisy was pleasantly surprised as the girl with the big open smile beamed back at her. With blue eyes, a mane of thick red hair, she was wearing a navy polo over faded jeans. No make-up. Big rounded teeth – full lips. Daisy instantly warmed to her.

They went through to the kitchen where they drank tea and chatted, laughing at Emmet's corny jokes. Nobody was saying very much, just enjoying the banter.

Daisy came to the conclusion that George couldn't have yet told Susan about the rumours. The girl was just too cheerful.

Finally, Daisy broke the flow. "Well, Susan, myself and himself have been friends for a long time. I'm glad to finally meet the love of his life. He had me tormented to meet you."

Susan shrugged her shoulders at the comment. "Early days and all that. You know, Emmet has filled me in on a few things. Not much, just enough to persuade me that there's nothing going on between you two. It hadn't entered my mind, of course. And why would it?"

They all laughed, Emmet's laughter sounding somewhat high-pitched.

The wording of Susan's comments hadn't gone unheeded by Daisy. So the girl wasn't quite the pushover after all.

Gathering her wits, Daisy replied, "Oh, did he now? And after I asked him to keep his mouth shut. Just goes to show you whose camp he's in."

Laughter again – the ice was broken.

Daisy made fresh tea for her visitors, pointedly asking them both if they took milk or sugar.

"You'd think at this stage I'd remember what Emmet took in his tea, but I don't."

Before Emmet could answer Susan answered, "Black with one sugar, mine's white no sugar. Thanks, Daisy."

Daisy couldn't help but admire this girl, who was going to have her work cut out for her with Emmet. But she seemed to have a strength about her that would definitely help to keep him in tow. Susan Doyle didn't appear to be the type to let a weak man take her down easily. Good for her.

"Susan, I think Emmet here was half afraid to be seen talking to me, in case you got the wrong idea. He and I are friends and will never be anything more. Even if the tongues in town were wagging."

Both women smiled as they got the measure of the other.

Emmet drank his tea, a sheepish look on his face. Leaving the girls to get on with it.

"Daisy, really, that never entered my mind. But, in any case, haven't we all a past? We're entitled to that without raking it up. But it's the future I'm interested in. Isn't that right, Emmet?

"Definitely – of course," said Emmet.

Not a pushover at all, thought Daisy. No pulling the wool over her eyes. Emmet was Susan's man. The past would remain in the past.

Susan felt comfortable, now that she had the measure of Emmet. She got him. Even if he had been with Daisy in the past, it was no longer the case. A man who would do anything for her – who made her feel like she was the most important person in his life. Emmet, she knew, didn't badmouth people. He made the best of every situation. He made her laugh and laughed with her. He had weaknesses – didn't everyone? He had followed Tom Arnold around for years like a lapdog because he could only see the good in him. But dropped him as soon as he had learned the truth of his treatment of Daisy. Yes, she would be holding on to Emmet. *But* … if she had an inkling that he would be anything other than friends with any women in the future, she would drop him like a hot cake.

The couple listened as Daisy began to speak.

"As you probably know, Susan, I was raised by my mother Rose O'Neill, in this house, my home. But I found out recently that I was, in fact, the baby found outside the church here in Ballygore in 1965. I'm telling you my age now."

Susan and Emmet smiled.

"I was dressed like a boy, all in blue. The day I was found was the same day that Rose began to care for me. She adopted me at one year old. That's the sum total of what I know for now, Susan. You probably know my ex, Tom Arnold, and the friendship that has always been there between Emmet and him. Emmet here had been trying to help me get out of that bad situation, which I have."

Susan reached over to Emmet, entwining her fingers with his. Obviously proud of her man.

Daisy carried on. "Tom never knew my story. Emmet tells me to go to the papers with it, in the hope that it will jog someone's memory. I don't care at this stage what I have to do. Rose, my mam, has passed on, so I owe nothing to anybody. So that's exactly where I'm at."

Susan eyes had welled up as she listened to the story.

"I'm telling you all this, Susan – I'm trusting you – because I don't want to be leaving you in the dark. And Emmet tells me that your brother is a journalist. George, is it?"

"Yes."

"Perhaps he could help?"

"I'm sure he could. And if he can't he'll know how to go about it. I'll talk to him for you."

"Thank you, Susan."

Daisy knew as the couple left that day that Emmet was truly smitten. Susan seemed like a nice girl who wasn't going to damage her future with him by being suspicious of his past. But she was definitely not a gullible fool like Daisy herself had been.

She and Emmet were well matched. Opposites.

Chapter 23

Instant Attraction

Ten days later George was shaking hands with Daisy. He had known her to see, but not well enough that he didn't have to be introduced. He wasn't as open as his sister, given his natural curiosities and suspicions about people.

Susan had told him in no uncertain terms that she and Emmet were going steady. He decided to let it sit, given the fact his sister seemed to be more clued in than he'd thought.

He could see the nervousness in Emmet as much as he saw the adoration in his sister's eyes, but he could also see that Emmet cared for her. Any entanglement that may have existed between Emmet and Daisy was well over. If it had ever existed in the first place. George was a realist. He would help the widow's daughter to find the truth. He loved investigating a good story. At the same time he would keep his eyes and ears open. Nothing much escaped George Doyle.

Emmet had introduced the two in the carpark of the

café. He told Daisy that Susan had thought it best to stay out of it. He said there was no need for her to know any more than she did. It was now in George's department.

"Daisy, this is George Doyle, Susan's brother. Susan has told him a little bit about you. So George here might be just the man to help you." Emmet laughed. "Well, according to Susan, there's not a thing happens here in Bally without George knowing about it." Emmet was talking too much, talking stupid, rambling on.

Daisy felt the need to stop him. But she would bide her time for now.

She liked the look of this tall man standing before her. She liked it a lot. Feeling butterflies in her stomach, she didn't know whether it was anxiety or attraction. He looked nothing like what she'd expected. Not exactly rugged as Emmet had said, but certainly not what she'd imagined an office-based journalist should look like. Broad shoulders with a strong neck – she liked that in a man. His soft tan suede jacket looked just right on him as did his check lumberman shirt. His curled strawberry-blonde hair sat loosely on his shoulders. His blue eyes held her own. You could tell he was Susan's brother.

"Emmet, are you off so? It's freezing out here – thanks a million," she said, waving at him, giving him the cue to leave. She didn't want Emmet around a moment longer. It hadn't taken her any time at all to realise that, like his sister, George was no fool. He was looking at her as if he could see right through her. Unnerving her. If he could make her feel like that, then Emmet wouldn't stand a chance in his company while she was around.

She was impressed as George took over – leading her to a table in the corner where they could talk – pulling a chair out for her – offering to close the sash window behind her back to keep out the October chill. A gentleman as well, she thought.

She waited until they had ordered coffee, then began.

"No need for small talk, I guess. Before I tell you about myself, George, I feel I should say something just to clear the air. Emmet told me about the rumours in the bar, about himself and myself. Not true. He was there for me during my marriage, when I needed a friend and God knows I did. Without hashing through that stuff – there's nothing going on between us."

Her eyes fixed on his. She saw his eyebrows lift in surprise at her directness.

She then began to tell as much of her story as she felt he needed to know. Being aware that it could be used to sell newspapers, she had intended on giving him just the basics for now. But she carried on confiding in him, more than she had intended. He had a way about him.

"George, I loved my mother Rose. She was all I had in the world. She loved me as her own. Finding out that I'm not her natural daughter hasn't affected me in the way that it could have. She gave me all the love and support in the world. In a way, although she kept the truth hidden from me, she prepared me in other ways for what is to come." Leaning closer to him. "Is it too much to wonder where my peculiar grey eyes came from? Or who I inherited my long nose from?" Trailing her finger down her nose. She looked into the bluest eyes which were glinting back at her.

Seeing the pleading in her eyes, suddenly George wanted to hold her.

He had listened to her tell the bones of her story,

looking at her intently. She hadn't shed a tear, while displaying strong emotion through her voice and her body language. He was at least a decade older than this girl who displayed the maturity of a woman well beyond her years. Without taking his eyes off her, he had nodded his head a few times to show her he was listening.

He noted that when she had mentioned Emmet Roche's name, there had been no emotion shown. He was impressed at her immediate effort to squash any rumours about herself and Emmet – it was obvious that some discussion had taken place. This girl wasn't one to hold back.

Daisy passed Rose's letter across the table to him – having folded it over showing only the part that she wanted him to read.

Quietly, he read the paragraph. He didn't open the page out. Handing it back to her, he was thinking that he must be going soft. This girl had just stopped him in his tracks.

He had no need to go public with her search yet. He needed to get home, pull out the wooden box to search through his notebooks.

The blue bag had jogged his memory – the blue washing bag. It had jumped off the page at him. That day when he had been hiding on his perch on the back wall of the church.

Putting his thoughts aside, he listened.

"I want to find out who gave birth to me and why I was dressed like a boy. I was left in a blue canvas bag. I can't help wondering – was I dumped because someone prepared for a boy? And surprise, surprise, I arrived instead – and so was abandoned. It might seem stupid to be going on about the baby clothes. In fact, I haven't had the courage to go to the attic for them yet. They've been up there long enough – another while won't matter."

"Daisy, can I interrupt you there? Who else knows that you were the baby found in the blue bag?" An image of Davie Keogh's face floated before him. He could say nothing yet.

"Just Emmet, your sister Susan and yourself now. That's it. Oh, and Thornton the solicitor. Mam is gone, Father Mac and the district nurse who were there on the day, gone too. I suppose there are people in the town that would remember the baby found at the church. But Rose said that because I was dressed all in blue they figured it was a boy in the bag. They were made none the wiser by the three people who knew the truth. So later no one realised I was the baby. I don't know if there's a record of it somewhere. Maybe there is, but you know what things were like back then – all shame and secrecy."

George leant forward, placing his elbows on the table.

His mind was elsewhere as she told him that she had been on to the church, which had nothing but a few lines. No details.

Almost certain that he had information in his notebooks, he wasn't about to jump in building up her hopes by mentioning it – not until he had seen for himself.

He would wait until the time was right – time to do his research.

"But surely there's some sort of a record about you being fostered by Rose. There has to be a file. I remember my own mam saying that Rose took in babies years ago. It was common knowledge at the time. Even I can remember seeing the widow rolling a pram around the town. She certainly stood out, proud and tall."

Daisy softly said, "And she was the most loving, kind mother." Then changing her tone, she went on. "If there are any records out there – do you honestly believe that they'll hand them over to me?"

"If the Health Board has a record of a baby being placed with Rose on the same date you were found, surely it's as easy as that to link the pieces. It doesn't give us much after that, but at least it's a start. There has to be some sort of a paper trail. We can put your story in print then, if we need to jog a few memories. Well, what do you say?"

"Jesus, the papers – that might be going a little too far for me yet."

"We could do it in such a way we wouldn't give away too much. I'm just covering myself as the eager journalist that I am. No papers then?"

He knew what he was doing – covering all angles – until he had his homework done.

Admiring his directness, she nodded her head.

Looking at her face, he decided to relent a little. "I have a feeling about this. I have some old records that I need to look through. I don't want to be giving you false hope here – just let me follow up on a few checks. It may be something, or nothing. I can't be sure. Let me take your number."

Daisy reached in her bag for a pen, feeling instinctively that this man was much more than a journalist. Hadn't he put the fear of God into Emmet? He was solid, not afraid to speak his mind. Good-looking into the bargain. She found herself hoping that it wouldn't be long before they would meet again.

223

Chapter 24

Denial

The phone was ringing in the hallway as she opened the front door.

"Daisy, how did that go? Was he suspicious? Are we off the hook? Susan seems well satisfied there's nothing going on between us."

"Um, yes. It's fine, I think." She didn't think it would help the situation to tell Emmet that she felt Susan was no fool and probably had his measure.

"Daisy, Jesus, I don't want to be saying too much over the phone. I never meant for any of this to happen. If I could only go back in time. Myself and Susan are right for each other and I wouldn't have it in me to hurt her. I don't know what I was thinking when we … well, you know … we were confused between friendship and the other. You get what I mean?"

"Look, I've enough to be dealing with right now, and actually George Doyle is being really helpful. So thanks for making it all possible. And Emmet, talk to Susan again. The two of you must keep quiet about me being the baby in the bag for now. George is going to have a look around to see what he can find. And I trust him not to let me down." Her tone changed quickly. She couldn't help herself. "I actually quite liked George. He seems like a bloke who stands on his own two feet without answering to anyone. I like that in a man. And he smells of musk and wild flowers."

Aware of what she was doing – she smiled wryly towards the handset, sticking her tongue out.

"Before you say it, Emmet – The age difference means feck all to me. As Rose would say, better an old man's darling than a young man's slave." She was taunting him.

He answered quickly, blurting out, not thinking. "What! You're joking? Your history in fairness – your past – as well as being a married woman. Jesus, what are you on about? George Doyle and you, you've got to be kidding me, right? In fairness …" Then quickly he changed mid-sentence. "There'd be no future in it – if that's what you're hoping for."

She spoke clearly. Disgusted. "Emmet, just remember, if I decide that George Doyle should be more to me, it's none of your business. One word. *Termination*. Do I make myself clear?"

"Crystal."

She could tell by the silence that followed that he was probably shocked at her outburst. No doubt he would be finding it difficult to believe that this was the same innocent girl that he had been so enamoured with.

She certainly had changed. She hoped that he regretted opening his mouth to deny her – he should have said nothing.

She'd expected far too much from him. Before he

could say goodbye, she acted. Time to put her plan in place. She would show him the true picture of himself.

"Look, just call over later on. I won't keep you more than a few minutes. There's something I have to show you. Two minutes. Seven o'clock and park at the back. I'll leave the back door open."

"Why –"

She hung up.

Not only had he brushed her aside and made nothing of the time he had spent with her, he had more or less said that she worthless – not good enough for George – mentioning her past – her history. Going out of his way to appear as the perfect man for Susan by belittling her in the process.

So he felt ashamed of their affair, did he? The cheek of him. Having chased her like a rabbit, until things got too much for him. Now he was trying to convince himself all he'd done was feel sorry for her. He had all but said she was tainted – used goods. He had as much as said she wouldn't be in the same league as a single woman. A woman such as Susan Doyle.

Well, she was no longer going to be undermined by men who used her and abused her. Her friendship with Emmet was losing its fervour. She would not be cast aside again like a used wrapper. Like rubbish.

Her plan would ensure that Emmet stayed on track in the future. And on track for Susan.

Emmet came to the back door at seven. She could see him from the upstairs window. The usual, wiping his feet over and over again on the mat. Flicking the moths away from his hand.

"*Hello!*" he called as he entered.

He sounded nervous.

"I'm up here, Emmet. Go on through to the front room. I won't be a minute, I'm just out of the shower."

Emmet sat down on Rose's mustard sofa.

Daisy appeared within a few minutes and sat down beside him, close enough for him to look uncomfortable. Wearing very little inside the short blue flimsy dressing gown, which opened up along her thigh as she moved closer still to him.

She could see that he couldn't make eye contact. He was too busy looking everywhere else. Daisy knew she had him where she wanted him.

"Sorry, Emmet. I forgot you were calling – it slipped my mind. Can I get you a coffee or a drink maybe?"

She went to stand up and, before he had a chance to answer, the gown she was wearing slithered to the floor. Bending over to retrieve it, her breasts were inches away from his face. She feigned embarrassment, attempting to cover herself. She watched Emmet, knowing that he couldn't ignore his instincts, aware that he wanted her badly.

He reached out, grabbing her by the arms. Pulling her across the sofa, he stood and undressed, removing all but his shirt and socks.

She did nothing, apart from making herself available to him. The excitement of controlling him had been foreplay enough for her.

It was over within minutes. She'd known it would be.

Rose's words came to her mind: *"Remember, love, it's the woman who holds the power in the end."*

She forced a smile – but not with her eyes.

Emmet would have forever to recall his shame and weakness.

She got to her feet and pulled her dressing gown on.

"Well, that was as I expected. You can get out now, Emmet. So, you will never hurt Susan. You felt sorry for me. You confused friendship with lust. *Bullshit.* You're as weak and shallow as they come. All I had to do was show a bit of flesh and you were putty in my hands. Listen and learn."

Emmet looked as if he couldn't believe what he was hearing. He sat on the edge of the sofa, trying to regain his composure.

"Women are not just easy targets to be used, abused and cast aside when the next one comes along. We're not there to be played by men. Emmet, you're no different to Tom. You were well met. The only difference is he's an alcoholic and a woman-beater. You're a user, a coward without balls. The ball is in my court now, Emmet. *And don't you ever forget it.*"

It felt good.

The following day the phone rang. She had been expecting the call. She held the phone to her ear, waiting for the caller to speak.

"Daisy, is that you?" A pause. "Daisy, just speak, so I can be sure it's you."

"Who did you think would answer?"

"Daisy, last night –"

"Yes, last night – I was surprised to say the least, when you ran out the back door so fast. You left your tie here, and your jocks. Don't worry, I'll keep them safe for you."

"Daisy, please, listen to me – I am here going fucking demented. What if Susan finds out – or worse still, George. He'll come after me big time, after she gives me the door."

"And you would like me to say what, Emmet? Should I say maybe that it never should have happened? Should I say I'm sorry you were so fucking weak that you couldn't resist a shag on the sofa with your bloody friend? Or maybe I should just say, 'Emmet, don't worry at all – it was just a huge mistake.' You choose!"

"You've proved your point. All I could see was Susan, going ahead into the future. I'm sorry – please don't mention a word of it – it will be our secret."

"I believed you when you said you were on my side – but you weren't." She had no notion of acknowledging his apology. He was a weak man in every sense. "I'll put it in the bag. Just like all the others, Emmet. One more won't hurt, will it now?"

The innocent Daisy married to Tom Arnold had long since gone. In her place was a woman who would not be played again. Having been told time and time again that her opinion didn't matter, she had ended up believing it. But her opinion would matter from now on.

"Oh, believe you me, not a word of this will pass my lips," he said. "The one thing you can count on is my word. Leave it at that. Bye."

Daisy felt relieved. She would hold on to his tie, just in case. The jocks she would burn.

Emmet had brushed her aside and made nothing of the time he had with her. Shame on him. She had regained her self-worth by showing up his weakness.

Emmet knew that he'd been played. Outsmarted. Like a fool he couldn't stop himself. She had used him. She might as well have stabbed him in the back.

How had it all come to this, he wondered. One day

Daisy was married to his best friend Tom. The next he was having a fling with her. Then nothing. Now all he felt was disgust and regret, knowing that he couldn't resist her. She had played him all right. Daisy had just lowered herself to the class of many other women he'd been with – sly, manipulative and out for themselves.

Susan was without doubt the safer bet. She mightn't be as thrilling or spontaneous as Daisy – but she was definitely safe. And his parents would approve – there was no dirt to be dragged out with Susan. No history that could throw up all sorts.

Two weeks later, on the last day in November, he got down on one knee to ask Susan for her hand in marriage. They'd been going out for six months. Once he had the ring on her finger, his fate would be secure. He'd have to say goodbye to any random thoughts he had of Daisy. Whatever the case.

Susan's eyes widened at the ring in the wine-coloured velvet box being presented to her by the love of her life. It was perfect, a petite solitaire, sitting on a thick gold band.

She couldn't take her eyes off it as Emmet placed it on her finger. It didn't matter that she hadn't replied. There was no need.

Finally she cried, "*Yes, yes, yes!*" and threw herself into his arms.

Emmet knew that she'd become his wife. It would all work out. They had a wedding to plan. But not for some time.

George smiled and hugged his sister when the couple told him the news.

Susan's mother was thrilled – and put a pound in the

Saint Anthony box. Her only daughter had cemented her future with a steady man at last. Emmet fitted the bill.

Emmet had one more call to make – before he could finally move on.

In the weeks that had passed, he had scarcely spoken to Daisy.

They met at the coffee dock in town. There would be no calling to the house unaccompanied. He had learned his lesson.

"To what do I owe the pleasure of your company, Emmet?"

"Ah stop, I just wanted to catch up." He waved at various people as they walked through the café. He wasn't going to be giving them anything to gossip about.

His meeting with Daisy was out in the open.

"Emmet, who are you waving at now. Will you get to the point and drink the coffee."

Holding her nose, she asked him what cologne he was wearing – she said that he smelled like a candle. He said that Susan had bought it for him.

Then he blurted it out. "Susan and I are engaged, since last night, and … I wanted you to be the first to know."

He looked at her, waiting for a reply.

"Not quite the first actually. George rang me first thing this morning to tell me the happy news. Congrats. I'm delighted for you both. She's a good girl." Meaning what she had said.

Emmet didn't know what to say. He hadn't slept a wink last night at the thought of telling her. And here she was now acting like an angel. He couldn't tell whether she was being genuine or sarcastic.

She couldn't help herself. Poking fun at him. "Aah, I must get you a little engagement present while I'm in town. You can collect it on your way home."

"Jaysus, are you crazy? I won't be going anywhere near your gate on my own, from now on. No problem meeting for the odd coffee in town."

"I'm joking."

He recognised the look in her eye. A look that had been polished over the past year.

"Seriously, Emmet." She leaned across the table, sliding his tie over towards him, making sure that there was nobody looking. "We are adults. We've had our fun. No blame, no shame."

Standing up, pushing the chairs back, they went their separate ways.

Chapter 25

Time to Act

Daisy woke up on a bright December morning to find her mood had lifted. The softness of the morning light warmed her. The sun as low as it could be in the sky. Feeling better than she had for some time, she welcomed the day ahead.

As she passed the attic door, she knew instinctively that she was almost ready to go up there. Ready to face the ghosts of her past. Now that she had put Emmet back in his box, she felt empowered – ready to move forward. But before she went to the attic, there was something she had to do.

George had supported her decision to have as many pieces put together before she held in her hands the one link to her birth.

She made the phone call.

"Hello, my name is Daisy O'Neill. Could I could speak to a social worker, please?"

"What's it in connection with?"

"It's about a baby found outside the church in Ballygore in April 1965. I am Daisy O'Neill, of 1 St John Street. I wrote to you ages ago and haven't heard anything back."

"Can you hold on a minute, please?"

Within a few minutes a social worker came on the line. Daisy once again repeated her story, asking if any records could be made available to her, telling the voice at the other end of the phone that she had telephoned a few times.

"Hold on now. Yes, I received your letter and you're on my list of follow-ups. So you're enquiring about archived records that may be here in the building since – what date did you say – sixty-five?"

"Yes."

"And the name of the … OK, I have your letter here in front of me. I need to do a little research and get back to you. Obviously any records, if there are any, would be strictly confidential. I can call to you, or I can give you an appointment to meet me here at the office. Whichever suits."

The woman at the other end of the phone seemed in a hurry to finish the call.

"Can you give me any indication as to how long all this will take?" Daisy said.

"I can't say much to you now. What I can say is that this is not as straightforward as it looks to you right now. It's not quite as simple as putting a few notes together and handing them over to you. The impact of such information can have astounding effects. The psychological aspects of delving into hidden pasts are never to be taken lightly. In my experience, dealing with family reunification and identity, people assume it's going to be all happy and light – the opposite is often the case."

Daisy had heard enough. "If I can interrupt you, I've just found out that the mother I thought I had for well over twenty years was not my birth mother at all. I was found in a bag, left beside the church gates. All I want to know is, have you any information on that or have you not? I don't need the big talk, no offence. My life has been turned upside down. I want you to tell me if I am wasting my time with you or not."

"I fully appreciate what you must be going through. But the chances are there are others around that will be impacted. How old are you? OK – 1965. About twenty-five? Twenty-six? Your birth family are probably still out there. We don't know who else is around or if she has remarried. If you have you siblings – if they know about you. Their feelings have to be considered." Her voice became more clinical. "Enough said for now. There is a process to be followed. I'm sorry I cannot tell you what you want to hear. But I will get back to you … say … in a week or so. Is that OK?"

"It must be, it seems."

Daisy felt the person at the other end of the phone didn't get it – didn't get her. She had talked about the feelings of others, out there. What about her feelings? Had the social worker any consideration for her? She had been left in a bloody bag – whoever left her there surely didn't have the right to be protected. Had they not lost that right on the 4th of April 1965?

Chapter 26

The Notebook

George Doyle lay on his bed in his mother's house. He needed time to get his head around the conversation that he'd had with Daisy. There was no better place to do so than in his bedroom, which had remained largely unchanged since he was a boy.

He looked around the room at the familiar wallpaper, green box shapes on a cream background. How many times had he lain there, tracing the lines on the paper with his eyes, from one side of the room as far as he could go – his fall-asleep routine as a boy, after writing up the daily events in his diary?

The heavy cream wardrobe had been a feature in the room for as long as he could remember. The room was uncluttered. His mother hated clutter. Some of the items that he had collected as a child were neatly placed on the single shelf at the far side of the room. A large magnifying glass beside a framed picture of Sherlock Holmes. A photo of his dad took pride of place, beside the row of army medals that he had been awarded. He missed his dad.

He didn't have to go far to find what he was looking for. He reached in under the bed, pulling out the wooden crate which held the small paper notebooks neatly in place. George liked to keep things in order.

It wasn't difficult to find the notebook. Each one was dated on the front cover. There it was. He'd found it. So, he had been twelve years old at the time.

His ability to recall was honed with years of practice and he'd had a strong feeling that it had been Davie Keogh who had let the woman out of the car. Now he had the proof in his hands.

He recalled the sound of the familiar engine of the car pulling up on the road, leaving the woman with the blue washing bag out, before taking off and circling around and back up Church Avenue, parking behind the half wall with the screen of shrubs behind.

George smiled to himself as he thought about his twelve-year-old self, hiding up on the wall. The memory of a man who'd realised his childhood dream of becoming a journalist.

Hiding from everybody – nothing hidden from him. He could still see the crowd coming out from Mass while he put his pencil and notebook back into his pants pocket, getting ready to come out of his hiding spot after the crowd had left.

As the people had gathered around the blue bag, he had to remain in his hiding spot longer than he ever had – he had run home faster than he had ever moved.

On the day he had been more concerned that the Devil had him or that his mother would kill him. His childish conclusion, recorded in the notebook, was that Davie Keogh must have been mitching from Mass and that the woman with the bag was a new "washing woman". But he had later written a big question mark beside this observation when Davie Keogh turned up again to his mother's door – with a new washing bag. The young George had then concluded that the new washing woman must have done a bad job and been fired by Keogh.

He grimaced at the irony. She had indeed been fired.

Prompted by his notes, he remembered seeing Old Father Mac and two women passing him by in the black Cortina.

His mother had mentioned something at the dinner table the following day – an infant boy had been abandoned outside the church. He hadn't responded – he wanted no conversation about the previous day. They had said a prayer for the mother and that was the last he'd heard of it.

 Now that he had the information, the difficult piece would be naming the man – telling Daisy and confronting Davie Keogh.

George had been around long enough to know there was no point in panicking. Rushing forward regardless. Yes – he had seen the woman getting out of the car with the blue washing bag. But it wasn't enough to go on. Not yet. His word against Keogh's? A twelve-year-old lad from the cottage on the Hill Road, the washerwoman's son, with the hand-me-down clothes, taking on the likes of David Keogh.

No. It would be George Doyle, the man, that would take him on. George Doyle who had been around long enough to see the likes of Keogh wiping the floor with people. Cruising around the town after dark, in his silver Jag, looking for easy targets. Women who were vulnerable no matter what way you looked at it. And Keogh whose head was so far up in the clouds that he no longer recognised his own people. Keogh thought he was above everyone else. Just because he had married up, he had notions. Well – George would bring him down to earth – he would unravel the dark secret he thought he had walked away from. It was the likes of Keogh who took advantage of people – but he hadn't figured on coming face to face with George Doyle.

He had agreed to meet Daisy just to keep an eye on Roche. But he had become smitten with her. He would now see it through to the end. Decision made. Time for confrontation.

He would face Keogh before going back to Daisy – he was fearful that Keogh would threaten her with all sorts. She had enough to be getting on with, contacting the social workers and doing her bit. He would tell her once he had confronted Keogh.

Chapter 27

Confrontation

Keogh was well over the limit the night that George decided to confront him. Waiting for the last of the punters to leave – drying glasses – then drying them again – he was taking a risk.

Confident that he would get what he wanted, without compromising, or losing the game in the process.

But he had to be careful on this one – this one was closer to home.

He watched David Keogh become more inebriated, answering "No problem" when he asked for one for the road. Keeping himself busy turning off the lights – pulling the plug on the Christmas tree.

Asking if he needed another. Tipping the optic twice.

Davie was well on but George had often seen him drive home in a worse state.

Mentioning how active the squad car had been around the town all evening. He had him. Keogh couldn't afford to lose his licence.

George offered to take the keys and drive him home – just as far as his mother's gate. Keogh would be safe enough to drive on home from there, once he was off the main road.

George's car could stay in Philly's yard overnight.

Keogh thought it was a sound idea, admitting that he was a bit under the weather.

Just as they were about to take off, George threw the keys on the dashboard.

"Well, Doyle? Are you going to start her up?"

George sat heavily back in the seat. Sighing.

Davie, wondering what the delay was about, said, "Are we moving, Doyle, or are we going to sit here all night?"

Straight to the point. "We'll move, Keogh, after you tell me about the day you left a certain lady out of your car. It was on a Sunday morning in April 1965, with a live infant in the same blue washing bag, that your good wife used to drop the laundry off to my mother. Does that jog your memory at all?"

Davy started to cough as he tried to catch his breath. "Wha'? What the fuck are you on about?"

"Don't mess with me, man. I have the whole story, which I will put in the paper for next Wednesday morning should you decide not to cooperate. Be very careful and think carefully before you answer." Thinking Keogh was about to choke, he tapped him hard on the back. "You see, Davie, you were seen by a person coming from Mass that morning. We have a witness."

Davie Keogh began to panic – he spoke in a rushed tone, barely pausing for breath. "What are you on about, Doyle? What the blazes are you on about? I haven't a fucking clue what you're talking about!"

241

"There was a witness on the day, by the wall behind the church. I have evidence to show it was you, man, driving Grace's green Volkswagen. You dropped a certain lady off with the blue washing bag and drove off. You appeared again around Church Avenue where you parked up behind the half-wall. You sat waiting for the same lady to sit back into your car – minus the blue bag. Davie, man, it wasn't the week's washing was in the bag, was it? It was a baby girl all dressed in blue. My source tells me the two of you drove off at high speed."

David was now speechless – trying to take in what he was hearing – trying to work out in his head how to answer without landing himself in it. He'd had one too many – he couldn't think. How did Doyle know?

"I don't know where the Gardaí would stand on this, do you?" George thought Keogh was going to throw up. But it was his own car, so what. "Do you want to hear more – will I continue?"

"Enough, enough – you're some bastard! You picked the right night to throw all this shit at me. Give me a day or two to sort it out in my head. Get the Christmas over with. I'm saying nothing, mind. Now fuck off out of my car. I'll drive on from here."

"One more thing, Keogh – if I hear you've contacted anyone to do with this – or open your mouth, I will see to it you're destroyed. If you think your solicitor buddy Thornton will help you, I will have his ass as well, for breaching confidentiality. Are we clear?"

"*Fuck off, Doyle!*"

George knew that Davie had sobered up as quickly as he ever had, as he opened the door to get out.

Keogh got out himself, looking as if he needed air.

Kicking his way furiously through the covering of rotten leaves that lay in his path.

"OK! OK! Look, I took the bag. I never thought this would come back to haunt me. It was a good deed. The girl was up the duff when she rented my flat in Spring Street. What are you on about? Must be twenty-five years ago or more. I dropped her off where she asked me, near the church. She wanted to leave the child there. It had fuck all to do with me and that still stands."

George had taken a risk that could very well have backfired on him. But he would not stand by and let Davie Keogh get away with it. He wasn't fool enough to make stories out of hearsay – the facts had made the story.

Davie Keogh hadn't exactly tried to deny it. He had him now where he wanted – he would make him pay. Daisy, he was sure, would not let him off lightly either, once she knew the truth. He would leave that side of it up to her.

Was Keogh Daisy's father? Who was the woman he saw getting out of the car? The answer lay with Davie Keogh. He was the only one alive who knew the identity of the woman.

He had admitted that she'd lived in the flats in Spring Street. The blue washing bag had to be the one that the Keoghs brought to his mother with the washing. His wife Grace would surely remember it if was. His own mother would probably remember it. Job done. Time to tell Daisy. But he had to be sure that his intentions were honourable, otherwise he'd be no better than that lot.

Growing up in Ballygore, one of the older of Keogh's children had been in the same class as George. He used to wish that his mother had the money to buy some of what they had. And the teachers were all about them. Old money, his granny had said. Apart from Davie Keogh, she said, who'd married above his station.

Their heads up in the air. They looked down their noses at the likes of George. Growing up, himself and Susan didn't have the smart clothes, the trendy hairstyles, or the elocution lessons. George Doyle was just the boy with the red hair and the hand-me-down clothes. His bag was a worn leather satchel. It had belonged to his father. The books inside were secondhand, given to him from the poor children's list at school. He had wondered what a day living their lives would be like. Now he wouldn't have them polish his shoes.

At Mass on a Sunday the whole family attended, looking as if they had stepped out of a glossy magazine.

"Well, Georgie, what was Jackie Onassis wearing at Mass?"

He didn't need to ask who his mother was referring to.

"Oh, Mam, she was wearing her clothes, same as always, all bright and breezy like a big flower. A big huge flower."

They had laughed at the good of it.

"Oh, for God's sake, George, I've seen her often enough to know that she hardly wears the same outfit twice. I wonder what she does with her castoffs? I've yet to see them in the washing bag. I'd say she sends them all in for dry cleaning. Would you?"

"Mam, that fool Keogh only gives me a lift when he's on his own, cos he's too much of a coward to pass me. But when young David and the other kids are with him, they pass me out, as if I was never on the road. Why would you be bothering what that crowd are wearing? Won't I have you looking a million dollars, when I'm running the newspaper?"

George had put out his arms to his mother. They'd hugged as if they hadn't a care in the world.

Chapter 28

The Meeting

Davie Keogh knocked at Thornton's side door. It was a wet January afternoon. Standing as close to the door as he could get, he was wishing now he'd brought the golf umbrella from the car – then realised there'd be little point – the wind would have taken it.

Having arranged to meet Thornton at the side door, he knew as usual he would be left waiting. But it was easier than going through the main reception desk – less hassle. The girls in the office were not privy to the casual deals between the two men. The less they knew, the better for all concerned.

He was wondering had this anything to do with George Doyle's stunt the week before. Very strange. Drunk and all as he was, he remembered every word that Doyle had said – and he'd mentioned Thornton's name. He felt uneasy – Thornton had said he needed to see him urgently.

Davie stepped in once he heard the click of the door

opening, shaking the loose rain from his navy wool coat. Thornton would be down in a matter of minutes.

Waiting against the edge of the hall table, he flicked through his hardcover diary where he kept up to date on the properties they were working on, chuckling at the thought of anyone else trying to make it out. He had his own scribble.

Thornton came down the stairs and ushered Davie into a small office. He didn't sit or invite Davie to do so.

"David, I have just a few minutes, I'm afraid. I have a client due any minute now. Something that dawned on me the other day. No 1 John Street where the Widow Neill lived – you know the one. The daughter moved back in after she died. Well, let's say it has come to my attention that there's a package of some value in the attic, that the daughter will be looking for."

"And why would this be of interest to me, John?" Davie knew Thornton was up to something.

"The reason I'm advising you is that I'm just ensuring there will be no questions asked about our little business arrangement – should things not be as they seem at the house."

"John, get to the bloody point, you've certainly got my interest now."

"You rented out Rose O'Neill's house for a few months until the will was sorted. Now, I can't go into the business attached to it, but I hope to God you weren't rooting around in that attic. Were you? A simple question. There's some sort of a panel up there where Mrs. O'Neill had left – let's say, items, for the girl. I'm just making sure that it hasn't been tampered with up there, before the girl goes to find them."

Davie composed himself as best he could – he still couldn't figure out the significance of what Thornton was saying. "Am I hearing you correctly, John? You're asking me if I tampered with some shite in the attic of the Widow Nail's house. Are you accusing me of something here?"

"I'm merely asking, David, if you have any knowledge of the package or not?"

"*Aah, for God's sake, John, give over!* I wasn't near the bloody attic. I'm nearly sorry now though that I didn't get wind of it sooner. It might have been worth a root around. What the hell is up there anyway?"

Thornton seemed relieved. Davie guessed that he was just covering his arse on behalf of the Daisy one. And some woman she was by all accounts. Just like her mother before her – odd as two left shoes. She must have had Thornton shaking in his boots.

The solicitor gestured towards the door, alerting Davie that the conversation was over. Why was it that every time he met Thornton, he made him feel like a working-class bumpkin?

Davie gave him a cold look. Thornton never left a stone unturned and always seemed to come out on top – even refusing to let him have the last word.

"By the way, John, remind me not to hire you as my brief any time soon. If I'd any skeletons in the closet – or indeed in the attic – you mightn't be the best in the confidentiality stakes. You know, it did strike me all right to have a look around that attic – but I didn't bother."

"That's that then. Just checking."

Suddenly feeing very brave, Davie went on. "One more thing, John. Should you be sharing a client's business at all? They could have you there, you know.

Were I to absentmindedly enquire of the girl if she'd found the package that John Thornton was banging on about ..."

Both men sniggered insincerely.

"David, my man. You and I both know you didn't hear anything from me. And if you're ever of a mind to say otherwise – a few years for embezzlement and misappropriation of funds might cool your whistle. My books are all in order. Be the shrewd operator that you are, now. Was there anything else to discuss? No, I didn't think so."

Davie left in a hurry, thinking that no matter how hard he tried Thornton was always a step ahead. He was nearly sixty years of age but every time he met Thornton he felt small. It seemed a bit odd – to be hauled into the office about a bloody packet in an attic in the widow's house. Thornton was as cunning as any man, but Davie couldn't make sense of this. Was Thornton covering up for something? Did he know more than he was saying? Or maybe he was just dotting his i's and crossing his t's like always. Probably. Davie felt relieved all the same. He hadn't been anywhere near the attic in the house, so at least there was nothing to worry about on that score.

Since Doyle had confronted him, he was becoming a bit paranoid. Waking up during the night in a cold sweat. Seeing Grace's big old blue washing bag looming over him, with a child's hands hanging out over either side of it.

He hadn't thought in a million years this would come back to haunt him. The bloody washing bag had been the cause of all this trouble. Who'd have thought it? The last think he wanted was for Grace to find out that he was mixed up in such a scandal. She wouldn't take it well and it could cost him dearly.

But he had his story ready. He wasn't going to get himself caught up in this. Molly Whatever-her-name-was had been one of his tenants and that was it.

No need to mention that he had paid the old woman off who had delivered the child. She wouldn't have opened her mouth anyway. Many a man's secret had been covered up in the town – and she'd been well paid for doing so. Who'd take notice of a dirty old woman, known for little else apart from backstreet abortions? They used to call her 'Knitting Needle', between themselves.

No. The child wasn't his and he'd stand up to whoever might say otherwise.

He would say the woman told him she was pregnant when she came to town. He had tried to help her out by giving her one of the flats.

It had been easy to put it out of his mind once he'd dropped her off at the station. As far as he was concerned, the child had been adopted.

He remembered talk of the baby boy being found in the bag. With Molly out of the picture, he'd held his head up and carried on. There was no talk after that. He'd never heard a word from her again. If he had, he would have ignored her anyway.

Payton – that was it, Molly Payton.

It had been so long ago he'd forgotten about it all until the bastard Doyle had brought it up.

Back then, it had taken him a while to figure out that the woman had been clinically insane.

Landing into Ballygore with a suitcase full of small banknotes in a big thick wrinkly paper bag. No one in their right mind would have believed her against him.

Hadn't he even given her enough money to tide her

over? What landlord would have done that? He remembered that the brother was to meet her on the day, in the waiting room at the station at the other end.

He would be taking care of her from then on – so she'd said anyway.

Women, he thought, you could never get to the bottom of them.

He stopped the car on the way home at the side of the quiet road, just for a minute or two, to get his thoughts together. A habit that he had got into, to clear his head, before facing Grace.

On this occasion he had it all sorted in his mind. So Thornton was raving about something in the attic. Nothing to do with him. George Doyle was trying to make out that he had fathered an abandoned infant. But that's all he had. He had nothing.

He could deal with whoever said they'd had seen him, when the time came. There had been no witnesses on the day, apart from the one Doyle said he had. He would call his bluff on that one.

He would give Doyle whatever information he wanted, as long as it didn't appear on the paper or the cops were involved. And no one knew where the infant had gone. It could be anywhere. Even abroad.

He guessed Doyle's angle was to have the story splashed all over the front page of the newspaper – but he had handled many a situation in his day and he'd handle this one as well. If it came to it, he'd pay whoever he had to pay to keep quiet. If there was one thing David Keogh was sure of – money talked.

Confident that he'd worked it out, he headed towards home. Feeling much better about himself.

Chapter 29

Finding Out

George had called to Daisy unannounced. It was Valentine's Day. Not being overly concerned with what he may have found out since she'd last seen him, she was pleased at the sight of him. Inhaling the woody scent of his cologne, she led him through the hallway.

"Sorry I didn't ring first. I decided to call and just got in the car. So here I am."

He handed her a miniature bunch of wild flowers – pink and purple crocuses and white snowdrops grouped together and tied in a bow with narrow yellow ribbon. He had taken it from his jacket pocket gently, without damaging a petal.

She was delighted.

"I couldn't call to you without marking the day. I picked them from around the trees at home. Happy Valentine's Day."

As he bent his head to kiss her on the cheek, she quickly turned her head. It landed as she'd hoped – right on her lips.

"Thank you." His gesture had pleased her heart.

In the kitchen George stood for a while with his back against the counter, watching her as she filled a glass jug with water and put the flowers in it.

"Tea or coffee?" she asked, putting the jug on the table.

"Tea would be fine."

As she filled the kettle and switched it on to boil, she told him that she'd had a call back from the social worker the day before – how disappointed and angry she'd felt by the woman's insistence that it would take time – that everyone else had to be considered – not just her. After waiting so long, all she was getting were condescending tones.

"I don't think I could be bothered waiting for them to check with every Tom, Dick and Harry, to be sure they won't be hurting their feelings. Jesus, the cheek of them! I think it's time to go public, George. I have to do my own search."

The time was right to tell her.

"I won't beat around the bush, Daisy. But I do have information."

She stopped as she was about to open the fridge, and stared at him.

"I've had it for a few days now but I just wanted to be sure that I had as much proof as I could before I came back to you."

Her face registered anticipation.

"It's going to be quite a shock for you. But I'm here with you, so you're not on your own."

She waited for him to tell her what he knew.

"I'll show you what I have but first I want you to promise me not to mention it to a soul, not to anyone. Especially not Emmet. Just to be on the safe side in case he mentions it in the pub."

Daisy sat down on a chair with a thud.

"Jesus, come on – will you tell me! I won't say a word."

George sat down, facing her across the table.

The man sitting in front of her was in a different league to Tom or Emmet all right, she thought. He wouldn't have acted without giving it due thought. He had proven himself to be a calm, patient man, not one to pounce on impulse. He'd had his doubts about Emmet and Susan – if he'd been too quick off the mark, he could have destroyed him. But he didn't – he bided his time.

Daisy trusted him. She felt safe, respected by him.

"Remember I told you that I've been keeping diaries, or notes I should say, since I was a boy. I suppose you could call it my hobby." He shrugged. "Well, one such note I recorded is from the 4th of April, 1965. I was twelve, hiding behind on the church wall here in Bally. Watching the comings and goings of the Mass goers – mitching from Mass myself at the same time. I remember the day well, because I was almost caught. I had recognised the sound of the engine before I saw the car come along Church Street and leave the woman out with the blue washing bag. Daisy, I recognised it. It was the same big blue bag that my mother was handed full of washing, every Monday morning, and collected a few days later, by the same man. It was that man who was driving the car that morning."

Daisy sat still. Too afraid to speak in case she missed the smallest detail.

George leaned over, laying his hand on hers. "The man who dropped the woman off with the blue bag was David Keogh, Daisy. It was Davie Keogh – the garage Keogh."

She stared at him in disbelief.

Davie Keogh?

As the name sank in, she thought her heart would burst.

"What? No ... George, don't tell me that ... Jesus, no ... please no ... that creep who called to my door a while back, trying to chat me up?"

With that Daisy's mouth opened. She held her stomach and dry-retched towards the floor, her head bent forward.

He gave her a towel to wipe her mouth, then filled a glass of water and handed it to her. She drank the water as he wiped the liquid on the floor away with a floor cloth.

After washing his hands, he came and sat in the chair next to hers. Then he pulled a well-handled notebook out of his jacket pocket and handed it to her.

"This is the actual note I wrote on the day. There is an in-depth version on the next page which I would have written later that night. The first scribble is as I saw it that morning."

Daisy opened it to the page marked with a red sticky.

The page was dated in heavy pencil.

Sunday April 4th 1965

Mass April – Position code CW.

Green volk number ZXT 456 woman brown coat with mams blue washing bag. He left her and bag near church. davy keogh drove off... Crowd came out ... all around the bag. cant get off wall. nearly fell. 15min davy back around block. drove off with woman. no bag. Fr Mac and 2 women have bag in Black Cortina VBY 333. Keoghs blue washing bag. Jimmy curtain robbed a paper.

Daisy looked at George in disbelief.

"So, is there a possibility that he could be my father? *Stop. No.* Don't answer that. I need to think about it but I can't think about it. *Jesus.* This is the worst possible news. He's the biggest creep ever. Jesus Almighty, is this what I ...?"

Too distraught to finish the sentence, she collapsed into his arms and cried into his shoulder. Great big bursts of tears. He comforted her, allowing her time to recover. Space to take in what he was telling her.

Eventually she managed to control her sobs and sat back. "Oh my God, so it was Davie Keogh all along and he renting out this place when Mam was in hospital! And the proof of it all hidden above in the attic. *Jesus.* Does that mean that I am related ...? No way! There must be some other reason he was there. Shur, he has kids older than me. I think I was in the same class with the youngest of them in primary school. I refuse to consider it's him. Of all the creeps in the town, I'm linked to him. And the woman ... my birth mother? Who was she?"

George sat there – letting her talk. Knowing that the information he'd just given her was anything but what she wanted to hear. Wanting to be with her – to be there for her.

"I would die if this got out – that bastard having anything to do with me. No papers now. No way. Not a soul. Keep this between ourselves until I've had time to digest it. I'm sick at the very thought of it. As long as he doesn't get wind of it, before I've time to see what I'm doing. Oh God ... maybe he knows already ... he came to my door late one night with a made-up story about damaging my wing-mirror ... and tried to invite me for a drink ... oh God, he must know!"

"You can't know that for sure. Let's take it a step at a time, OK?"

He couldn't tell her now that he had already confronted Keogh. He would tell her when she had calmed down.

As the day passed, Daisy let the information sink in. She wasn't sure she believed that David Keogh was any relation of hers. But she did believe that George had seen him drop the woman off with his wife's blue washing bag. Could it have been her birth mother?

It would be a long road ahead, that was for sure. In less than two months she would be twenty-six. No longer the gullible fool of a girl who believed everything she was told. With every setback she had come forward with a strength she never knew was in her. Now was not the time to give up. She would ask every question she had to ask, to get to the truth which had been denied her all these years. No more lies and secrecy.

She realised that being angry with Rose wasn't going to get her anywhere. Her childhood had been filled with love. Her mam had provided that love, giving her the skills she was using now, to face the truth.

Daisy believed George when he'd told her that he'd stay by her side on the path to her birth family, whoever they were.

The shortest journey, which she had to take on her own, would be the most difficult one. The attic. Months had passed. George had offered to go up there, to check that it was still there – seeing that Keogh had access to the house. It wasn't as easy as that – she had declined – too much had happened – she would go up herself but only when she was ready.

No one could understand how she felt. How could

they? How could they know how she dreaded the thought of coming face to face with the only physical link to her birth. Afraid that once she found the package, that it would all end there, right in that moment. The longer she waited it out, the longer the anticipation would last. There was a strange sort of comfort in it – impossible to define – but that's how she felt. She was in no doubt that the packet was safe up there – Rose would have made sure of that. It was her life and her decision. Knowing that it was there – waiting for her – gave her purpose in the days ahead. Purpose which did not include Davie Keogh.

Yes, she would go into the attic alone. On Rose's first anniversary in March. It seemed like a fitting plan to her. She would go look for the package on March 27th.

Standing at the grave on the day, she spoke easily to her mam. This time there were no tears.

"Mam, it's me, Daisy. Can't believe it's been a year with all that's happened. You are my mother – my true mam. And thank you for loving me. Times aren't great, but I'm stronger. I'm off home now to go to the attic – I couldn't all along – so stay by my side. You've always known I hated spiders."

She told Rose that she loved her. Telling her again that she was her mam no matter what the future held. Telling her that at last she had found herself a man she knew Rose would approve of.

"Don't worry, Mam, we'll be taking it easy. Very easy. He's quiet but confident. I know you'd approve. I just feel it."

Locking the front door behind her, she walked up the stairs. She was ready. Feeling the strength of Rose's spirit, she reached for the makeshift ladder that John P had

258

made years ago. She climbed into the attic. Nervous but ready.

George had given her the most important piece of the puzzle – nobody else would have had that information to give her.

She had thought about letting him go to the attic with her. No. She had to do this on her own. Needing to be there as she had been on the day. Alone. Wanting to see and feel the past in her hands. Maybe feel close to the person who had placed her in the bag.

She moved around carefully, having pulled the light-cord immediately inside the attic door. She could see the feathery spiderwebs against the light as she went forward. For once she didn't mind. Brushing them out of her way, she thought about how considerate John P was – he had thought of everything.

She knew exactly where to go – to the far corner to her right, where the low sloped ceiling met the wooden ledge. It was just as the letter had stated. The ledge looked intact as did the wall.

Pulling a three-legged stool underneath her, she sat down, so that her eyes were facing the ledge. She pressed down hard on the corner. A small section of the ledge lowered immediately. The wall panel below opened with a click.

"My God!" she said aloud.

She hesitated but then reached inside. She rooted around. It wasn't an easy task. She had to extend her arm – not knowing what might be lurking in there. She shuddered. Kneeling now on the floor, trying to ignore the dry dust around her, she placed her hand on something.

Pulling the object towards her and out of its hiding place, she saw she had the parcel in her hand.

She could feel her heart thumping.

She banged the cupboard door shut.

Clutching the tightly bound parcel to her chest, she could feel the swell of emotion building up inside her as she climbed back down the steps to the top landing. She was wondering what had been going on in Rose's mind all those years ago when she had hidden the packet up there. Going straight to her bedroom, she laid the dusty plastic package down on the white cotton bedspread, not caring whether it marked it or not.

It had taken her long enough to have the courage to go look for it. She had imagined all sorts – certainly imagining it to be of significant size. It was much smaller and lighter than she'd expected. Tightly wrapped in grey plastic, it was bound together with tape. She removed the sticky tape piece by piece, then wiped away any residue of dust.

She walked away from the bed – looking back at the parcel – before going back again. Without lifting it off the bed she then opened it quickly. Inside was a blue canvas bag, which had a coloured scarf looped and tied around its handles. She pulled open the bow of the scarf and looked inside. Inside were several small bundles wrapped in tissue paper.

On top of them lay a letter. She was shaking as she picked it up, recognising her mam's handwriting. She traced her fingers over the paper then read her mother's words.

Daisy,

I sincerely hope it is you who are reading this note. If not, I appeal to whoever you are to put the parcel back where you found it. This parcel is for my daughter, Daisy O'Neill, who will be aware of its whereabouts.

*Love, I have no explanation for you except to say that you
must know I have loved you to the end of the world and back. I
trust you have read the letter that I have given to Thornton. For
fear that you are not the one to find this parcel, I will not give
away too much in this letter, just in case.*

*There were three people there on the day – myself, Father Mac
and Nurse Jean, both of whom I know have since passed. The
social worker in town at the time assured me years later that
whatever notes that she had taken, once she became involved, will
be available to you once you are ready to ask for them.*

*These are yours, Daisy, and all that I have from that day –
there is nothing missing.*

God Bless you always
Mam

Daisy cried as she read and reread the letter.

Typical Rose, she thought. Just in case the parcel fell into
the wrong hands, she had said little more than she had to.

She opened the tissue-wrapped bundles. There was a
crochet matinee coat with matching pull-ups in blue. A
blue babygrow as well as the thick soft wool baby blanket.
A white towel. A plastic bag which held a blue soother, the
teat of which was old, swollen, and dried – attached to a
large nappy pin. A small clear plastic envelope containing
a holy picture trimmed with yellow, which read "*Lord
protect this baby from harm*". A small glass baby bottle
completed the contents. Picking up the tiny matinee coat
she held it to her face and breathed in deeply. It smelled as
it might have done, had it still been in use.

A yellow-and-white motif of a daisy had been stitched
onto the sleeve with black wool thread. The stiches big
and roughly sewn. The baby hat was blue wool, which

261

had been lined with a white cotton cap, stitched again in the same rough black thread.

The blue canvas bag itself was unusual to say the least. It wasn't even a decent bag – it was, as George had said, a blue washing bag. Davie Keogh's bloody washing bag. But nothing like she had ever seen before. She filled it, placing the baby clothes back inside before tying the scarf in a bow, trying to imagine what it must have looked like on the day.

Walking towards the mirror, she carried the bag, looking at her reflection – trying to get a sense of the person who had placed her in it, twenty-six years before. Trying to imagine what it was that Rose had seen as she first approached it. Feeling pity. Pity for the shame of a long time ago – and the repercussions into the future. Pity for the woman who'd given birth to her, who couldn't see a way out. One thing was for sure. The name 'Daisy' had been given to her by her birth mother and hadn't been lost along the way. She could feel the connection.

She cradled the bag close to her chest. "So this is who I am," she said aloud, laughing and crying at the same time.

Lying on the bed, she tried to visualise the baby girl, all dressed in blue, by someone thoughtful enough to stitch a light cotton cap inside the outer one, to prevent the wool from irritating her baby's delicate skin. The woman who had abandoned her must have been desperate.

The phone was ringing in the distance, bringing her back to the present.

"Hello, Daisy, long time no see, it's Anne here, Anne Dwyer. I ran into Susan Doyle at the weekend when I was home. She told me you were back in town. Just thought I'd give you a call to catch up."

"Oh Anne, great to hear from you! And thanks for the card when Mam died. I meant to get in touch. Sorry, but it's not really a good time. Can I give you a call later?"

"Fine, Daisy – please do – we have a lot to talk about."

The café was packed. It had taken her a week to get back to Anne. She'd told her that she'd meet her there at eleven. Her friend already seated, waving furiously at her from a table by the window. It must have been three years since they had been together, but she had changed little. The same honest smile for Daisy, as if they had met yesterday.

The women hugged each other.

"No way, Jesus, no way! Where's Daisy? Who's this model standing in front of me? I can't believe it! Daisy O'Neill – you look like a million dollars. What have you done with yourself? Seriously, you look fantastic. Your coat, your boots. Wow!"

"It's the good life, Anne. I'm back at my mam's – but you know all that from Susan, I suppose. And about Tom." Laughing to herself at Anne who never could hold back once she got started.

"Daisy, we didn't know what to do. He was intimidating myself and Bernie – but we couldn't say anything to you – you adored him. Would you have believed us if we'd told you at the time?"

"Intimidating you? How?" Daisy asked, not sure she wanted to hear the answer.

"He was making a play for the two of us, except we didn't even tell each other for ages. I was plain scared of him and Bernie was blaming herself."

Daisy was hearing what she had already begun to

suspect. He had isolated her not only from her mother but from her two best friends as well.

"He made several passes at Bernie in your flat. She had to stay out of his way after that. With me, he just used to leer at me, eyeing me up and down in a lewd way. What idiots we were! Took us ages to figure it out – that's what he'd wanted all along – to scare us off. He played us like fools." Anne's eyes filled with tears.

"Anne, for feck's sake! Will you stop! I was the fool. He'd no respect for me – none whatsoever – but I couldn't see it. I could write a book on it. Ye weren't the only two. He made sure my mother was out of the picture as well. That's what these cowards do – isolate their women so they've full power to do as they like. Think about it – if I'd had family and loads of friends around he wouldn't have got away with half the stuff. He'd have been under the spotlight – I was just an easy target. The bruises I healed from – breaking me away from my mother I will never get over. But I'll get him in time and, when I do, he won't know what hit him."

Daisy knew that she came across as being angry and revengeful, but she didn't care.

She saw the look on her friend's face, knowing that she could scarcely believe it was the same Daisy as before sitting there with her. Yes, she looked different and she sounded different. Very different. The old Daisy wouldn't have said boo to the cat.

"Anne, look, it's gone, it's over – there's no going back. He's more than welcome to as many women he can manage at one time. But I fear there won't be too many in the queue and it won't be me and I doubt if it'll be you."

Daisy smiled at her friend as a sign of acceptance that

the truth was out. Both women giggled. They carried on talking, as if they'd never been apart.

The two friends became close again. Meeting every weekend for coffee when Anne was home, speaking on the phone in the time in between. But Daisy made a point of not discussing what she'd found out about her birth. George was her sole confidant now. She had learned many a bitter lesson on her road to trust. She would share her story in time.

She became part of a wider group of friends whom she met through Anne. Bernie was back in touch. She hadn't seen her since Rose's funeral Mass. And then it had only been in passing. Life became fun – she had her friends back. Places to go, people to see. And a man to confide in.

The three friends would meet in one of the pubs in town, mainly at the weekends when the girls were back in Ballygore.

One such day, as they sat laughing at Bernie telling tales on her latest date, a voice from behind her interrupted her story.

"Oh hello … Daisy, isn't it?"

Daisy recognised Karen Boland – she knew her to see her. And who didn't?

She certainly stood out in the town. Looking as if she was in from out there. Hanging around the likes of Tom and his buddies. A racegoer, big into the horses.

Daisy remembered Tom saying that her husband was half an eejit – dull as dishwater. A dope that she had married for his money. Karen made up for him, with her voice as well as everything else. Loud and high-pitched. Her shoulder-length hair the colour of hay, if not the texture as well, her face red and weather-beaten, her skin showing the tell-tale signs of an outdoor life, without moisturiser. Daisy thought she might be better placed on a ranch in Texas. Or maybe in a mart, rounding cattle into pens. She wasn't quite sure which.

She was wearing a long wax coat to her ankles – browny green – hard to tell the colour. Was it grease or dirt? Daisy couldn't make out. Maybe both? It looked as if it smelled. Below it was a pair of brown cowboy boots with horrible rhinestone embellishment on the sides. Classy.

Daisy had never really known her well enough to say hello. She would never in a million years have considered her to be anything other than a racing acquaintance of Tom's. She certainly wouldn't have considered her to be competition. Until Emmet had let it slip that Karen had been with Tom that night in the hotel when she had gone to bring him home. She had disturbed them. That awful woman had been hiding in the wardrobe all the time – listening to her as she pleaded with Tom to come home. No wonder he couldn't get Daisy out of the room fast enough.

"Well, girls, are ye out for a cuppa? I haven't seen or heard of you for an age, Daisy. How's the hubby keeping? I haven't seen him either since the point-to-point in Laytown."

Daisy's eyes narrowed, her contempt for Karen Boland obvious. "Sharon, isn't it? This is my friend Anne. And Bernie –"

Bernie was busy stifling a laugh, her eyes settled on Karen's ridiculous boots.

"It's Karen, not Sharon."

"Oh, *hellooo*, Sharon," said Anne with a big exaggerated smile. "Have we met somewhere? I'm trying to think where I know you from. You're awfully familiar."

Anne turned and gave her friend a knowing wink, outside of Karen's line of vision.

"It's *Karen*. Not Sharon! And that could have been anywhere, dear. Myself and my man travel the length and breadth of the country – always on the road."

"*Hmm*. I know where we met now, Sharon."

Daisy didn't know what was going to come out of Anne's mouth but she knew by the look on Karen Boland's face that she wasn't going to like it.

"We met in a pub in Clonleen when yourself and Daisy's ex, Mr. Arnold, were pissed drunk, up at the bar. Having a good old snog and the whole place in stitches, watching the get-up of the two of you. You don't remember, Sharon? But I bet Daisy remembers the night all right. The night he didn't come home." She looked directly at her friend. "I couldn't tell you at the time, Daisy. You wouldn't believed a word of it."

"No, Anne, probably not," Daisy answered honestly.

"I thought as much. But you believe me now."

Karen took off without a word, the studs on her boots hammering the timber floor.

"*I'll be sure to tell Tom you were asking for him. Sharon!*" Daisy called after her. "*That's of course if I'm ever unfortunate enough to lay eyes on him again!*"

The woman continued quickly towards the door, her face purple with anger, sweating with the shock – the waitress chasing after her – she had forgotten to pay her bill.

"Bitches, bloody bitches!" she muttered under her breath.

The three women laughed their heads off.

Chapter 30

Payback Time

Daisy bumped into Tom now and again in town. In the beginning her heart would race when she'd see him coming towards her. Always between pubs – walking out of one pub – heading towards another.

As the months went by it didn't have the same impact on her. She got used to it to an extent. She wondered if he was still working? Had he ever truly loved her? Asking herself why she even cared?

Sometimes butterflies in her stomach – sometimes not. If there was no way past each other, they'd stand and share a few words. Words without meaning – words neither would remember. Sarcastic tones – condescending tones – depending on how drunk or sober he was. Sometimes old familiar tones, ones which made her feel confused. More often than not they just ignored one other. There was no normal. Tom's lifestyle hadn't changed.

She knew that once it had registered with him that she wasn't coming back, he'd have moved on, his pride intact.

She'd heard that he'd rented out the house – she supposed that it was to cover the mortgage.

Emmet had told her that he was staying at his mother's now and then – or in his car. Knowing Sally, she wouldn't put up with him for too long. And Tom wasn't one to be under her scrutiny – no – he wouldn't have any woman, even his mother, lording it over him. Sleeping in the car was a bit of a shock to her – she wasn't that cruel to be pleased that anyone had to sleep in a car. But he didn't need to.

Karen Boland opened her front door in such a hurry that it bounced back and hit the wall behind it. She couldn't believe her eyes when she saw who it was.

Tom Arnold. Standing on her front step, looking dirty and dishevelled, brown beer stains at either side of his mouth, his hair greasy, tie knot loosened down his chest. The shirt he wore had yellow stains down the front and its dirty collar suggested that he'd been in it for days.

His suit looked shiny and wrinkled. He was carrying a white plastic carrier bag in his hand. She could smell him from where she was standing at the door.

Karen could see that he was not in a good place.

"Arnold, what the hell are you doing here at my door? What the fuck? William is gone out to check the lambs abroad in Littleduff. He'll be back by five."

"Karen, I've nowhere else to go. Staying at the mother's on and off – but I don't want to be going over there in this state. I was wondering if I could come in for a while. Just for a quick wash and a change of clothes?" He held up the white plastic bag to show her.

"Are you for real, Arnold? Now, fuck off right this

minute, back to little Miss Daisy and don't ever come near my door again. My marriage isn't going to fall apart because of a quick ride now and again which, by the way, I will deny – just in case you are thinking of badmouthing me around the place. Now crawl back into whatever dirty hole you crawled out of!"

Stepping back, she closed the door in his face.

"Fucking halfwit – and in broad daylight," she said aloud. "We'll see who's in the wardrobe now, bollocks."

Karen knew what she was about. She certainly wasn't going to let Tom Arnold, or anyone else, destroy what she'd worked hard for all her life. Respectability. It hadn't been easy being married to a man who had little interest in her, outside of her strength on the farm. But she was Mrs. William Boland and nobody was going to take that away from her. She decided there and then that she'd finished with Tom Arnold.

Never again, too risky. And the state of him, he looked like a bloody tramp! Even talking to him now was a liability. William mightn't be that clued-in – but she wasn't about to get careless.

She watched through the open window as he walked away from the door with his head bent. She heard him shouting back at her "*Fucking fat bitch!*" as he sat into his car. Kicking out whatever chip bags and cans were on the floor of the car, once he sat in. Leaving his rubbish behind him, he took off at a speed that matched his temper.

"Fuck him," she said aloud.

Tom hadn't expected Karen to be exactly delighted to see him, but he had expected to be able to get around her.

After all the brandies he'd bought for the cow.

All he'd wanted was to use her bathroom for a few minutes. If he'd been hopeful of more than a wash, he could forget about that now too.

He had no other option but to go back to his mother's house. He would throw the mother a few quid for his keep and try to keep himself to himself, until he got a place.

There was no chance that Daisy might come around, he'd known that since the day he'd tried to give her the piece of paper with the number of the marriage-counselling service. He would have been willing to give it another shot. But no. She was having none of it. The bitch.

He sniffed under his right armpit – he badly needed a wash.

His mother opened the door. She looked as if she was on her way out.

"Well, Tom, I thought you'd disappeared – but I guessed you'd turn up at some stage. Are you at work at all these days?"

"I'm down to a three-day week – so what – happens to the best of us – no harm with all that was going on. I'll be back on full time soon enough, once I get settled."

"Well, you stink to high heaven. Go up and run a bath before you clog up the place. And turn off the immersion when you're finished. We don't want to be running up the lecky bill. I'm in a hurry – pick up as you go – I'm nobody's maid."

"For fuck sake, Ma, I got rid of one bloody nag. Don't you start on me now, the minute I land in the fucking door." No wonder his father had left, he thought, shaking his head.

He walked through to the kitchen. His mother followed. He was anything but happy. He could feel the rage rising inside him. Bloody women. But he knew better than to have a go at his mother.

"If I'm going to be staying here for a few weeks, it'd be best if you just keep out of my affairs. I'm telling you now, Ma. But I will give you one thing – you were right about that bloody parasite. A right leech is all she was. I bought her a house, a car, put clothes on her back – and she still wasn't happy. Who was it that rescued her from the fucking Widow Nail as well? And that's the thanks I get. She fleeced me."

Sally Arnold looked at Tom blankly for a second, trying to indicate to him that she'd been listening. She hadn't. Letting it in one ear and out the other. Typical man, even if he was her son. She'd seen his temper – it didn't take a whole lot to rise him. But she knew how to deal with him – take no shite from him. He'd always been an angry child, a handful from the start, and here he was, feeling sorry for himself. She had the measure of him all right – he was just like his father before him, drinking every penny he'd ever earned, leaving her to go out to work in whatever bar would give her the hours. And then roaring and shouting at her when she'd arrive home, making out that she was off with every Tom Dick or Harry in the town. When he'd fecked off to England it was a relief. She'd done her penance or so she had thought.

He had left owing money to half of the town, leaving her to pay it back. All in her name. Dreading the postman, every other day she got letters from the bank demanding their money. Well, good riddance. Useless excuse for a man.

Now it looked as if his son was heading down the same road – shouting and roaring – blaming everyone else for his own cock-up. That Daisy one was no angel and that was for sure. But at least she didn't have the life that she herself had had. No. Daisy had stayed at home sitting on her arse doing nothing. Cute enough to run off though when the money was wearing thin, when Tom was down on his game. Well, tough luck – Sally wouldn't be picking up the pieces for anyone. She'd reared him – she could do no more. She wanted to ask him about the rent. No free dinners. She decided against it for now – she would bide her time. She'd no intention of letting him settle back into her home. If his job went through the drink, then he'd better have a place of his own sorted or she'd be stuck with him. That was not going to happen. The sooner he found somewhere the better. The community welfare crowd would pay the rent for him. But if he was staying with her and the job went, then she'd be in trouble, she'd be stuck with him. Used to her life as a single woman, responsible for none but herself, she wasn't about to give it up for Tom. Maybe he'd feck off to England like his father.

Off out the door to the darts tournament, she wondered why she ever had children in the first place. This mother business was overrated.

Chapter 31

The Psychiatric Ward

Daisy decided that waiting for the social workers to get back to her was futile. She would move forward on her own. Full steam ahead. And George was becoming just as obsessed as herself.

Who'd have thought it? The man she'd expected would spread rumours about her affair with Emmet turned out to be the only man she could trust. Her support. Knowing instinctively when to come forward and when to pull back. He didn't try to fill her head up with nonsense, just giving her the facts. Telling her that David Keogh had squealed like a piglet. And squeal he had. She figured he must have gone full throttle after David Keogh until he'd given him what he wanted.

He had given George the first name of the woman who had dropped the bag at the church. He claimed he could not remember her surname. That was all George needed to get him started. It took George a while to come up with her surname. But he had. Payton. Her name was Molly Payton.

When Daisy had heard the woman's name first, it had been both strange and familiar at the same time.

She thought it had a nice ring to it. Saying it over and over again.

"Molly Payton. Molly Payton."

"Daisy Payton."

Anyway, Rose had adopted her so she was legally Daisy O'Neill. Speaking aloud, she said, "My name is Daisy Jean O'Neill."

She and George had searched as much as they could, looking for any mention of Molly. Nothing. Molly was nowhere to be found in the telephone directory. For a while they had thought that she was dead. But there was no record in the death register. And she wasn't in the register of electors.

But now they knew why. Molly Payton was a long-term patient in St. Ultan's. A psychiatric home. That was a profound shock for Daisy and it had taken her few days to pull herself together again, with George's help.

Keogh then belatedly came up with the brother's name – James – and they found a James Payton in the phone book.

So this James Payton was her uncle then? Must be. He certainly hadn't given her that impression when she'd rung him. Very matter of fact – odd that he didn't question her or even ask her why she wanted his sister's details. Just told her that his sister Molly was in St. Ultan's. He said he'd give her the phone number, if she'd hang on for a minute. He found it and Daisy took it down. End of conversation.

Daisy called St. Ultan's in advance of her visit, explaining that she had got the details through James Payton, Molly's brother. George had advised her to sound

275

confident on the phone as if she was familiar with the Payton family.

She told them that she hoped to visit the following week, half-nervous in case that they'd refuse her request. They asked if she was a relative. She said she was. She wasn't going to say 'Oh yeah, I think this poor woman is my birth mother. She left me in a great big washing bag and just walked off with the local gigolo.'

She felt in her bones that the woman was her mother, despite occasional misgivings when she wondered if David Keogh was to be trusted or believed at all.

Standing at the gates of the psychiatric hospital, she felt scared at the thought of what she might find. It had been an easy enough decision to make – she wanted to meet the woman who had abandoned her. She wasn't looking for reasons, or excuses, or great displays of emotion. She just wanted the truth.

George had wanted to accompany her but she had said no. This she needed to do herself.

Approaching the steps of the hospital with trepidation, her heart was beating fast. She had never in her wildest dreams imagined a place such as this as holding the key to her past.

After reading Rose's letter she had often tried to imagine what her first meeting with her birth mother would be like. It didn't look like this.

The door loomed large in front of her as she hurried up the steps. It was now or never. Her backpack held the blue bag she had been found in over twenty-six years before.

Inside, she was given directions by the receptionist. A nurse would meet her once she got to the top floor. Up one flight of stairs, around the corner, up a second flight and up once more, half a flight. The nurse was waiting, a bunch of keys in hand. One door. Eerily quiet, the nurse unlocked it. Locking it again once they were inside. Nodding at a colleague who sat at a table behind a screen – hard to make her out, with all the scratches on the perspex. More doors opened and locked again.

Daisy felt uneasy. More than uneasy. Frightened.

She was inside the ward before she knew it. No warning.

On the way up from the ground floor it had seemed normal enough – normal enough, she imagined, for a psychiatric hospital – but not this. Seemed like a world away from the world outside.

Her first instinct was to leave. She couldn't.

Forcing herself to listen to what the nurse was saying to her, she was aware that she was gaping at those around her. Women. All women. Older women. Wild eyes. Dead eyes. Staring – making sounds. Feral sounds.

Once she had advised Daisy on how to behave with Molly, Nurse Cahill busied herself in the room. But staying close. Checking that the women were secure in their chairs. Two rooms. Some in beds – others not.

She thought that there were about eight women in the ward but she couldn't focus enough to count them. The smell was strong. Pungent body smells. She was half-afraid to breathe deeply. There was little air in the room, the one window small and barred from the inside.

The sounds pierced through her. One terrifying scream. Another joined in. Babbling like children. They stared at her, someone calling "*Lady, lady!*" Another scream. She couldn't tell where the sounds were coming from – none of the faces looked responsible.

Looking around, she could hardly believe her eyes, wishing now that she had taken George up on his offer to accompany her. This awful world, hidden away from the other wards at the top of hospital. Out of sight. Was she in a prison? The fluorescent light was bright enough to light up every corner of the room.

Molly Payton was sitting in a faded check armchair, unfazed by her surroundings. Her thin white hair was held off her forehead with a child's red plastic clip. She wore a faded yellow knitted cardigan, many sizes too big for her. The shapeless dress she wore was patterned with large flowers of muted shades. Her legs swollen and without cover, the skin dry and cracked. Her bare feet were purple. Her toenails were thick, yellowed and dry, reminding Daisy of seashells from Galway that Rose had stuck onto a wooden box at home. The backs of her hands were purple and swollen, her nails discoloured, tough and long.

She was holding on to a grubby cloth baby doll with a plastic head – rocking it.

Daisy knew instinctively that she was the doll that Molly held in her arms.

Looking into the old woman's eyes, there was no need to wonder any more if she was her birth mother. The woman stared ahead, her eyes deeply set. Slate eyes, identical to her own. Rose had often said that her eyes were the same grey as you'd see on a heron's back. Her nose was straight, pointed at the tip, the same as her own. This woman was her mother. No doubt.

The nurse told Daisy that Molly had tried to bite some of the staff when they had attempted on several occasions to take the doll from her to wash it. The doll was filthy.

Worn and well used. It had no distinctive features left, apart from its shape.

Molly had been given the doll by one of the nurses some years before when she had noticed that Molly would be at her calmest when she sat rocking with her arms held as if cradling a a baby. It hadn't been hard to work it out.

Daisy's emotions took over as she knelt before the woman she knew to be her birth mother.

She could feel the nurse's presence close behind her. Then the nurse leant over to whisper, "Speak gently to her now and no sudden movements. Admire her baby if you like. You won't get a response, dear, but she has shown herself to understand more than you'd think, at times. Say what you have to say."

"Thanks. I will take my chances."

Daisy leaned as near to Molly's face as she could.

"Molly, hello. I am Daisy."

Molly looked up, making eye contact with the girl in front of her. Quickly looking back again at her baby doll. Humming a tune which Daisy recognised, an old tune.

"Daisy, Daisy, give me your answer do, I'm half crazy all for the love of you, It won't be a stylish marriage ..."

As she hummed, Molly continued to look at her doll. She'd made her choice.

The tears were silently falling down Daisy's face. She let them fall.

"Molly, I am your baby, Daisy," she whispered.

Then realising that Molly had her only comfort in her arms, as she had done for all these years, she relaxed with her birth mother and her baby doll. Humming the song along with Molly, the two women merged in the tune that linked them together

Not wanting to cause upset, Daisy stood up slowly, telling Molly that she would come back to see her soon. The old woman continued to rock, to sway, humming her tune, as her daughter walked away.

Daisy beckoned to the nurse that she was ready to leave the ward. She had seen enough for now. It was time to leave.

Nurse Cahill escorted her off the ward and down the narrow stairs, taking her firmly by the arm.

"Listen, love, I don't know the ins and outs of all this. But let me tell you that visiting Ward Three too often is not to be encouraged. It upsets things for the patients. Poor Molly is as happy as she can be, as long as she has her baby doll to rock in her arms. Whatever is in her past should remain there, as there's little hope for any future for you, with her. Do yourself a favour, love, and leave her be. Just get on with your life for both your sakes."

Daisy looked coldly back at the nurse. She stepped back before she spoke.

"My birth mother is sitting back there in your so-called Ward Three," she said. " She's wearing clothes that wouldn't sell in a jumble sale, a child's plastic clip in her hair, rocking an old baby doll that she thinks is me. I have just met the woman who gave birth to me and you're telling me to forget it." She could feel her temper rising. "I will tell you now, yes, I will be back. And if that doesn't suit you and those who pay your wages, ye can all go to blazes. The next time I call, your eyes might have opened and that ward might be in a better state than I've seen it today. It's nothing short of abuse. I'm sure my good friend, the journalist, will have a field day, looking around your Ward Three!"

"There's no need to take that tone with me, miss," the nurse responded, giving as good as she got. "I have been here for over thirty years and it's far from easy, I can tell you. Try telling that to the management. We all saw it one time as you did today. Believe me, the passion for change soon disappears when it falls on deaf ears again and again. You walk in here like the madam that you are and expect to see a picture of what you see in your own head. Talk as we walk. There should be three nurses on duty – we are lucky to have two."

The nurse gestured towards an armchair on the corridor.

"Sit and calm down a bit. I am well aware that it must seem strange up there. But it's normal for the patients. Believe me, it's the best situation for women who are here for good reason. Nobody goes up there, except those of us who work there by choice. These women all have families, you know. Molly's not the only one with a history. Yes, families, who conveniently choose to forget that every one of the women up there has a past. Outside of here."

Daisy let the nurse speak. She could hear the frustration in the woman's voice.

"They are placed here because their families could not or would not look after them. Promises are made but soon forgotten. In my experience family members are so relieved that their relatives are here, they stay away, afraid in case they will be landed with them. Some are too ashamed to admit that they're related to them. The stigma attached to being mentally unstable. Most of the families don't even try to communicate with the women up there. For whatever reason, intentional or unintentional, the women have had no visitors and haven't had for years. Explain that to me, if you can?"

Daisy opened her mouth to speak, but she stopped – suddenly she had nothing to say. The nurse had made her point.

"Call before you visit again and we can look at giving you a little private space with Molly, supervised of course. Molly has been in the top ward now for well over twenty-five years. And you, my dear, are her one and only visitor. Go home now and have a think about it. She won't be going anywhere."

Nurse Cahill headed back to her charges, shaking her head in disillusionment, taking in what the girl had said.

Molly and the others might not be dressed in presentable clothes. It was hard enough to dress them in the first place. They were dressed in clothes which made it easier for the staff. The clothes were shared, hanging on racks in the back room. Each day after breakfast the women were dressed in whatever clothes came to hand. No belts or ties. Small buttons were a nuisance. There was no order, day clothes or night clothes, whose clothes, it didn't matter.

Some of the women had a 'calmer'. Molly's was the doll, her baby doll. If Molly wasn't holding the doll by morning, she howled like an animal, a disturbing sound which eased the minute the baby doll was placed back in her arms.

The girl had come to find her birth mother. And it hadn't been difficult to put two and two together as she watched Molly and the young woman. The resemblance between the two was uncanny. No old photographs needed here to prove the likeness, thought Nurse Cahill. In the job for thirty years, she'd seen it all.

But the fresh eyes on the ward had unsettled her.

Retirement was looming and she was ready for it. On the wards below, where visitors came and went to the shorter term patients, it was a very different scene.

Nothing to be had in mentioning to the girl that she remembered the day that Molly was first admitted. Remembering the milk stains on Molly's blouse and the bloodstains on the seat when she had got up to leave the room. Today she had looked into the eyes of the child Molly Payton had given birth to. She had felt the connection between the two women.

Who spoke Molly's truth on the day all those years ago when she came down to take her to the ward, where she would remain for the rest of her life? Nobody.

It hadn't been her brother and that was for sure.

"Maybe this one might prove to be genuine."

She decided there and then to stay out of it. The girl would have to search for her own truth.

Chapter 32

The Reunion

Molly Payton had been moved from the children's home at the age of seventeen. The nuns had placed her in the convent laundry at the rear of the school in town. She had improved enough to be able to interact with those around her.

The death of Sister Angela had allowed the young girl to be more sociable and coherent than she'd been in years. Molly had kept her bag of dried plants but was not inclined toward making the brew. When she had managed to make it, the taste had been bitter and distasteful. Spitting the bits out of her mouth, she thought it didn't taste the same as she'd remembered it. As the contents dried up, her dependency on the brew lessened. She found the musty smell from the bag disgusting. It looked more like dead pieces of bark and rotten mushrooms than anything else. Throwing its contents out, she saved the brown bag as a reminder of the kindly nun that had helped her.

She was more lucid and aware than many had ever

remembered – everything about her had woken up. She had been on her own prescribed medication for some time but without her magic tea to supplement it she was a changed girl.

Mother Superior had been pleased to see the girl was improving. It was only a matter of time before she would see the last of her. She placed her in the smaller laundry with the intention of moving her on, once she had been shown the ropes by the women.

She disliked the child to the extent that she could hardly bear to look at her. Once she got the measure of her ability, she would arrange for her to be sent away as far as possible, to one of the bigger laundries.

For now, Molly would continue to live on the grounds of the school.

Happy in her new job, Molly realised she had a contribution to make, working with four local women who came in from outside, paid for their work by the nuns.

She was taken aback at first when the other women included her in their conversations. Molly had to respond loudly enough to be heard, whether she liked it or not, as it was noisy from the moment the first of the machines were switched on in the morning. The women had to shout to be heard.

When the nuns were around, conversation was stilted.

Her job as the newest girl was to take the soiled linen from the large wicker baskets and transfer it to the huge washing drum. Two large wringers sat beside the drum. The washing board was four times as big as any she had seen before. She scrubbed the worst of the linen against the corrugated glass, up and down until the worst of the stains were gone, using a large stiff scrubbing brush for the more stubborn ones. Slow at first, she soon got the hang of it.

The women kept going all day, from nine in the morning to five in the evening, catering for the well-off households, convents, and priests' houses in the area.

The smell of sour, damp laundry in the mornings would be less noticeable as the day went on. Sheets in the morning, tablecloths and pillowcases in the afternoon. Steam everywhere. The smell of starch permeating the building by evening.

The women treated Molly as one of themselves. Once she knew what was expected of her, she was as hardworking as the best of them. They knew that the girl lived at the back of the convent and that she had been raised in the home. It was obvious she wasn't the brightest star, but it didn't matter to them. They were long enough around to know not to comment. Taking her under their wing, they became very fond of Molly Payton, finding her gentle and eager to please.

The girls who were usually sent to them from the children's home didn't stay there very long. They were being prepared to move on to the bigger laundries – testing their skills and learning new ones before they were ready to move.

The laundry women were like a family, except that there was never a cross word between them.

Biddy Butler, the eldest of the women, was a spinster in her fifties. She had by her nature taken charge over the years. Instead of the standard navy apron, she allowed herself the privilege of wearing a patterned apron, wrapped around her and tied at the waist, falling to just above her knees. It set her apart from the others. Her overdyed black hair was plaited and pinned up at the back of her head.

The nuns didn't challenge her, either about her choice of uniform, or about the fact that she had an obvious air of defiance about her. Biddy had been around the nuns for as long as she could remember, she knew how to handle them. Outside of the laundry, she cleaned the ground floor of the convent in the evenings so considered herself to be well established with the order.

The other women had a genuine liking for their elder, showing respect for her with small unspoken gestures. The women had a small boiler which was used to make tea once a day during their break. It was an unspoken rule that Biddy's tea was made each day by one of the others. Always.

Any questions that needed to be answered were directed towards Biddy, who was always happy to help. The women never questioned her refusal to comply with the apron rule.

They themselves wouldn't dare wear anything other than the plain navy aprons that had been provided by the nuns.

Josie, in her thirties, was large as life with a sense of humour to match. Being a skilled seamstress, part of her job was to check the laundry for rips and tears.

Francis was barely four foot ten, her size not matching her ability to do as much of the heavy work as the others. She had thinning fair hair. The others poked fun at her, in an effort to coax her into washing it.

"Fanny, did you wash that hair with a bucket of black oil again?"

Francis gave back as good as she got. The women enjoyed the banter amongst themselves.

The gentlest of the four, Phyllis, was closer to Biddy in age. The two were inseparable, both in work and outside.

Once the women got used to Molly, and she to them, she found herself opening up about matters which hadn't registered with her in years, recalling the past. She didn't understand how her memory had returned. It had crossed her mind that it may have had something to do with Sister Angela's tea.

She told the women about the day her world stopped, when her twin, James, disappeared from her side. James, she told them, had been boarded out and sent to work on a farm a couple of miles from the town – she had remembered the nun telling her that.

The two older women would talk on their way home of their fondness for the girl. They didn't want to see her spending her life out there in the laundries without experiencing a life outside. Agreeing that Molly Payton had never been given the chance to show her worth to anyone, they felt protective towards her.

She had been with them for six months.

The nuns would enquire how the girl was coping. The women took it on themselves to say that Molly was slowly learning. They didn't want to let her go. Wanting to drag her time with them out as long as possible.

"Not quite there yet, sister."

Biddy and Phyllis decided to make it their business to look for James. If her brother knew where she was heading, he might well get her out of there and away from the nuns.

All they had to do was get their hands on the Reverend Mother's heavy black ledger, which held the details of all the children in the home.

Their plan was that Biddy would insist that she

needed an extra pair of hands, to give the office a good clean. Phyllis would then keep watch. Having seen the book many times, Biddy had often had a peek when nobody was around, even though Reverend Mother insisted that the door to her office was left open while Biddy was cleaning. If she wasn't in there herself.

So Phyllis would clean the floor in the hallway, moving the metal mop-bucket around with the side of her foot as she went – ready to give a cough, if one of the nuns appeared on their way towards the office. Nobody did.

Biddy skimmed through the ledger. Noticing that the details of the children who had left the home weren't nearly as complete as the entries.

She found what she was looking for. In alphabetical order for the year 1940.

"Molly and James Payton entry July 1940. James Payton signed out by Mother Superior on Thursday, March 18th 1943, boarded out to Mr. and Mrs. James Bates at their family farm. Bates Farm."

Biddy closed the book quietly, as she'd heard Phyllis cough. Then she remembered that Phyllis was always coughing from the cigarettes. But she had found what she was looking for.

The two women walked arm in arm towards home, smoking the best cigarette of the day, Phyllis coughing away and laughing at the same time. The information didn't need to be written down. Everyone knew Bates Farm.

The women knew their jobs were at stake if they were ever found out. And neither of them could afford that, Biddy warning Phyllis that this was strictly between the two of them. It wouldn't be shared with the other women in the laundry and especially not with Molly.

The two friends decided to send a note by post to Mr. James Payton, care of Bates Farm. Even if he had left Bates farm, they'd surely know where he was.

Phyllis would pen the note, dictated by Biddy. Due to her lack of formal education, the nuns assumed Phyllis to be illiterate – she was glad that she had never made them any the wiser.

Biddy's handwriting could be easily recognised as she signed in and out for the laundry on a daily basis. Phyllis's small rounded writing would not be identifiable.

James. Your twin Molly is working in that laundry behind St. Martha's school. She is free from the home. You can get her out. Make contact.
   Signed
   Teeny Crowe

The women figured that the chances of them being found out were next to nothing. Nobody had that much of a brain to work out who Teeny Crowe was. Bates farm was less than ten miles away – as the crow flies.

One week later, Molly had been called to the convent office to be told that her brother was waiting in the parlour to meet with her.

The meeting was formal and stilted. Once introductions were made, the two looked at each other as if they'd never met before. Too much had happened over the years for the twins to be as they once were, neither understanding the effects of the trauma on that day long ago. James had become a young man who depended solely on himself. He didn't show emotion or know how to show it. He was lacking the courage it would take for him to rekindle his lost emotion towards his twin.

Molly said nothing – she couldn't look at him.

The following morning just before nine, Biddy lit up her third cigarette of the day at the front door of the laundry, as she always did. Waiting for the door to be opened from the inside. She had a sense there was something in the air.

Her sense was proved right when, with a clank of the lock, the red metal door opened.

It wasn't the usual laundry nun – it was the head nun herself, Reverend Mother, standing in front of her.

Biddy quickly put her cigarette out between her thumb and forefinger. She wasn't about to waste it just because the head nun was there. Back into the front pocket of her apron, she'd finish it later.

"Good morning, Mrs. Butler. I thought we'd have a chat before the others arrived in."

The nun walked back inside toward the laundry room, saying, "Molly Payton will not be turning up for work today, or any other day for that matter. There was an incident last evening. I don't know how I thought that girl was fit for any type of work."

Biddy followed, making faces, sticking her tongue out at the nun's straight back. Rolling her eyes.

Once inside, the stern-faced nun turned to face Biddy. Her face giving nothing away.

"Molly Payton had a relapse which none of us were expecting. She had been doing so well. Her brother James arrived at the convent last evening to see her. Right there in front of us all, she lost control of whatever sanity she had been surviving on."

"Oh sweet Jesus!" said Biddy, blessing herself. She was feeling shocked and guilty at the same time. Her cheeks reddened. Her part in getting the twins reunited had caused this. But she'd say nothing. She knew if she did her job was gone.

"Poor girl, Mother. Shur all we can do is say a little prayer for her. Will she get back to us at all, I wonder?"

"Mrs. Butler, it's unlikely the girl will ever return. Her breakdown was completely out of the blue. She is not to be trusted around the laundry machines. Where would we be if she caused an accident?"

"What way did she break down, Mother?"

"She went to the washroom, having made a holy show of herself in front of her brother, refusing even to look at him. He took off straight away, after bringing all that trouble to the door of the convent. She was found sometime later, in … let's say, a distressed state. Meeting him must have triggered the weakness in her. She will get the help she needs in Ultan's. Now, Mrs. Butler. Her replacement will be here Tuesday morning at nine. That's all there is to say about it. I've already said too much."

The nun put her hand on Biddy's arm to stop her from replying.

"Just tell the others she will not be returning here."

"Poor Molly, and she was coming on so –"

"Now, Mrs. Butler, the decision is final. It was made in consultation with the doctor and the girl's brother. He was on the telephone again this morning. Look at the upset this must be causing to poor Mr. and Mrs. Bates, who have been the only parents the boy has ever known. That's all now. Tell the others and not another word about it after that."

Biddy stood for a moment, knowing that she was

beaten, and so was poor Molly. Herself and Phyllis had tried to do something good for the girl. It had worked against them.

She blessed herself one last time before going back to meet the others as they turned up for work. She would tell the women and say no more about it. Biddy Butler knew her place.

Chapter 33

Retribution

Daisy lifted the phone. She'd spent a long time mulling it over in her head. If she didn't do it today, she didn't know when she'd have the nerve again. She would have to confront Davie Keogh herself.

Having talked it over with George, she had told him that she was finally going after Keogh. She dialled the number slowly, she didn't want to get it wrong. It had been an easy number to find – it was there scrawled along the side of his garage wall.

Daisy had rehearsed what she was going to say to him. She had written it down to have it in front of her. Ready for anything he might throw at her, she hoped her voice wouldn't falter.

The ringing tone stopped. The phone was answered. She had almost hung up.

"Hello?"

"Hello, is that Mr. Keogh?"

"Yes, yes, it is, David here."

In the best voice that she could muster, she spoke slowly and succinctly. "I am sure you will well remember me. It's Daisy, Tom Arnold's ex-wife."

She heard him cough as if to clear his throat.

"Yes, Miss Daisy, what can I do you for?"

She paused, letting him laugh nervously for a moment.

"Firstly, Mr. Keogh, this is not about you calling unannounced to my home at almost midnight some months ago. I have other business to discuss with you. You are aware that I was left my mother's house here in town?"

"Yes, Daisy – can I call you Daisy? Is this about Thornton –?"

Daisy cut him short. "No, it's about me!"

"Oh. You have me now, dear. I'm not sure what this is about. Call over if you want. I'm here at the garage all day. Or will I call up to you?"

"No, not after your last visit, Mr. Keogh. We can meet at Thornton's office. I will make an appointment."

"Shur, why would we be dragging John Thornton into this? Can't we chat between ourselves?"

"Mr. Keogh, I will set up a meeting at Thornton's. I want him there too. I assure you, it will be in your best interest to be there."

"Of course, love, set it up so – let me know the details. I will be chatting to Thornton myself anyway and we can take it from there. I've someone here now so I have to go. Bye now and thanks for the call."

Strange, she thought. Keogh hadn't really pressed her on why she wanted to meet.

Chapter 34

Introductions

George introduced Daisy to his mother casually in town four days before Christmas. People everywhere rushing in and out of shops, picking up the last few bits. Rain and wild winds kept people huddled in doorways.

Perfect timing. A quick introduction on the street between Daisy and his mother followed by an invitation for Daisy to come to tea at his house the following day.

He realised that his mother would have more than likely recognised Daisy around the town anyway. She would also have to recognise the fact that her only son was going out with Daisy and no one, not even her, could get in his way.

His mother wasn't the type to say a bad word against anyone and she certainly wouldn't risk hurting Daisy's feelings or indeed his own. As an Irish Catholic, the fact that Daisy was another man's wife would certainly bother her. But she'd get over it. That would have to be his mother's issue. Not his.

The women had greeted each other warmly on the street – there had been no embarrassing silences, no awkward glances. The following evening, back at the house, George, his mother and Daisy sat around the kitchen table, as if they had known each other for ever.

He needn't have worried. His mother had welcomed Daisy into her home, telling her she was as welcome as the flowers in May, giving her a warm hug by way of greeting. George felt pleased when she had added that she had known Daisy to see over the years. And she knew her mother well. She said Rose O'Neill was nothing short of a walking saint. George smiled to himself with pride at his mother's warm attention to Daisy.

What he knew she didn't say was that Sally Arnold's son was a waster, a cheat and a wife-beater. That she knew Rose's heart had been broken when Arnold had coaxed this girl away from her before subjecting her to years of bullying – to a dreadful life that would have been far outside the radar of Daisy's childhood experience. There was no need to worry that his mother would start a line of questioning now. She had the answer before her, sitting right in front of her in her own kitchen. Georgie was happy at last and she knew it.

When he heard his mother inviting Daisy over for Christmas dinner, he smiled at her, recognising the gesture, and the manner in which it had been extended. Daisy accepted.

Daisy walked up the steps to Thornton's office, taking a seat at reception until he came to call her in. There was no sign of Keogh as yet. She had rehearsed what she was going to say. Having decided in the end to confide in

George, the couple had discussed it, making sure that all angles were covered. But she insisted on going it alone.

John Thornton came out within a few minutes, his glasses as usual sitting low on his nose. Daisy couldn't help but notice his long flashy tie, which looked out of place on him.

"Ah hello, come on in now. David Keogh has just arrived before you."

"Thanks, Mr. Thornton."

In the office, Thornton invited her to sit beside Davie, while he sat behind his desk. He assumed that the meeting about to take place was to do with the girl's property. The widow's house. He had no reason to believe otherwise.

"Now ... what can I do for you today? I have your file out as you can see, ready and waiting."

"Oh, thank you, Mr. Thornton, but the matter I have come here today for has nothing to do with my house or money. I wanted to see David Keogh here, and I want you to witness what I have to say."

"Now, Daisy, I'm not sure that this is right," said Thornton. "As you well know, I haven't been prepared beforehand or been informed of your intent."

"Oh, but you are well aware of where I'm coming from, Mr. Thornton. You've seen the letters. You've talked with Rose, my mam."

David remained quiet. He was not about to open his mouth until he knew exactly what this was about. But he didn't have a good feeling about it.

Putting her handbag on the desk in front of her, Daisy removed an envelope and slid out three colour photographs, larger than the norm. She handed a copy to each of the men. Looking at them, there was no recognition on the face of either man.

"Now, Mr. Keogh, I'm unsure if you are aware that I was not Rose O'Neill's birth child. She adopted me in 1966." Turning her own copy of the photo towards Davie, she continued, "I was found in this blue bag, wearing these blue clothes, outside the church here in Ballygore on April 4th 1965, Does this ring a bell? Yes? No? Mr. Thornton, as you know, the package that I recovered from the attic was in fact the baby clothes and the bag as they were on the day. I fully intend to get to the bottom of this through the papers, or the radio, or the pulpit, wherever I have to go to find the truth."

Davie was changing colour. She thought that he was going to have a heart attack. He held his chest, then raised his hands as if to hold up his head. He looked as if he couldn't believe what he was hearing. He sat there with his mouth open, staring at her.

Thornton stared at him.

Looking directly at Davie, she continued, "Well, you were seen dropping my birth mother off, carrying this blue bag which had me inside. Does the name Molly Payton ring a bell at all? And, I have a witness, believe it or not. So if you are considering denying this, Mr. Thornton can take note of your response."

"Now, Miss O'Neill, this is rather a shock for all of us," said Thornton, "and I sincerely wish that you had forewarned me of your intention to challenge this man here. I must firstly say that I do not and have never acted in matters outside of a small bit of business with David here. However, I am your family solicitor and in this regard we need to stop this meeting for now – until we all have had time to digest it. Particularly David Keogh here, as you are making a serious accusation against him."

"Oh, Mr. Thornton, what do you take me for? I am here today simply to state that I have a witness who is willing to come forward, to give an account of what they saw on that Sunday in April after Mass. I'm merely advising David Keogh that he was seen driving his green Volkswagen car, dropping my birth mother and the bag off. Should Mr. Keogh need, as I am sure he will, to enlist a solicitor of his own to look after his own legal affairs on the matter, I am here to notify you of my intention, expecting Mr. Keogh to respond in due course."

David Keogh was green in the face. He could not speak. He had nothing to say. It was obvious that he was in shock.

John Thornton looked at him and said, "David, you do not appear to be in the best form to respond. Am I to take it that you do not accept what Miss O'Neill is saying?"

Davie responded quietly and slowly – it was difficult to hear him. "This conversation better go nowhere else, until I've had time to digest it. I am saying nothing. I'll be in touch, John, once I've made contact with a brief of my own."

He stood up and walked out.

Daisy thought that Thornton had a face on him that would stop a clock.

"Well, Miss O'Neill – your statement, I would say, has certainly had the desired impact. I had no idea that you were about to throw that one out there. So, we need to be clear what it is you're saying here. Are you suggesting that Mr. Keogh is your biological father? Or are you saying that he simply dropped off the person who left the baby, yourself of course. As, if you are, it will have serious repercussions for a lot of people, not in the least yourself. As your legal representative, I have to warn you that you need to be one-hundred-per-cent sure of your witness, as you have just accused the man of something that could damage him irretrievably. I suggest that you gather whatever concrete information that you have and make an appointment to see me independently of Keogh. He will no doubt need to get his own legal affairs in order, independently of myself. I must also advise you to speak of this matter to no one – it will be best not to do so at this point."

"I am well aware, Mr. Thornton, that this is a civil matter as it stands. Unless of course it can be proven that he forced my birth mother to abandon me. However, I will await a response from David Keogh and, yes, we will take it from there."

Daisy left the office. Confused that she didn't feel any better or any worse than she had before. There was no relief.

Later, as she relayed to George what had happened, she thought that she even felt a little sorry for Keogh, now that Thornton had mentioned to her the likelihood of lives being ruined over this. She had no interest in causing upheaval in the lives of the Keogh family, but he was most certainly accountable.

George had reminded her that he had the number, make, and model of the car and the mention of the bag that he knew to be the same as the one that Mrs Keogh used to send the laundry to his own house. And she herself had the evidence now. There was also the fact that there were many, many notebooks, which George had compiled over the years, all with the same level of detail and dates that wouldn't take long to convince a judge that the writings in the notebook were genuine and of their time.

They decided to wait ten days to hear back from Keogh.

The next day the phone rang in the house.

"Daisy, David Keogh here. Regarding the conversation in the solicitor's yesterday, I want to discuss it further, but as I said to you, I will not do so until I engage a brief of my own. John Thornton cannot represent both of us. Failing that, you and I can meet along with your witness, if you wish to discuss the matter. We can do so at a place of your choice. I suppose what I am trying to say is, if you are up for it, we can leave out the legal people and save ourselves a lot of time and money."

"Well, to be honest, Mr. Keogh, at this point I haven't thought about what the next step is going to be. It's unlikely that it's a criminal matter – more civil I would say. I have the proof as I see it and my witness is not shy about coming forward, so yes, I will think about meeting you and bringing in the witness. Where did you have in mind?"

"I'm easy on that score. Needless to say, I was very upset at what you had to say. I will leave it to you to chat about it to your witness and get back to me. I will not be discussing the matter from my end with a single soul and certainly not with Thornton. We have a business life to take care of. I have no intention of letting that go."

"Well, OK then, why don't you call to the house here – you know well where the front gate is. I will arrange to have my witness here. Then there will be no confusion."

"Hold your horses there now, missy. Do you expect me to walk into a house where two people are lying in waiting? That'd be like leading a lamb to slaughter. And may I ask who the witness is? Have you gone to the papers already? I know well you have, because that Doyle fella has already threatened me – weeks back. Look, what about meeting somewhere more neutral, more private."

Daisy could feel her body stiffen. What the hell had George been doing accosting Keogh? And he hadn't opened his mouth about it, to her. But she would have to leave that alone for now. "I don't consider that you are in any position to be taking over, or making decisions here. Do you? Be here at five o' clock tomorrow evening. I will decide where and when we will meet in this regard. Don't you think I have waited long enough to find out who the hell I am? Five o'clock. Be here."

Daisy put down the phone with a bang.

When George called to her later in the evening she told him what had happened.

"You'd better be careful with that fella. I will be there of course and it isn't as if he's going to say anything incriminating at this point. He'll be coming here to find out more. He wants to know who the witness is and how credible the person is. I'd say he thinks that you've come to me to print it."

"Yes, he mentioned that. And he also mentioned that you'd gone after him. Jesus, George. I wish you'd told me. I really needed to know that, before I met him. I felt like a right fool when he mentioned it on the phone. Just as well he couldn't see my face."

"I was going to tell you, Daisy, but thought it best to keep it quiet, given that you'd enough on your plate to deal with. But I never mentioned your name to him, or Rose's. But he probably doesn't know what to think after my little chats with him. No doubt he'll be afraid of his

303

life that I will print it and ruin him. No harm – he's an awful clown. And he's up for some shock when he realises that I am the witness."

"But what if he denies it, based on the fact that it's a twelve-year-old child's account?" she asked.

"Don't worry, guilty people make mistakes you know – he won't know whether he's coming or going. The fact is that we have the proof and it's up to him after that. If he's just going to deny it, we'll threaten him with the law. The case of an abandoned baby with the poor mother in a psychiatric home ever since. No way will he want that to become public. Particularly when it involves such a vulnerable woman as Molly. Daisy, even Keogh isn't stupid enough to take a chance on being questioned. Just to be sure, I'll record the conversation."

"No, George, please don't. He might cop what you're doing and I don't want to take that risk. We'll say what we have to say and hear what he has to say. We're not idiots. And I'm well able for him."

Of that, George had no doubt.

Five o'clock sharp, David arrived at the front door with a stack of brochures under his arm as if he was calling to look at the property. Sensing the fear in him, Daisy led him through to the kitchen, where George sat waiting. The blue bag sat slumped on the table, the baby clothes inside.

David didn't seem to notice George for a second as his eyes were drawn immediately to the bag. Then he looked at George.

"What the fuck!" said David, looking more bewildered than anything. "I should have bloody known you were in on this. With all your bullshit and blackmail and me telling you like a half eejit how to find Molly Payton's brother! I only knew where he was because he was in the fucking telephone directory. No secrets there, Doyle."

"Mind your language, man, in front of the lady. Take a seat." George took the blue bag from the table and moved it to the sideboard.

"What the hell has this to do with you anyway, Doyle, apart from your bloody threats to splash it all over the paper? I know you like getting your gossip ready for that rag you're working for. So where's this witness? I will only talk to him and Miss Daisy here."

"That would be me, Davie man. It was myself who sat on the church wall that morning, watching you drop off the woman with the blue washing bag. Before you say anything else – I will tell you exactly how I know what I am talking about."

David looked stunned. "Go on then, you bastard. I won't say another word."

George removed the little brown notebook from his pocket. Opening the page which he had marked with the red sticky note, he handed the notebook to David.

Davie read it before throwing the notebook back in front of George.

"All baloney, Doyle. Do you take me for a complete fool? I'd expect nothing else from you! Yes I told you I dropped her off – she was a tenant in the flat and so what? I was only giving her a lift."

"Make all the excuses in the book, say what you like but no one here is listening to you," said Daisy. "I wonder would your wife like to take a look at the bag – and indeed the baby clothes inside? I don't think you quite understand, David. You see, I never knew that I wasn't

Rose's child until lately. I have the exact details of how and where I was found. Rose left it for me and I have it in writing. And I know that it was you. I can tell that alone by the look on your face."

"You know fuck all."

"Oh, I wondered over and over again why in God's name my birth mother had dressed me in blue – 'twas hardly to match the bag. Then it dawned on me."

George took over, seeing the strain on Daisy's face. "Keogh, the fact that the townspeople figured the child in the bag was a boy was actually in Daisy's favour growing up – they never connected her with the baby in the bag. The only person who knew the baby was a girl, apart from her mother, was you. You knew because it was you who supplied the clothes for the baby. Your son Oliver was born a couple of months before Daisy was found. We know this because he was in the same class as Daisy all through school. And anyone can apply for a birth certificate these days, man. So, I'd say that you took the clothes from your own house and gave them to Daisy's mother to dress her in. That's why she was dressed like a boy. There was no other possible reason, other than the availability of baby clothes at your house."

David looked like he was about to pass out, feeling as drained as he knew he looked. Guilty. For the first time in his life he was stuck for words. Thoughts of his life being turned upside down bombarded him. He couldn't think quickly enough or sharply enough to get himself out of this. These two wanting answers. And wanting them now.

He regained his composure – he was no fool – the last thing he was going to do was be forced to admit what he knew, or worse be blackmailed by them. He had too much to lose.

"OK, so let me get this straight." He paused. "So, you two here, snarling at me like a couple of dogs, have come up with this notion that I had something to do with this child, left outside the church in that blue bag." Then, looking directly at Daisy, "And you're saying 'twas yourself in the bag." Looking from one to the other, he knew he had no choice but to deny that he had any part in abandoning the infant. "All the evidence you have is that of a child's notebook. Do you honestly think a court of law would believe a kid from a impoverished background – above me, David Keogh. I gather you are aware that my eldest is studying to be a solicitor – and the wife's family are all professionals. I'll wipe the floor with ye!"

"Oh, we figured you'd be in denial mode so we've kept the best bit until last, David," said Daisy. "I found my birth mother in a psychiatric hospital in Dublin. I've met with her. Yes, I found her through her brother James. So, thanks for that, David. Molly Payton has been a patient in St. Ultan's psychiatric hospital since April the fifth, nineteen sixty-five. Ring any bells for you? So she is another witness."

Davie stood up sharply. George stood up as well. He thought Keogh was going to hit her. Instead he walked straight out the door without saying another word. The front door banged. He was gone.

"Daisy, just let him off. He needs to go away and have a long hard think about his part in all this. Let's not jump to conclusions just yet. There's a strong possibility that he is your bio–"

"*Stop it*, don't say it, George. Even if he is, he was not my dad. I have no memory of John Pat and how could I – but he was my dad and the memories of him handed down to me are far more special than anything that bastard could offer me. I will never look on him as my father."

"Right – let that go for now. One thing I ask is that we keep it to ourselves. Keogh certainly won't open his mouth, unless he looks for legal advice. He can't use Thornton, as he's your family solicitor involved in the O'Neill affairs for years. He won't go to his trainee son. He will have to go out of town. So just to be on the safe side, don't mention this to Thornton again until we see what Keogh comes back with. Thornton is as cute as a fox at the back of it all even if he has been your family solicitor for years."

"I won't be saying it to anyone. Jesus, what about Emmet? He knows more than he needs to."

"Leave Emmet to me – he's so tied up now with Susan, he won't do anything to jeopardise that. I have my eye on him and he is well aware that I have."

Daisy saw the look in George's face, making her feel just a little uncomfortable.

"Oh, forget Emmet," she said, heaving a long sigh. "You're right. But warn him. He's a friend after all. He was there when I needed him. I have you now, George, and you are all I need to help me through this." Aware that she sounded patronising, she leaned in closer to him.

The doorbell rang. Daisy went to answer it. She viewed the the caller through the peephole and called back to George.

"*It's him, George, he's back! He must have been outside all the time!*"

Davie walked straight past her through to the kitchen.

"Right. How much is this going to cost me? Come on. How much are ye looking for? A grand, two grand. Ten grand? Go on. Name it."

Georgie pressed the button on his mini-recorder, which sat waiting in his jacket pocket.

"So. You're offering money now, David. Ten grand, did you say? Are you saying that you do believe the word of a twelve-year-old boy after all? By the way, that notebook is only one of the many journals I kept since I was ten years old. All written clearly, albeit in the handwriting of a child. I'm sure there are ways in today's world of proving that the diaries are authentic. In fact I'd put my career on the line for it."

Davie held his two fists above his head. "Yes, it was me who left that crazy woman out of my car with the blue bag. The woman who you say was your mother, Molly Payton, lived in one of my flats in Spring Street for a few months. I told you that weeks ago, you prick!" He looked at George who remained silent, letting him speak. "She tried to pin it on me at the time – but I knew well she was pulling a wild card. She was pregnant coming to town and then tried to make out it was mine. But I never had sex with her. I knew it couldn't be mine so I realised the best thing was to leave the baby where it could be taken care of. She knew that herself – that she wouldn't be able to take care of it. So I got the washing bag from home. The baby clothes were already in it. The wife must have been getting them ready for someone. They were perfect and Molly didn't seem to care what the colour of them was. They fitted the baby and so she dressed it up in the clothes."

He looked at Daisy, who nodded her head in disbelief

as she watched the man who had held her beginnings all this time.

Davie continued. "I only did it cos I felt sorry for her. She wasn't well, the woman. As cracked as a brush. I found the number of her brother in her handbag and called him for her. I never mentioned that she'd had the child. I was in the phone box with her when she told him she wasn't well. He made the arrangements after that. I drove her to the church and then to the station. The brother collected her off the train to take her back to the nuthouse. Where she belonged."

Daisy felt her eyes filling with tears as David Keogh continued to deny that he was her father. At least that was something to be grateful for, but did he have to be so cruel in the process? Either way, he would never have the privilege of being named as her dad. Molly Payton was her birth mother all right. To Davie, she was just a loose woman, up for it, worthless.

"So, David, you're saying that Daisy here is not your biological daughter, but that it was you who dropped her mother off at the church, here in Ballygore, on that Sunday in April 1965, with the baby."

"Yeah." He nodded. "Yes, yes, it was me, I told you already."

"But did you not also tell me that night in Philly's yard that you'd been with her?"

Davie couldn't remember what exactly he had said that night. Doyle was confusing him. Had he already admitted to sleeping with the woman? Had he mentioned it that night when Doyle put it up to him in the car park at Philly's? He had been jarred and he wasn't sure. He must have had.

"Look, she was well pregnant coming to town – eyes wide open looking for a fool of a man to claim the child."

"But you haven't answered my question, David. Did you not already tell me you had been with Molly Payton?"

David stared. "Hold on a minute, Doyle! Jaysus, if I didn't know better, I'd say you were taping me. You're asking me questions like a bloody detective. You are, you bastard! You're taping me."

George removed the recorder from his jacket pocket – pressing play for a second to check that he had what he wanted. He had.

"You bastard! Give that to me!"

David tried to grab the recorder but George shoved it back in his pocket. "All mine, Keogh!" he said.

Daisy was devastated after hearing David Keogh talk about her birth mother in such a demeaning manner. Poor Molly would never be able to stand up for herself, or even understand any of this. Daisy's mind was made up and this time there would be no room for procrastination. As Molly Payton's daughter, she would stand up for her, she would be her strength. And her voice. Wondering what hell she must have gone through, now at the far end of her life, rocking her baby doll, refusing to let it out of her hand. Molly Payton had felt the pain – there was no doubt in Daisy's mind.

Yes. She would destroy this excuse of a man.

Desperate now, David appealed to Daisy. "Daisy, love, listen to me. I am not your father. Your mother got pregnant with some other fellow. She was well up for it and I don't say that lightly – she just wasn't mother material."

"Enough of that now, David," said George. "Whether you are or are not Daisy's biological father, time will tell.

Keep your money for now, until Daisy here has a think about where we go from here. Oh, and if we get a sniff of you discussing this with a soul we will take you to the cleaner's. But that's highly unlikely, David, isn't it?"

David stood up to leave once again.

As he walked to the door, George asked, "By any chance was Thornton involved back then, in the letting of the flat to Molly? I could ask him myself, or if you know the date that she came to town?"

Davie was caught on the hop – without thinking, he answered spontaneously. "I know well when she came to town because the wife had buried her aunt the week before, and it delayed doing up the place. The aunt had been living in the flat to be nearer the church. That was at the beginning of August, builder's holiday. I remember because I couldn't get a builder in and had to do the work myself. The Payton woman moved in about a week later. I couldn't believe she was in such a hurry to take the place without seeing it."

David realised too late that he had been tricked.

"Or was it? Let me have a think about it."

George was too quick for him.

"Do the sums, man. The woman could hardly have been pregnant coming to town."

David Keogh cursed aloud as he left the house.

Daisy ran upstairs to the bathroom. George could hear the sound of the toilet flushing. He knew that she was getting sick.

He waited for her to return to the kitchen. He would persuade her to put it on hold for now. They needed time to think.

"Oh my lord, to think that that lowlife could be – what am I saying could be – he bloody *is*, my biological father!

312

If Molly wasn't pregnant coming to Bally and he was sleeping with her, well, the sums sure add up. George, would you mind leaving me be now – I need to be alone to come to terms with this."

"Of course, Daisy, have all the time you need, just remember that you are not alone. I will be behind you all the way." He held her face in his hands. "Daisy, I will mind you."

Her head was reeling with the information she had to consider. Recalling also a time when the two other men from her past had spoken the same words to her that George just had. "I will mind you." If there was one lesson that Daisy had learned – she would be letting nobody mind her again. Never again would she be weak enough to take the word of any man who offered her the sun, moon and stars. She felt confident and well capable of holding her own, in facing the likes of Keogh, while feeling sick to her stomach at the thought of this excuse for a man being related to her by blood. Worse still, he had denied Molly, an obviously vulnerable woman, just for his own ends. She knew that George was there for her but she also knew that it had to be her and her alone that would act against the man that had ruined Molly Payton's life.

She had loved her mam and in her heart she would always be her true mother. But she had felt a strong bond with the sad distracted woman who had given birth to her. She knew that she would not stop until she was at least satisfied that the man responsible would feel the pain.

Chapter 35

Sweet Revenge

Two weeks to the day, Daisy walked brazenly into Keogh Car sales in Ballygore. He had seen her coming and had come to meet her, trying to prevent her from coming any further into the building. Too late. She walked straight past him, into his office. He closed the door. It was lunchtime and there was nobody else around.

"I hope, David, that I have picked a good time for you. I've decided that, yes, I will accept your offer of ten thousand pounds. In cash. And if the money is not dropped in my letterbox by the end of the week, I will visit your wife, before giving George the go-ahead to print the story. Simple."

She changed her tone then, now speaking gently, thinking of the pain that he had put Molly through.

"You didn't imagine that you would get away with it, did you? Molly certainly didn't, but then again you knew that."

He stood there facing her. "I tell you the woman is a

liar. We might have been together a few times but there is no way I'm the father of the … your father. I've practised birth control all my adult life. Ask my wife, she was the one insisting on it after the lads were born. I'm sure you don't want to hear the exact details? But I will do the decent thing – rather than having it said that I didn't help you out. How will I know that it's settled then?"

"You won't ever know, as long as I am around. And, oh, by the way, Thornton better not be in on this or I will take him down as well. So say nothing to him about the payment. Should you utter a word and it comes back to me, which it will, I will make the whole story public. Your name will be ruined and nobody will buy a car or rent a property from a man that could do what you did. As for your family –"

"Enough, enough. I hear you. You're blackmailing me."

"No, David, I am merely coming to collect what has been rightfully mine for all of these years and, before you reply, I would advise you strongly not to deny me again. Or deny that you used Molly. As, if you do, I can become so unreasonable that you won't know whether you're coming or going."

"All right, I"ll arrange the payment. It won't be easy, mind, but I will do it. God almighty, I almost feel sorry for Arnold. How did a nice young girl like you turn out to be such a manipulative controlling bitch, who'd go to the ends of the earth for revenge? And you're telling me I can never be sure you'll keep quiet and that you might even come back for more!"

"Oh David, you will never be sure, never as sure as I am that you made my poor mother pregnant, before destroying her."

"Jesus, I'm sure of one thing – I've three at home and there's not one of them that have the cunning in them that you have. There's no way in hell that I'm related to you."

Daisy told George what she had done. There would be no discussion. Ten thousand pounds for now. Later she would go after the house where she was born, in Spring Street. Daisy felt a sense of accomplishment and control and, better still, she liked it. Deciding not to share these feelings with George, she left it as it was.

The thick envelope holding the money came through the letterbox at the end of the week.

She acknowledged it by opening the small window and nodding at the man as he closed the gate.

She stayed away from Thornton, knowing that she made the right decision to keep him in the dark about her arrangement with Davie Keogh. And it was small payment for what the bastard had done. Thornton could stick to what he was good at – arranging the legal stuff.

Daisy had one more trip to make, back to the hospital to see Molly. Making sure that she would get the best of care that money could buy. Davie Keogh's money – he certainly owed her that.

Molly appeared just the same to Daisy, as if time had not passed since she had last seen her. Except for the cardigan, which was just another faded garment. Rocking her baby doll, she didn't seem to be fretting or anxious. She was calm.

The only changes that Daisy could see around the ward were what must have been left of a few Christmas decorations which were still stuck to the wall. Paper chains. Sitting on the table behind the Perspex screen sat a Christmas tree. A two-foot-high half-bald tinsel tree, too old and too damaged to create any sort of festive atmosphere. She wondered had there even been Christmas cards, realising then that she hadn't send one herself. Too quick to criticise, she thought.

Daisy had made the trip alone, ringing ahead to make an appointment to see the psychiatrist, after first spending time with Molly. Having made the decision that she wouldn't be calling her mam, or mum, or mother, all of which had to be reserved for Rose, she would call her by her name. Molly.

"Hello, Molly, it's Daisy, your Daisy."

The woman sat there rocking her baby doll.

"Molly, I am your little girl, remember, your baby. Daisy."

No recognition from her. Daisy wondered if she was just unsettling Molly as her grip tightened on the doll. Nervous, ready to attack if anyone came close enough to take it from her. Easy to imagine that on this occasion she wouldn't be giving her baby up without a fight.

After spending some time and crying more tears, Daisy realised that it was as the nurse had said. Molly had lost her ability to communicate. She couldn't process facts or time in her mind. Nothing. The only connection between this woman and herself was the baby doll, which represented the greatest heartache of them all.

The damage had been done, to an already damaged woman who could take no more. The only people that she had ever loved had been taken from her. Each time leaving her more vulnerable than before. She had been taken advantage of by David Keogh and possibly many more. She was locked into herself. All they could do now was to keep her comfortable and calm. As long as the doll was replaced while Molly slept, that was the best that they could do to keep her calm. Daisy would send on a new baby doll to her. Yes. The nurse had been right in suggesting that visiting Molly might cause more distress than anything else. But she had plenty time ahead to think about that one.

She went and spoke with the psychiatrist. After that, she had to accept that in all likelihood Molly would never change.

And what was she hoping for anyway? For her memory to come back? To be filled with the pain of all she had lost? Or for her to recognise her daughter for a second, just one second? To give her a hug? Yes, yes, please – but no. Daisy knew that it wasn't about her now. It had to be all about Molly. Molly had her baby doll to hug all she wanted. She seemed contented.

Once Daisy had enquired about a private arrangement for her, it was clear that things would be at least more dignified for her. Respectful.

She would be moved to the private wing, where she would have her own room, as well as whatever therapies could be recommended for her. Music – Molly must have liked music at some point. Even water, her skin was dry and cracked in places. Stimulation, photos. Proper clothing. A proper chair to sit in, to hold her safely. A television in her room. All at a cost, but the money was there. Daisy would visit occasionally, making sure that she was being cared for in the best facility that money could buy. And she would remember to send Christmas cards, birthday cards.

The ten thousand pounds would foot the bill for the foreseeable future.

In the meantime, she had every intention of going after Keogh again. She hadn't quite finished with him. She would take the house of flats in Spring Street from him, the flat where he had taken advantage of Molly. If Keogh objected, she would just go after one of his other properties. Or maybe two. The property would be used as collateral for her birth mother's care, well into the future.

When the time came, it went smoother than she had ever thought possible. Keogh was like putty in her hands. He didn't put up a fight. But she figured that losing Number 6 Spring Street wasn't such a big deal to him, if it meant that the problem would go away.

Chapter 36

The Proud Father

Thornton had been walking out of his office when he met David Keogh on the stairs.

"John, can I have a quick word?"

"David, I trust whatever it is, it's to do with your property profile. Because, I can't advise you on any other matters relating to Miss O'Neill. Don't ask me. Do we understand each other?"

"I'm just transferring a property from the company portfolio."

"Come on up."

They went back to the office and sat down.

"John, it will suit me just fine if you don't ask me any questions. I will be transferring the title deeds, from the company file here, to a private individual. Number 6, on Spring Street. The deeds are here in the company portfolio? No questions asked."

Davie could tell that Thornton was edgy – guarded in case their little money-earner would be threatened.

"Just one question – is it a gift or a purchase?"

"It's a purchase, the money has been paid cash to my private account. I want you to do the necessary. The contact solicitor is McCarthy and Crowe on Merrion Road, Dublin. The sum paid is ten pounds. Just forward them on."

Thornton raised his eyebrows but Davie knew that the solicitor would know better than to comment.

"No questions, you say. Well. As long as it's all above board. Any harm to ask who the buyer is?"

"Molly Payton, she is a ward of court. Her next of kin is Miss Daisy O'Neill. You may be surprised to hear that I'm selling it for ten pounds. You know yourself it's better that way. Put it like this, John, I'm just settling a score that I should have settled years ago. I'm playing it right for a change."

"Right you are, David. You know what you're at. I will take a look later and get the deeds out to you. Best if I send them on to yourself and you can finalise it through your own solicitor."

Thornton stood up, and David picked up on his cue to leave.

Just as he got to the door, Thornton said, "Oh by the way, there is a property in Main Street that I want you to take a look at. Quite spacious, owner gone to a nursing home, only son in the States."

"So it's business as usual then, John – I'll be seeing you."

David had realised that if he didn't comply with the girl's request, he could lose far more than one of his properties. Should Grace get wind of all this she would certainly take him to the cleaner's. And the boys would disown him.

So the house in Spring Street would be signed over to Molly Payton.

Whether or not he was the girl's father, he had landed himself in this unholy mess. And if the girl was his, she could indeed contest his will after he had gone.

Although, she'd have some fight on her hands at that stage as Grace's crowd and the boys would do everything in their power to deny her. And deny her they would. His very own flesh and blood or not.

Maybe she really was the daughter that he thought he'd never have. Time would tell, he had no doubt. Yes. It had been the right decision.

It had dawned on Davie all of a sudden. He had done a lot of thinking of late – thinking about the girl – how she reminded him so much of someone. It had tormented him, but he couldn't for the life of him figure out who it was. It had struck him after she had cleverly demanded and succeeded in taking the house in Spring Street from him.

Calculated, determined to have her own way. Confident enough to bulldoze her way through, to get what she wanted.

Himself! He had seen himself in her.

Now that he began to take notice of her antics, she seemed to have more of him in her than any of his own boys had.

The daughter that he thought he would never have.

David visited Daisy once again after signing over the deeds. He called to the house unashamedly. There was no longer any need for excuses.

Daisy was on her own. She ushered him in, telling him that this would be the last time he was to call to her home uninvited. He understood.

Smiling at her, feeling like a different man. He apologised, admitting to her that he hadn't given Molly any consideration. Or any respect.

"Daisy, I'm sorry. I've come here to say just that I've been a proper bastard. I suppose I couldn't let myself believe that I was the baby's – *aham* – your dad. It was easier for me just to deny it to myself. Too easy. Until I watched you the other day and saw myself looking back at me."

"Now, now, David, I wouldn't go that far. We can still go ahead and do a paternity test, but I think that we both know what the result is going to be. Let's just leave Molly with the dignity of us knowing that she was not a whore or a loose woman. She was a woman whose loneliness and mental state made her vulnerable to those who preyed on her, and you were high up on that list. Say it!"

"I know. I admit it. I will do whatever I can, love, but I ask you for now to keep Grace and the lads out of it, as I need time and a plan as to how I will tell them. If you want me to?"

"What I want, David, is not for your family to find out. I have my own family, a life of being protected and loved by Rose and John P's memory. All I want from you is that the woman who gave birth to me lives the rest of her days in the new facility that she has just been placed in. Funded entirely by you. She will have the best of what private care can offer and you will be paying for it. I don't want or need your money – Rose has left me enough. The ten thousand will pay for her care. No insurance will cover the cost of what I have in mind for Molly. She has already been a permanent patient for far too long long. And one thing is for sure, my birthmother, Molly Payton, will not be turning up in the likes of the county home any time soon. So we'll just have to wait and see. Won't we? The house in Spring Street can be sold when the time comes."

David Keogh looked with new-found pride at the carbon copy of himself.

"The woman you got pregnant will be as comfortable as she can be for the future. You owe her that and a lot more. So we understand each other? Other than that, there will be no statements made, or stories told. And it's much too late to be playing daddy to me."

"Oh, did I ever think the day would come when I would be standing here looking at myself. I will not breathe a word to a soul, how could I? Grace is a decent woman who probably didn't deserve to be married to a bastard like myself. And the boys are good. I've messed them around enough as it is. If you decide that you ever want to tell my family for whatever reason, give me warning. I know I'm in no position to be looking for favours, but if you could?"

Daisy nodded, hardly believing the change in David Keogh.

The two shook hands before David walked out of the house.

Davie felt lighter than he had felt in a long time. He felt like the weight of the world had been lifted from his shoulders. He had made a few mistakes over the years and had paid well for silence. This was different. The girl was his and he had no doubt about it.

He cringed, as he recalled the night that he had called to his own daughter's door to put it up to her and all for a bet.

He knew well that Arnold had been rough on the girl – from what he'd heard, she had taken more than her share of beatings from him. His own Grace was at peace at home, with every comfort and enough money to buy whatever she fancied. One thing was for sure, he treated his wife with respect. He would now make sure that Arnold paid for the distress that he had caused Daisy. His daughter. It had been one thing to hear that Arnold liked to keep his women under control. But the tables had turned.

Nobody would harm a hair on Davie Keogh's flesh and blood and get away with it.

Chapter 37

Job Done

Tom had just left his mother's house on the Old Road to go to work. It was the first day back after the Christmas holidays. A little worse for wear, having hit the whiskey hard the night before. But he was glad to be getting out of the house and away from his mother. Arriving at the main door, he saluted whatever workmates were around. Feeling a bit uneasy he carried on through the building, wondering if the drink was making him paranoid. Was he imagining it, or were people staring at him? Paul Jones, his boss, was at his office door as he passed.

"Tom – can I see you for a few minutes?"

"Morning, Paul – what can I do for you?" Tom hadn't a notion of what to expect, thinking that as it was just after the New Year maybe Jones was putting him back on a five-day week.

"Take a seat, Tom. There's no easy way to put this, but as I arrived at the desk last Monday morning, there was a packet waiting for me, which I have kept for you to take a look at."

His boss picked up a large brown padded envelope from behind the desk.

From it he took a note written in black ink and a pair of what looked like the company's overalls. He handed Tom the note.

It read:

Tom Arnold is a thief. He has been stealing from you for years. Bragging about it to his pals in the pub. He has been making your work coats and selling them to some of your customers on the side. Proof – check invoices for Steward's factory. Call Dan Steward and ask him how many of your own overalls did he sign for in the last order. Call the glove factory and ask them the same question. Now check out the overalls in the packet. The name tag says COATS BY THOMAS. Do your own investigation.

"So, Tom, what do you make of all this?"

Tom just stared at his boss. He needed time to figure out how to answer. And there was no time.

"God, Paul, I haven't a notion what this is all about. Are you accusing me of something here? Should I get my solicitor like? Should I be worried?" Tom threw back his head and laughed, expecting that Paul would do the same.

He didn't.

"Oh Tom, I'm afraid it's bigger than all that now. I've had the weekend to do the maths and have a think about it. It took me a while to figure out what was happening when I checked back over the orders. Look at the latest example. Steward ordered forty overalls. Here's the order, dated Oct 3rd. Here's the invoice. Received twenty. Paid for twenty by cheque. How come? What happened to the other half of the order? Twenty overalls. Should I ring him now while I have you here? Steward has done nothing untoward to the company here. Of course the tax man may take a different view with whoever is responsible."

He passed the sheet to Tom who picked it up, reading it in silence, knowing that his game was up.

"It seems, Tom, that there were two invoices, each for twenty coats. Except that the second invoice isn't our own. Is it? And Steward wasn't about to cover for you when the chips were down. He sent me a copy. Take a look for yourself."

Tom recognised his own attempt to imitate a company invoice.

"And these tags are not from our company, Tom. Are they? Looks like someone we know has been running a sideline, making and selling an identical product, using their own tags. Sending invoices separately to the companies and picking up the payment, which does not appear back here – neither does the invoice."

Paul Jones had been careful not to directly accuse him until now.

"What do you have to say, Tom? Or should I call you Thomas? Jesus, how long have you been at this? Don't worry, we know who the two machinists are, making their few bob on the side. Those two will answer also. But it wasn't either of them who sewed on those tags. Hannah Waters has come clean. You had the girls run up the coats in their own time. I myself trained you in, Tom, and as far as I can remember your first job here was as tag-sewer, and good you were at it too."

Tom slumped back in the chair.

"The game is up, Tom, and no one is as sorry as I am. You've had it good here and you would have had it better.

I have decided to give you two options. I can bring in the law or you can resign."

Tom cleared his throat. "You bollocks, Jones! I worked like a slave for this company. Bonus my arse – all I ever got for my years of service to this company wasn't worth a curse. The wife liked the good life, I couldn't afford to keep her, so I set up a little business on the side. So what? I ordered my own tags, got my own business and sourced my own fabric. Well, mainly. So I made a few extra products and sold them on. I don't owe this company anything – only for me there would be no business. I brought the business in, and it was my personality that rolled in the customers. I have made this company."

"And now you can leave this company," Paul Jones said.

Tom shifted in his chair as he considered his next move. He needed a drink. Badly. He couldn't think on the spot. No point in continuing with a conversation that was going nowhere. Jones was not a man to back down once he had his facts straight. He was probably jealous of him, that was it, envious because he was so well regarded in Ballygore.

"Well, Tom, it's up to you now."

Tom decided to try a different tack.

"Paul, look, I wasn't going to say, but things haven't been going well at all on the home front. You know Daisy my wife has left me. She left me with woeful debts, which I have been trying my best to repay. She had gambling problems and you can imagine the sorry mess that was. I admit that I created my own little company, but I have never taken what wasn't mine to take. I worked hard here in the company and outside in the evenings and weekends for myself. So where's the crime? A bit of material here and there. The petrol. Wear and tear on the car. I will stop it immediately, if you give me a chance, Paul. One chance."

"Trust, Tom. Trust is the issue. You know darn well that you have used the company whatever way you could, to support your own sideline. I have met with the senior management and, as I have said, you have two options and now two minutes to decide. As for your wife, the rumours are all around the factory. They say that your wife was black and blue on more than one occasion. Bruises which, from what I hear, were well visible. I'm a family man with three daughters myself and I have my own opinion on the kind of a man that'll beat a woman."

Tom had enough. He wouldn't be bowing down to a man he had no respect for. His mother had told him to be wary of Jones, who came to head up the factory. Church of England, mad for work. Sally had said that the likes of him would work a person to the bone. But Tom knew that he couldn't compete with Jones, and threatening him with a solicitor's letter for defamation of character might just backfire on him. The way things were going for him, his best bet now would be to keep a low profile.

"OK, mister. I will walk out of this office, after I offer you my resignation. Don't worry about a reference, save that for someone who needs one."

Paul handed him a resignation slip, Tom didn't bother to read it, signing it at the bottom of the page where his boss had tipped with his pen.

"Any money owed to you will be send on to you by the end of the week. There is a clearcut case here for the police, but I am giving you this one chance. No police, as long as you dismantle your current business. Goodbye, Tom. And a happy New Year."

Paul stood up, as did Tom. Neither man offered his hand. One man disgusted, the other man disgraced.

Tom walked out of the building for the last time. Meeting some of his colleagues on the way, he talked as he walked on. "Lads, ye can have it all now. I've had an offer too good to refuse, I'm out of here. *Sláinte!*"

Workers on the factory floor turned their backs to him. Lowlifes, he thought. Bloody lowlifes. Bottom line was that he was better than any of them. And they knew it. Today wasn't the day to let them see Tom Arnold being tossed out of the job he had worked so hard in. And after he had put in a good word to get the jobs for half of them. Some of the women sitting at their machines kept their heads down. He hadn't thought that they'd hang him out to dry, but someone had and when he found out who the bitch was that had squealed on him, he'd break her bloody neck.

Good riddance to the lot of them.

He drove straight to the River Hotel bar. He had a plan which he needed to execute before word got out. Seeing Tobin the hotel manager standing at reception, he called him aside before expressing his interest in the nightwork as advertised. Explaining that the wife had cleaned him out, Tom told him that he needed a bit of nightwork to pay off the debts that she'd left him with. The manager couldn't refuse him. Wasn't he one of the lads himself?

Within a few minutes Tom had landed himself the job. It wasn't quite what he had in mind but it was better than nothing and he wasn't exactly in a position to argue. It would do him for now until something better came up. If Tobin had heard that he'd got the push from Jones he mightn't have been so willing to take him on. So the timing was perfect. The men shook hands on the spot.

Tom would start within the coming days.

Entering Philly's bar, he could see Simon and Keogh in the usual spot, deep in conversation. Philly was shuffling about inside the bar.

"Well, lads!" said Tom as he slapped Keogh hard on the back.

"Tom," answered the two as they turned around to face him.

"Listen, lads, I've just come from the job. I decided there and then to hand in my notice. Too much old shite going on and the bastards wouldn't agree to the new contract I wanted. So I quit. Tobin at the River had been tormenting me to do a few shifts over at the hotel, as a night manager. I've taken it now, so ye're the first to know. Philly, give the lads a drink there and a brandy and pep for myself."

"Oh, that'll suit you, Tom," said Keogh. "Or will it? Will the night work not be tough enough?"

"Not at all, shur a change is as good as a rest, they say."

Tom paid for the round, standing beside a man he felt he could trust. The man who had given him the best advice on how to set up his own business. Best to keep him onside. Davie Keogh. A shrewd operator.

Chapter 38

The Future

George had suspected for some time that Philly might be getting forgetful. Doubling up on orders. Placing orders for stock that he had previously refused to carry. Then, not ordering what they needed. Having repeated the big Christmas order in February – he knew for sure that all was not well with Philly, who was blaming the reps for messing up the orders. George kept a close eye on him as he realised himself that his memory was slipping. Apart from that, he just wasn't as switched on, or as interested anymore in running the small hotel bar that had been in his family for generations.

Previously, calling George aside, he had made his intentions known to him. The bar would go to George as soon as Philly decided that he couldn't manage any more. Philly had stipulations. He would remain living upstairs for as long as he could manage. George was to arrange for him to go to the nursing home at the far side of town, once he felt that Philly wasn't able to live on his own. He would sign the bar over to him now, if George was to return to Ballygore permanently. The two men had talked about it often enough over the past few years. George could become freelance, still submitting to the paper that he worked for. In effect it would widen the scope of his work.

Philly was getting worse. Losing things. Small things. Every day.

"Lad, I've watched you since you were a small boy with that notebook of yours, hovering around watching everything. You know this old place is yours, yours to let or manage, or sell, when I lose the plot completely. You've been like a son to me."

George couldn't deny the vacant look in Philly's eyes. "Phil, don't be talking like that now, I'm here as always, to give you a hand. You know that. Don't be giving up on yourself, you've a long way to go yet before you retire." He could feel his eyes water. He smiled at the older man with fondness. "Phil, I do understand what you're saying, I have your back and always will – of that you can be assured. Say no more for now, there's no need."

The men looked at each other and nodded in understanding.

George had certainly plenty to think about. Would he remain on as a journalist in the city, continuing to come back to Bally at the weekends? He didn't think so. Or would he take up Phil's offer to run the bar, returning home permanently. Sounded like a plan. Marrying Daisy wasn't an option just yet – he knew that she didn't feel the same as him about marrying in a registry office. She insisted that she wanted to go back in through the church door, the same as she had the first time. But this time as a happy bride. He didn't think it was about religion. But it didn't matter to him where they married. Or if they married. They could live in sin.

Susan looked as if her mind was elsewhere as she left the hair salon in town, bumping straight into Daisy. The two girls stood laughing with their heads thrown back.

"Hi, Susan, I suppose you're busy with the wedding plans. How's Emmet doing? I can't believe it's months since I laid eyes on him and we all living in the same town."

"Oh Daisy, Emmet's just fine. Like myself, he's doing his bit preparing for the wedding. But never mind us. What about yourself now and my big brother – should I be telling my mam she'd better get a second outfit?"

Daisy could feel her face redden. She didn't know how to answer the girl as she didn't quite know herself. George and herself had made a commitment to each other, but she didn't want it getting out, just yet.

"Hold your horses there. I'm still waiting to hear about my annulment."

"No offence, Daisy, but can you qualify for an annulment given that … you know … ye were like … you getting pregnant and all that?"

"Ah, you see, an annulment can be granted on any of three grounds. I have him on the 'I didn't know certain stuff about him before I married him' – I won't go into it here, if you don't mind."

"Oh, so there's hope for my poor brother yet. Mammy would be delighted, Daisy – she's mad about you. It wouldn't take a whole lot now for her to buy the second hat."

"Time will tell, Susan. Go and enjoy your wedding preparations and I'm glad that Emmet has found the perfect bride for himself. I know ye'll be very happy."

"Funny how things work out in the end, isn't it, Daisy?"

"It sure is, see you soon – the four of us must have a get-together before the big day."

The women went their separate ways, Daisy, safe in the knowledge that there was no animosity between them. Whatever had happened between herself and Emmet was just a memory, left behind in the past.

She felt excited at what was to come. She had enquired about a Church annulment. If she were to marry George in the future, the venue would be their choice. Her choice. And she couldn't do that if she was still married in the eyes of the Church. Not that she was a practising Catholic, but she wasn't going to made feel inferior by limiting her options. Yes. She would get her annulment and walk back up that same church aisle in Ballygore. But this time wearing the most beautiful wedding dress that she could find. With the perfect man by her side.

Chapter 39

The Man in the Black Jacket

The man in the black jacket released the heavy bolt on the front door of the River Hotel. He could see through the peephole that there were a few people standing outside, trying to get in for a late one.

Checking before he opened the door, he recognised Emmet, standing in the dark with three others. He figured that one of the women must be the new one that Emmet had gone soft on. He hadn't seen him in an age.

"How'ya, Tom," said Emmet. "Just in for a late pint – we rang ahead and got the say-so, from Tobin."

Reaching behind him, he took Susan's hand and he walked in past Tom, towards the bar. No need for introductions. Behind Susan, George held Daisy's hand as they stepped in.

"Well, Tom, we hope there will be no hassle," said George. "We're here for a drink. I'd heard you were here. Haven't seen you in Philly's for some time."

Raging inside, Tom directed them in past him. He

wasn't going to lose the only income that he had by starting anything with Doyle. Daisy could fuck off, he was well rid of her. Doyle, he would fix in his own time.

Daisy held her breath as she passed in front of her ex-husband, the man who had been her world only six years before. Recognising the silent fury in him, her heart started to thump. But she had done it, she had shown Tom that she had moved on. George Doyle was her man now.

She didn't expect him to acknowledge her. He didn't.

He had his job and had no intention of losing it, she knew. She'd heard that he'd moved into a small bedsit at the back of the hotel. He was hanging on by a thread.

The letter was easily identifiable when it dropped through Daisy's letterbox on a wet Friday morning. A white business envelope. The result was finally back.

Whether or not he was her biological father she would never have any attachment to him, paternally or otherwise. As long as there was plenty of money in the account to cover her birth mother's expenses, she had no need for David Keogh.

She hadn't mentioned it to George that she had driven to Limerick to give blood, for proof of paternity. It had taken long enough for the results to be returned – the samples had to be sent abroad for testing.

Daisy would explain to George in good time, depending on the result. Keogh had visited the same clinic in Limerick on the same week. She had insisted that they travel separately, even though he had offered to travel with her.

Envelope in hand, she wasted no time in opening it. Ignoring most of what the letter said, she was only interested in the dark print underlined at the bottom of the page.

The paternity test no. 23464 shows that Specimen A can be excluded as the paternal father of Specimen B. The likelihood of paternity is 0%. Specimen A is therefore absolutely not the paternal father of specimen B.

While it was as she had suspected deep in her gut, to see it in writing was a different matter.

She chuckled to herself, a long satisfying chuckle, that brought with it the sadness of realising that even though David Keogh wasn't exactly the father she would have wished for – at least she would have felt like she knew who she was.

Placing the letter in amongst the baby clothes, back in the blue washing bag, wrapping the lot in the same plastic that it had been found in, she headed straight for the attic, where she once again released the latch, opening the panel. She placed the items, as well as Rose's letter, back in their original hiding place. As far back as she could reach. Safe.

He had paid and paid well for his part in covering up the circumstances of her birth. She would keep him in her sights for a long time to come.

The End

Printed in Great Britain
by Amazon

62859690R00200